DRAGON STORM

THE DRAGONWALKER BOOK 5

D.K. HOLMBERG

If you want to be notified when D.K. Holmberg's next novel is released and get free stories and occasional other promotions, please sign up for his mailing list by going here. Your email address will never be shared and you can unsubscribe at any time.

www.dkholmberg.com

CHAPTER ONE

The edge of the forest had a certain stink to it, a scent that came from decades of detritus, but it was more than that odor drifting to Fes's nose that troubled him. There seemed almost a heaviness to the air, a weight that hadn't been there before. It mixed with the haze drifting out through the trees, a haze they referred to as the Dragon's Breath, and with that, Fes felt the energy humming within him.

The forest was alive with power. Most of that power stemmed from the dragons, energy, and heat that radiated from their massive forms, helping conceal them within the forest itself. Fes could see through the haze, but doing so required that he use his Deshazl magic—and he wasn't entirely certain that he wanted to right then.

"You don't have to sit with me," he said to Jayell, who sat beside him.

She smiled, taking his hand and squeezing it within hers. She had been something of a constant companion ever since the Damhur had last been defeated. It was almost as if she feared how he might react were she gone.

And he did fear. He worried what might happen if the dragons were attacked. It wasn't a difficult thing to imagine the Damhur bringing more people across the sea, using their Called Deshazl and throwing countless numbers at the empire. The dragons were enough of a prize that they would do whatever it took to succeed. So far, their absence had been striking. Another attack had to come, but when?

"Would you prefer that I didn't?"

"I know that you would rather be training with Azithan."

Jayell only shrugged. "There's plenty of time for us to be training."

"Has he been helpful?"

Jayell had left the fire mage temple and had abandoned that side of herself. Only, now with the Damhur attack, there was a need for her to do more—which meant that she had to learn to be more.

Azithan had willingly worked with her, helping her understand how powerful she could be. From what Fes understood, she could be *very* powerful in time. He didn't like the idea of using her for that potential, but they would need someone like her the next time the Damhur attacked. They would need to be ready, and it would take everything in all of their powers to be ready.

"You haven't cared to ask before now."

"I've cared. I just haven't asked before now."

"Azithan has been working with me as much as I could expect him to."

Fes frowned at her, shifting from one foot to another before turning his attention to the forest again. The steady haze reassured him that the dragons were still here. "That doesn't tell me anything."

"It tells you that he's been working with me, and seeing as how it's Azithan, I can't really expect much more than what he's offered."

"He knows that you have potential."

"Potential means only a little," she said. "Azithan cares about results."

"When it comes to the dragons and what we need to be doing, we'll need all the potential that we can get."

There was a moment of silence, then Jayell asked, "Do you miss working with *them*?"

He closed his eyes and took a deep breath, inhaling the smells of the forest. Not only did the decay and earthy scent fill him, but there also was a smoky quality, and he suspected that came from the dragons themselves. The visions that filled him when he slept were likely tied to that, though the dragons would never confirm it.

"I hate that I learned when I did."

"You hate what you learned or that they were the ones to teach?"

Opening his eyes, he studied her. With her dark hair, she could almost fade into the shadows of the forest, but that didn't suit her. She was meant to stand out. "Both, I suppose. They taught me how to use my power to harm, and I hate that they were the ones able to teach me so much."

"Still, it's useful."

"It is. The same as you working with Azithan."

Her brow furrowed and she looked as if she wanted to say something more but refrained. "How long do you intend to remain here?"

"Should I not?"

"There are other things that need to be done," she said.

"The others can take care of those things." The Deshazl here were fully qualified to ensure the safety of the village, especially with Arudis working with them.

"The others don't have your experience."

"I'm not so certain that my experience amounts to much," Fes said.

"Your experience is what allowed us to survive the Damhur attack."

He swallowed. Every so often, he would feel the effect of the Calling, almost a remnant of it. It was likely nothing more than a memory, but it still troubled him, filling him with a sense of dread every time he was aware of it. How long would he continue to have that sensation? How long would he struggle with his awareness of the Calling? Would there ever come a time when he no longer could remember what it felt like to have Elsanelle demanding his compliance?

Even when he had complied, there had been a part of him that had known exactly what he was doing. As likely as not, that had been her doing. She had *wanted* him to know and had wanted to torment him with that knowledge.

"We got lucky," Fes said. "I worry what will happen when they bring real power to bear. I don't think they believed we pose much of a threat. How could they, when the empire has only had fire mages for protection? But they've been warring with the Asharn for centuries. They have far more experience fighting than we do and far more knowledge about the Deshazl abilities."

That might be what bothered him the most. It wasn't so much that he struggled with who taught him but that with everything he had learned about his abilities, he was still playing catch-up to the Damhur. They knew far more than he did about the kind of magic he could utilize against them. He had managed to surprise the Damhur once, but he doubted he would be able to do so again. Now it was not only the Deshazl who needed protection —it was the dragons.

"The fire mages will keep us safe. They have always done so."

Fes considered Jayell for a long moment. If only it were so simple. He wished that the fire mages could do exactly what they had always claimed they were capable of doing and that the fire mages really *were* the protection the empire needed, but he was all too aware of how the Deshazl magic cut through fire mage magic, and with the number of Deshazl the Damhur controlled, it wouldn't be difficult to do.

"I think we have to be prepared for the possibility that the fire magic won't be nearly as effective as we hope. During the last war—"

"You don't know what happened during the last war."

"I can infer from what we *do* know. And the last time, the Deshazl hadn't been controlled."

"Only the dragons."

"Which is why we have to hide them. Protect them." Maybe move them north to the Dragon Plains, though he wasn't sure how effective that might be.

"The fire mages—"

"That's not my responsibility. That's more Azithan, or even you."

"I'm not sure that I am the right person to participate in that."

"You're a better person than me. I might have faced the Damhur, but the fire mages aren't particularly fond of us."

"It's more you than us," she said smiling. "You *did* break into their temple."

"Like you didn't participate in that."

"I'm different. I've been a part of the temple before."

Fes grinned at her. "You're different because they want you to return."

Jayell looked around, giving Fes the feeling that she avoided his gaze. "For the most part, I have."

He still wasn't certain whether Jayell was pleased by the fact that she had returned or whether she still regretted it. When he had first found her, she had abandoned the fire mage temple and had begun to follow the Priests of the Flame, searching for answers that she hadn't been able to uncover otherwise. What would she have done had Fes never found her? Would she have remained with the Path of the Flame? Fes suspected that she would have, and it was possible that she might have been happy to do so. Following him had brought her into a world that she had not been a part of, but then, following him had helped return the dragons, and that was something the priests had long sought.

"You're only in as deeply as you choose to be."

"When it comes to Azithan, I don't know that is true. He has a way of pulling me deeper, regardless of what I might want."

"There is that," Fes said softly. Azithan had done something of the same with him. How much had Azithan planned for all of this? He had suspected Fes's ability from the beginning, even using it to ensure that he obtained lost dragon relics. What more might he have anticipated?

A distant rumbling caught his attention, and he turned, looking deeper into the forest.

"You can go," Jayell said.

"I'm not sure that was meant for me," he said.

"Still."

"The timing is strange."

"The dragons have been gone from the world for a thousand years. I think they are permitted to be strange."

Fes chuckled. "I suppose you're right."

"Go. See what they want from you."

Fes squeezed her hand and headed deeper into the forest. At the edge of the trees, some of the faint moonlight had managed to filter in, but the deeper he went, the more he encountered the haze all around him. It reminded him of what he had once experienced on the dragon plains, the same haze that had disappeared when Azithan claimed the last of the relics from the plains. That haze made everything difficult to see, but he was able to detect the presence of movement around him. Somewhere nearby, the dragons waited.

The rumbling had been for him, something of a summons. It wasn't the first time they had summoned him. In the weeks since the Damhur attack, the dragons had asked for him to join them in the heart of the forest. It was the reason he had remained behind, waiting when others had returned to Anuhr. The emperor had departed, though he had made several trips back, wanting to spend time with the dragons, hoping to connect with them in some way.

As he neared the heart of the forest, he slowed. Somewhere nearby, he could find the ancient Deshazl city, but none had spent any considerable time there. Arudis had made it clear that the dragons didn't want anyone else within the city now that the Damhur had been pushed back. Fes—like everyone else—had visited and had spent considerable amounts of time within the city, but he had never stayed overnight. The sense he had from the dragons was that they didn't want him to. Even though he had saved them, they were still reserved.

Another rumble echoed through the forest, drawing his attention. He turned to it, heading deeper into the trees. They had veered away from the city and stayed within the forest itself. Other than himself, he didn't detect anyone else. Maybe the dragons had only called to him. And it was a calling—or a Calling. Whatever else he knew about it, Fes was certain that there was a summons within it, drawing him toward them at the heart of the forest.

But why?

There came a rustling nearby, and he turned to see Arudis joining him. The older woman had her silver hair pulled back, and she moved easily through the forest for someone her age. A gray robe flowed to her ankles.

He should have detected her, though maybe the Dragon's Breath made that difficult. He hadn't spent that much time attempting to use his Deshazl ability while making his way through here. Perhaps that was a mistake.

"I wasn't the only one who received their call," she said. "I suppose I shouldn't be surprised."

"Why do you think they called at this time?"

Arudis frowned. "With the dragons, anything is possible. You know as well as I do that there is very little we understand about these ancient creatures."

They fell into a comfortable silence as they followed the sense of the summons. After a while, Fes glanced over at her. There seemed to be something of a path leading through the trees, so he followed it, keeping his eyes on what was directly in front of him, as the haze made it difficult to see anything else. "Is it only the two of us?"

"I don't know. It's possible."

"Is the emperor..."

She shook her head. "He returned to Anuhr a day or so ago."

"And Azithan remained."

"Azithan and Jaken."

That last was strange—almost a strange as Azithan remaining. Jaken was the emperor's son but also the captain of his Dragon Guard, and as such, he needed to be with the emperor, especially given the danger of war, but he had stayed within the forest almost as much as he had stayed with the emperor.

Presumably, he wanted to understand the Deshazl and what it meant for him to have that connection—and possibly, that power. While he certainly wanted to help ensure their safety, the real reason was likely that he wanted to have more time with the dragons. In that, he was much like his father.

"Will either of them have been summoned?"

"I doubt that Azithan will be. He isn't Deshazl."

"He's not Deshazl, but he is a powerful fire mage."

"I'm not certain the dragons approve."

"The dragons allowed the fire mages to use their connection, their bones, to protect the empire," he reminded her.

None had asked the dragons whether there was an issue with the fire mages using the power of the bones, but eventually, Fes would need to know. If the bones could be used to return the dragons, would they risk that by allowing the fire mages to draw power from them? Maybe the priests were right all along.

"They did, but since their return, the dragons have been less than impressed by fire mages. I think Azithan has recognized that and has made no attempt to push them. It's probably for the best."

They reached a clearing, and the sense within Fes told him that he should wait there, so he did. Arudis glanced at him, nodding. Her sense of the summons must have been similar, but there was no sign of the dragons. If they were out there—and considering the nature of the summons, Fes believed that they were—they hadn't yet arrived.

More rustling came, and Fes looked over to see Jaken stalking through the trees. Azithan followed, and Fes arched a brow at him.

"Fezarn," Azithan said.

"You received the summons?"

"I followed Jaken."

"I'm not sure the dragons will be pleased with your presence," Arudis said.

"The dragons don't get to choose where I go. It is my responsibility to ensure the safety of those within the empire. The dragons happen to be within the empire, so it is my responsibility to ensure the safety of Jaken. Would you have me do otherwise?"

"I would have you recognize the dragons have suffered long enough."

"And they remain crucial to ensuring the safety of the empire," Azithan said.

Arudis opened her mouth as if to argue, but she wasn't given the opportunity. Another rumbling echoed through the forest, cutting her off. This time, it was close, and Fes looked around.

The dragons were near.

He glanced up, but they wouldn't be coming by the sky. As much as he longed to see dragons flying overhead once more, it wasn't safe. They preferred to remain hidden within the forest, using the trees and the haze to conceal themselves. It lessened them somehow, though he understood the need for it. There was safety in their concealment, and it was safety that wasn't found in any other way. If they didn't remain hidden, if they would have flown overhead, it would have caused chaos throughout the empire. Already it would be difficult enough to convince people that the dragons didn't pose a significant threat. After centuries spent telling a particular story, changing it to another would be difficult.

The trees bent, and the blue-scaled dragon appeared. He practically slithered into the clearing. He was enormous, though not as large as some of the dragon bones Fes had seen. He kept his wings folded up against his body, and his scales glittered in the moonlight. Heat radiated off him, and there seemed to be almost a faint glow beneath his scales, enough that he practically pushed back the shadows of the forest.

The dragon looked at each of them, snorting. More of the haze erupted from his nose, little more than steam that billowed out, filling the clearing before retreating.

"You summoned us," Arudis said, bowing her head. There was something reverential in the way that she addressed the dragon. The Deshazl who knew about the dragons all felt much the same way.

Fes struggled to feel the same. He respected the dragons, and he wanted them to have their autonomy and their ability to fly, but they weren't creatures to worship. As far as he knew, they never had been. So for the Deshazl to now treat them in such a way, it was almost as if they were acting more like the priests.

It was still better than how the emperor treated the dragons. He looked on them as if they were a tool, a weapon, and it wasn't because they might not be those things, but they were *more* than that. Why didn't the others see it the same way as Fes?

"There is a presence," the dragon said, his voice rumbling.

"What kind of presence?"

"One that draws on me," the dragon said.

Fes frowned and focused inward, looking for a sense of a Calling. There had been no sign of the Damhur in weeks, long enough that he had allowed himself to relax, though they wouldn't have been able to destroy all of them. They had stopped the main thrust of the attack, but there would be more. At least now the Dragon Guard was involved, searching for signs of them, working with the army, but the Damhur could move stealthily and didn't need massive numbers to cause trouble.

While focusing on a Calling, he felt nothing. "I don't detect anything."

"Do you believe that you would?" the dragon asked.

Fes sighed. When Elsanelle had used her powers on him, she had been subtle enough that he hadn't been able to detect it. It was possible they were able to do something similar now. "I don't know."

He turned to Arudis, who frowned and closed her eyes, her hands clasped in front of her. Dressed in a gray robe, she stood out within the forest. She exuded peace as she stood there, leaving her eyes closed as she searched for evidence of a Calling. It was the same thing that Fes had done, though Arudis had more experience with it. She had come from Javoor, much like Fes, but she had known it as an adult whereas Fes had only known it as a child, and his memories were gone. Any recollection of a Calling that he'd had before the recent events had faded, leaving him to know only his time within the empire.

He should be thankful that he'd not been raised within Javoor, that he hadn't needed to suffer, and he was, but a part of him wondered what he would have been like had he grown up there. Would he have been Called, controlled the same way as some of the fighters that he'd encountered? Or would he have been like Arudis, somehow finding a way free? Or possibly he would be like one of the Asharn, men and women who had descended from the Deshazl who had managed to escape and had mastered their abilities in ways that Fes still wished he could.

"I sense nothing," she said softly.

"Perhaps it is not meant for you," the dragon said.

Fes stepped forward. "We will protect you. We have done it before, and we will remain here, ensuring that you are safe. The Deshazl protect dragons."

"And the dragons protect Deshazl." The dragon snorted, flames billowing out before extinguishing, leaving Fes with an afterimage burned into his eyes, like a memory of the fire. "Yet we grow weary of remaining hidden."

"It is safest," Arudis said. "Either you remain here, or you head north, back to where the dragons once called home."

"That is not our home. That was a place of dying."

Arudis frowned. "I thought it was a sacred place you had once shared with the Deshazl."

"It was shared, but it was a place where we hid, and a place where we died. We would be free."

Fes studied the dragon. He wanted the same thing. He wanted to help the dragons find freedom and to once more soar overhead, but he also agreed with Arudis. It was dangerous for them to do so.

"I will search for what you detected. For now, it's probably best if you remain here, staying where it's safe."

"We will come with you," the dragon said.

Arudis shook her head. "That's not a good idea. You know what—"

The dragon roared, a gentle rumble that rolled through the forest. "It will not happen again. Now that we know, we can be ready." He shifted his gaze, lowering one golden and glowing eye down so that he could look at Fes. "And this one will work with us. The Deshazl protect the dragons."

Fes swallowed. If there was a Calling, the dragon wanted him to be responsible for ensuring their safety? He had a hard enough time ensuring his own safety, but then he *had* managed to stop the Damhur once before. Working with the dragon, he was confident he could do it again. What choice did he have?

"We'll need to make preparations so that we can ensure your safety," Fes said, looking over at Jaken. Would he go with them?

"I'm not sure how much longer we can wait," the dragon said.

"We need to make preparations to ensure our safety, too," Fes said.

The dragon huffed, and steam came out of his nose, billowing around him, almost a sense of annoyance. "We will wait."

The dragon stared at him for a moment before slipping off between the trees and disappearing once more into the forest. Fes had already learned that if the dragon didn't want to be tracked, he would be unable to do so. He had tried before and had failed; each time he had ventured after the dragon, he had grown disoriented, lost in the haze, wandering until he managed to find some vague familiarity. He suspected that were the dragons to want to, they could force him to wander endlessly.

"What do you think he detects?" Azithan asked.

"Perhaps it's nothing," Arudis said.

"If the dragon detects a Calling, we do need to investigate," Fes said. "If the Damhur have returned—"

"They should not have risked returning," Arudis said.

"The Guard has discovered nothing. They are not here." Jaken stared after the dragon with a longing in his eyes.

"Don't you think we should question what he *does* detect?"

"They lost one of the Trivent. It will take time to replace her."

"What if they have come thinking that she's still here?" Fes asked.

Arudis stared into the darkness, her gaze locked on the place where the dragon had disappeared. "That would be… unlikely."

"Why?"

"The Trivent lead the Damhur. They are the strongest among them. I am surprised one of the Trivent risked themselves coming here in the first place."

"For a dragon…"

Arudis sighed. "Perhaps that is true."

"And if they have once, what makes you think they won't do it again?" Fes asked. Elsanelle's calling had been nearly impossible to ignore. Another—or two—like that would be truly impossible.

"If they do, then we are in danger."

"We, as in the empire?"

She pulled her gaze away, focusing on Fes. "We as in the Deshazl. The dragons. All of us. The rest of the Trivent is as powerful as Elsanelle."

"We defeated her once," Azithan said.

Arudis turned to him. "We defeated her because she didn't think that we were capable. And if they begin to work together, we will find the challenge more difficult than what we can survive." She took a deep breath, seeming to calm herself, and started back toward the village at the edge of the forest.

Fes watched her go before turning to Azithan and Jaken. "It troubles me that they would attack again so soon."

"Perhaps they haven't," Azithan said.

"The dragon detects something."

"The dragon has been alive for only a few months," Azithan said. "It's possible that the dragon doesn't fully understand what it's detecting."

Fes turned to Jaken. "Do you have trouble knowing when there's a Calling?"

He stared at Fes for a moment. "No."

"Neither do I." He turned back to Azithan and found his hand going to the hilt of the dragonglass sword he carried. The daggers he once had worn were long since lost, and he thought that the memory of his parents had been lost with them, but since learning of his history, learning that he had come from a place outside of the empire, his connection to his parents had changed. He thought that he understood himself better than he had before, and thought that he understood his potential better, too.

"You would have us follow the dragon?" Jaken asked.

"I would have us search for evidence of the Damhur. We knew that they were going to threaten an attack. We thought we would have more time, but perhaps they were ready for this."

"If they were ready for it and already press their

attack again, then we are in far more danger than we thought," Azithan said.

Fes looked back out into the forest, his attention drawn toward the spot the dragon had last occupied before disappearing. He couldn't shake the sense that Azithan was right. Worse, the nagging feeling that ate at his belly made him worry that perhaps he had overlooked the effect of the Calling the dragons now felt, something that he should have known how to detect.

And if the Damhur managed to get to the dragons, the war would be over before it even truly began.

CHAPTER TWO

The camp was busy. Fes remained on the outskirts, hesitating to get too involved but knowing that he needed to. That was the whole point of being here. They had wanted him to have greater involvement in training the other Deshazl, though he still wasn't sure if that was something he should do or not.

Nick glanced over. Darkness wrinkled the corners of his eyes, and the youthfulness had faded from his face, almost as if it had never been there. That troubled Fes in a way that reminded him of just how much everyone within the camp had been through. It wasn't only he who had suffered, though he had been through significant struggles facing the Damhur, ending up Called the same as the rest of them. Fes was unique in the fact that he had come out of it with increased skill. That was what he was trying to impart to the others, preparing them for the inevitable moment when the Damhur attacked again.

"What is it?" Nick asked as he approached.

"Everyone is doing well." There were several dozen of the Deshazl working on the outskirts of the village, all of them training with swords, and all of them working with their Deshazl magic, trying to increase their capability with it. If they could manage to do that, they would find themselves much better prepared for the possibility of another Damhur attack.

Many of the Deshazl within the encampment had already begun to master the art of ignoring the Calling. Arudis had been teaching them to focus their minds, something that she was particularly skilled with, whereas Fes had demonstrated skill with honing his Deshazl magic into something like a weapon. Everyone needed to be capable of that, though he still wasn't sure if all would be able to do so.

"Everyone understands what's at stake."

"I'm not even sure if I understand what's at stake," Fes said.

"You're the one who has been teaching us."

"I worry, Nick." He glanced over his shoulder, turning his gaze to the forest in the distance. The sense of the dragons came from deep within it, though it was faint. The haze, the Dragon's Breath, wasn't visible from here, though he could almost imagine that he could see it. "The dragons detect something off," he said.

"A Calling?"

"I don't know. They don't know, either, and the dragons are determined to prove that they aren't susceptible to the Damhur Calling, but—"

"But they are."

Fes nodded slowly. "They are."

"What's it like?"

"What's what like?"

"Speaking to them. What's it like?"

"Uncomfortable. Frustrating. Disheartening."

"Why?"

"I think mostly because I feel as if there's more to be doing. The dragons need our help, and I want to do everything that I can to ensure their safety, but the longer that I work with them, the less certain I am that I'm going to be able to protect them." He turned his attention away from the forest. "Arudis tells me that the Deshazl of old had a way of communicating and connecting to the dragons, but I just don't feel that I have a good understanding of it yet."

"You're closer to it than anyone else."

"Maybe." Fes turned his attention back to the Deshazl who were working. "What can I help with?"

"You being here helps quite a bit."

"I doubt that my presence matters all that much."

"You doubt it? You're Fezarn! You're the one who defeated the Calling. You're the one who saved the dragons."

"We had help. Were it not for the Asharn, we wouldn't have defeated the Damhur." And it was more than just defeating the Damhur. It was a matter of stopping the Deshazl controlled by the Damhur, both those who came from the empire along with those who the Damhur had brought across the sea. "If they bring numbers, we might need help again."

"They haven't brought any numbers, Fes."

"I know, and that bothers me."

"I think everything bothers you," Nick said, smiling.

It was his first show of emotion, and Fes couldn't help but smile along with him. "Not everything bothers me. Just people who think to Call us and who seem to know the secrets of the empire that we don't even know."

"Will you help the new recruits work on their Deshazl magic?"

"That's why I'm here."

Fes approached the nearest grouping of Deshazl. He'd had a hand in rescuing all of them, and that made him feel particularly responsible for this group, especially over the Deshazl who had trickled into their camp. The people he had rescued had already been abducted once, and many of them had suffered under the Damhur, some of them to such a degree that they wouldn't even speak of it. Fes wondered what they had been through, but very few of them were willing to share those experiences, and knowing just how awful most of those must have been, Fes was loathe to push them.

"The great Fezarn," Sarah said, smiling widely as she watched him approach. "Arudis finally convinced you to come and speak with us?"

"I'm not sure that Arudis had so much to do with it. It was more that I figured you needed my expertise."

"What expertise is that? Is it getting dragged off by the Damhur, or do you think to share with us your great expertise in losing weapons?"

Were it someone else, Fes might not laugh, but with Sarah, he knew what her intentions were.

"Is there anything that I can help with?"

"You can help me understand how you hold your Deshazl magic out around you."

Fes focused on his Deshazl connection, drawing from deep within him. When he first had known about his link to that side of himself, he had used it in a rush, drawing upon rage and anger to give him the strength needed to be effective, but over time, he had learned that wasn't necessary at all. Instead, what was required was to focus on the way that it burned within him. It made sense considering the way his connection was bound to that of the dragons, and because of that, he shared the fire that flowed through those magnificent creatures.

"What do you detect when you reach for your magic?"

"I don't detect much," she said.

"How is it that you reach for your Deshazl magic?"

"When I feel it, it's little more than a stirring within me." She scanned the other Deshazl working, most of them fighting. "I know you told us that we needed to draw from our anger, but it doesn't always feel like I have the necessary anger to draw from."

"I didn't mean that you needed to draw from only anger. Partly that is how I draw upon my magic, at least how I used to, and I figured that it would give you something to think about when you're trying to use your own magic."

"You no longer use anger?"

"It's different for me. Ever since I was Called and held captive, I understand how to hone that connection much better than I did before."

"What did they teach you?"

There was something Fes had been trying to work on, knowing that if he could understand what it was that the Damhur Deshazl had done, the way that they had worked with him, coaxing his power out of him, then he might be able to share that with the others. And if he could, they could generate enough of a Deshazl resistance that hopefully would give them a chance.

Even if they trained all of the Deshazl within the camp, he still didn't know if they would be enough. He'd seen how many Deshazl the Damhur had managed to Call, and it seemed to be all too easy for them to draw that power. Unless he and Arudis could teach this group how to resist the Calling, there would always be that danger to those he would protect.

"Some of what they taught me came from the hold they had on me. They Called me, and because of that, they forced me to focus in a way that I don't think we can force anyone here to replicate."

"Even if you ask Azithan to help?"

It was something that he'd considered. And Azithan would likely do it, mostly to make sure that they were able to resist the Calling as much as possible. As far as he knew, Azithan had been working with Jaken, wanting to ensure that he could recognize the Calling. More than anyone else within the encampment, Jaken—and the emperor—were the closest to pure Deshazl. The rest were not quite as pure-blooded. Fes didn't know if he was a pureblood Deshazl, but given his connection to his abilities, and the way that he could slice through fire mage magic, he suspected that he was as close as there was.

"Azithan helped as much as he can, but even he is limited in how much he can do."

"We could always capture another Damhur." She smiled, and Fes shuddered.

He had tried that approach before, and it had very

nearly backfired on him, leading to a dangerous situation. "I'd like to think that we don't have to deal with them."

"That's just it, isn't it? We don't know when we will again."

"No," Fes said. He took a deep breath, focusing on the Deshazl magic within him. "How about we do something more productive?"

"I would like that, and so would the rest of them."

He joined Sarah as they made their way into the larger group. They gathered around him, listening, and there was a part of him that felt almost as if he didn't deserve their attention. They all focused intently on him, even Nick, and Fes had already shared with Nick everything that he thought he knew. Then again, Nick had managed to withstand almost everything Fes had.

"Sarah tells me that we need to work on honing your Deshazl magic." He looked around. Many of them had dragonglass swords. There had been a time when he believed that dragonglass weapons were rare, and perhaps they still were, but after facing the Damhur, claiming dropped weapons, the Deshazl now had a significant supply of them. It wasn't that the dragonglass weapons allowed them to carve through Deshazl magic any easier than anything else, but it did help them focus their Deshazl magic, which was what he wanted. "When I was first learning about my connection to magic, I used a pair of daggers that I had. I sensed my power through them and allowed that to be my focus. I think that if you were to do the same, maybe it would allow you to draw that power out."

"What if we can't even draw the power out?" The question came from Nina, and Fes smiled over at her.

"If you can't, then we will continue to work with you to do everything that we can to help you figure out what your focus is." His smile widened. "I doubt that you need to find rage the same way that I did."

"You don't think that I have the capability of having rage?"

Nina took a step toward him, and Fes smiled. She was tall and slender and carried herself with an authority that she had earned ever since her rescue. "I am certain that you can find the necessary rage," he told her, "but I am more certain that perhaps you have another way of finding a focus." He swept his gaze around the gathered Deshazl, quietly counting them. When he reached thirty, he stopped.

There were more within the village, but not so many as to provide significant numbers. Why hadn't he realized that before? "Many of you will have another way of reaching your Deshazl powers. Maybe the key for some of you is recognizing that power is connected to the dragons, whereas others may need to find something else that burns within you. Maybe it's not rage but a sense of injustice."

Nina was watching him, and he thought that triggered something within her. Taking a deep breath, he focused on his Deshazl connection, honing it tightly. He pushed it out from him, letting it flow outward, crashing into the ground, where it exploded softly. There wasn't much force to what he released, but there hadn't needed to be. That was what he wanted them to know.

Someone took in a deep breath. "Was that fire magic?"

Fes couldn't tell who was speaking, but he shook his head. "I had something of a similar reaction the first time I encountered any of the Damhur using their magic like that. I thought that only fire mages could release it in such a way, but though our magic is similar, it's not the same."

"How is our magic similar?" This came from Walden, an older, slightly heavier set man with a thick mustache that held a remnant of his lunch.

"If you think about it, both of our magics is tied to the dragons. Ours is directly tied, and we share that same power with the dragons, whereas the fire mages use the remnants of the dragons themselves to generate their magic. We are related, though not the same."

"They require destroying the dragons for them to have their strength," Nick said.

"They require the dragons to allow them to use that power," Fes said. He watched Nick and realized that he'd made a mistake in not working with his friend sooner. Nick needed him, though he probably didn't even know that he did. Nick felt as if the fire mages had stolen his sister away, and there was a part of him that still raged at the fact that they hadn't found her. It was something that Fes should have done long ago, if only to ensure that his friend had an opportunity to know what happened to her. "As far as we know, the dragons let the fire mages use their remains. As far as we know, the dragons wanted them to."

He waited for Nick to challenge him, but he clenched his jaw and said nothing.

Fes took a deep breath, stepping back and joining the others. "Why don't we practice? We can work on honing our connection to the Deshazl magic and releasing as much as you're capable of gathering. It won't be much. Focus through the dragonglass and see if you can aim it at the ground. Nothing more."

They began to separate. Sarah stayed near him, watching him.

"What is it?"

"They respect you, you know."

"They respect the fact that I have a connection to power that they want."

"It's more than that. They want to fight the same way that you were able to fight. These people were all Called by the Deshazl, and all of them know what it felt like, and none of them want to experience it again. They would do anything to avoid it."

"If it comes down to fighting the Damhur, I don't know that we have enough power to overwhelm them."

"We will figure it out, Fes. We're getting stronger. And we are learning to fight so that we can be of more use."

He shook his head, smiling at her with a hint of sadness. "It's not that I don't think that you're not of any use. It has more to do with the fact that from everything that I've seen, the Damhur have far greater numbers than what we will manage."

"We still have the army. The Dragon Guard. The fire mages."

"And yet, during the Damhur attacks, so far it's only been the Deshazl resisting."

She watched him and finally turned away, joining the others.

Fes stared for a while before retreating, backing up to observe. Every so often, he felt a flash of power and was rewarded with an explosion of earth. For the most part, it came from people he had expected would be able to demonstrate their connection to their Deshazl magic. Nick was strong, but he lacked control. Sarah would occasionally release a powerful blast. A half dozen others would do the same, but not nearly enough that he felt confident in their ability to pose much of a threat to the Damhur.

Turning his attention back to the forest, he looked outward, nervousness rolling through him. If the dragons were in any danger, would he be able to defend them? It would come down to him and perhaps the very few others who had managed to reach their Deshazl magic, but there wouldn't be many able to defend the dragons. So far, the Dragon Guard hadn't participated that much, nothing more than sending a few brigades out through the outer edges of the empire, searching for signs of the Damhur, but there were none. Fes had little doubt that they would encounter more, and probably soon. The fact that they had repelled the Damhur once meant nothing.

"You seem troubled, Fezarn."

Fes spun to see Azithan watching him. How had he managed to sneak up on him without him realizing it? The fire mage was skilled, and he had quite a bit of talent with stealth, but Fes hadn't detected anything, and there had been no sense of fire magic.

Now that he was aware of Azithan, he could feel the fire magic flowing off him and wondered if perhaps Azithan were revealing it intentionally, wanting him to know that he was there.

"I'm troubled by the dragons."

"What is it about the dragons that troubles you?"

"What if there is a Calling that they have detected?"

"Have you detected it?"

"That's not how it works."

"I am perhaps more aware of how it works than you."

"And you are saying that because you have the ability to Call?"

"Yes."

"You don't have the same subtle touch that the Damhur manage. They can work so stealthily that I'm barely aware of their presence within my mind." It was easy enough to remember what it had been like when Elsanelle had Called him. He hadn't even known until the connection had burned out of him. She had been there, and he had known that she was going to be there, but there was nothing that he was able to do about it. "If they don't want anyone but the dragons to be aware of it, they probably won't be."

"They suffered a great defeat. There is no reason for them to attack again so soon."

"What if it wasn't a great defeat to the Damhur?"

Azithan arched a brow. "You destroyed one of their leaders."

"One of three. And the other two are equally powerful. I imagine there are others who are nearly as powerful, all waiting to take over for her." That was what troubled him the most. The Damhur had centuries of experience with their Calling, centuries of controlling the Deshazl, and here he had only begun to learn about his abilities. How could he ever hope to defeat them? "All I want is to help prepare the Deshazl to be able to withstand the Calling, but I worry that we don't have enough numbers—or strength."

"What are you getting at?"

"I don't know. I know the emperor is willing to send troops sweeping through the perimeter of the empire, but the Damhur don't need to move in massive numbers to be effective."

"They are the only ones ensuring our safety."

"The fire mages?"

Azithan said nothing, and Fes shook his head. The fire mages weren't fighters. They preferred to collect and control power and had never shown any inclination to do much more than that.

"The fire mages might be called to do more than what they have shown so far, Azithan."

"Those within the temple already have begun preparations."

"What sort of preparations?"

"The sort that matter only to fire mages."

"You do know that I can ask Jayell?"

"And Jayell has taken herself away from the temple. Train your Deshazl, Fezarn. I feel that is valuable, but perhaps there are other ways for you to be valuable, too."

"And what ways are those?"

"As you seem to have a connection to the dragons, you

have incredible value to the empire. The emperor would like to use that."

"Use that. You say that in a way that strikes me as far too similar to the way that the Damhur would use my abilities."

"And yet, you would be providing service to your empire."

"That's just it, Azithan. If what I've learned is true, I'm not a part of the empire."

"The empire has welcomed you within its borders."

"The empire hasn't always been welcoming." He didn't need to tell Azithan how he had barely survived his first years on the streets within the capital. Azithan might have rescued him from that, but he had kept him in part of the danger, not saving him from that lifestyle. Then again, had Azithan done anything differently, Fes might never have known about his Deshazl connections, and if nothing else, he was thankful that he had discovered his abilities. They were important to know, and it was essential to truly understand who he was.

"The empire provides a place, but it doesn't always provide safety. For that, you must act on your own behalf. I've seen that you are more than capable of doing so, Fezarn."

"What would you have me do?"

"You could protect the emperor."

"I'm not sure that I could do anything that Jaken cannot."

"We both know that is not true. As does the emperor."

"You want me to move the dragons to the capital."

"As I said, you have a certain connection to them. If they were in the capital, they would be easier to defend against the Damhur."

"And if they were in the capital, then we run the risk of them attacking the people of Anuhr if the Damhur succeed in Calling them."

"That is why you must protect them."

"It's too dangerous. I think keeping them here in the forest is safest."

"You think keeping them near the Deshazl is safest, but the emperor and Jaken are both Deshazl, Fezarn. Do not forget that."

"I haven't, but has the emperor forgotten that he is Deshazl?"

"He has not."

Fes breathed out heavily. "I will think about it. While I do, why don't you and the other fire mages offer to provide a certain protection to the Deshazl?"

"We have no need for such defenses here. The Damhur have not shown themselves."

"Yet."

"You expect them to?"

"I trust what the dragon has detected. If there's a Calling, I'm willing to do whatever it takes to ensure the dragon's safety."

"And that safety would be provided by the capital."

"I said that I would consider it."

Azithan watched him, looking as if he wanted to say something, but he bit it back. There was a time when Azithan wouldn't have, but in the days since Fes worked directly for him, their relationship had evolved. Maybe it had changed for the better, but Fes wasn't always sure that was the case. He certainly felt as if he had changed for the better, though perhaps even that, Azithan would argue as well.

He turned his attention back to the Deshazl, watching them as they worked. Every so often, there came an explosion of power, and with that explosion of power, he felt a surge of pride. They had learned from him, and the more that they worked, the more they could continue to learn, and eventually, he believed that they would be able to control whatever connection to power they possessed.

The only problem was that he didn't know if it would be enough. And if it wasn't, how did he hope to protect the dragons?

CHAPTER THREE

Fes awoke in a cold sweat. He looked around the small building he'd claimed within the village. His head throbbed, pounding with heat and pain. It was more than heat and pain that troubled him. Once again, a vision had come to him, a dream that had been plaguing him. In that dream, dragons had flown overhead, swirling in the skies, free in a way that they were not now. One, in particular, had flown higher than the others, one with scales of a deep purple so dark that they could be black. In that dream, Fes felt as if he should help them, and yet… there didn't seem to be any way to truly help them.

"It's okay," Jayell said, looking over at Fes.

She was sitting near the hearth, coals barely glowing and reminding him of the heat coming off the dragon. Fes sat up and rubbed the sleep from his eyes. As he did, he couldn't shake the image of the dragons from his mind. As much as he wanted to, it was there, staying with him, burned into his memories.

"What happened?" she asked him.

"I had a dream," he said.

"Another one?"

He nodded. "It's like the others, only they seem to be getting stronger."

"Dreams of dragons. You know, when I was still with the priests, they would have considered you blessed."

"I don't feel particularly blessed." He rested his hands on his lap, staring down at them. He steadied his breathing, and as he did, he searched for any evidence of a Calling. In the time since the attack, he found himself doing so less and less, but after a vision like that, having an image of the dragon in his mind, he couldn't help but reach for that sense, even more so after the warning the dragon had given.

There was nothing, and he knew that he was making too much of it, but between his vision and what the dragon had told them, he couldn't shake the sense that he needed to do something more.

"You might not feel blessed, but at least you get to see the dragons flying in your dreams."

He glanced up and smiled tightly. Jayell shared his feelings about the dragons and, much like him, she wanted to see the dragons flying once again. It wouldn't be possible unless they managed to remove the Damhur threat. Until that time, there would be no way for the dragons to safely fly.

"I'm sure if you torment yourself enough, you would be able to have the same vision."

"It's not a torment, is it?"

"It's something," Fes said. He stood and started pacing, making his way around the small room. There were only so many homes within the village, and everybody had to share. Jayell shared with him, and though they were something more than friends, they hadn't taken it any further during their time in the village. Every so often, Fes considered trying to push for more of a relationship with her, but when he did, he hesitated. He didn't want to disrupt what they already had, not wanting to lose her, but with a war coming—and it *was* war—did waiting even make sense?

"I think we've been spending too much time in the village," Fes said.

"You said we had to wait for Jaken and Azithan to decide when we would depart," she said. "And then you wanted to sweep along the south to ensure the Damhur hadn't returned."

He sighed. That had been the plan. They would go and search for evidence of a Calling. The idea was to keep the party small, make it so that they could easily move, and hopefully limit the possibility of others getting

Called. None of them wanted to deal with the chance of having to attack one of the Deshazl. It happened often enough since Fes had first rescued the Deshazl that he wasn't about to be responsible for it happening again. He had saved them, and they deserved the opportunity to remain free, not worried about when the next attack would come. More than that, these people were not soldiers. They were his friends.

"I don't like the waiting," Fes said.

"I know you don't. Ever since I met you, you've been the kind of person who likes to be active."

"It was hard even when I was in Anuhr. I never liked sitting around and waiting for a job."

"I have a hard time imagining you sitting around and doing anything," she said.

"There were times when I had no choice. Azithan didn't often have jobs, and once I started working for him, others didn't hire me."

And he hadn't needed to take other jobs. Not really. Once he started working for Azithan, the pay had been good enough that he was able to be selective, and because of that, he had been able to choose which tasks he would take on. Especially the last few, with money beyond what he ever would have imagined possible—which reminded him that he needed to go to Carter when he returned and get his money back from her.

"It's not so much that we're sitting around," she said.

"I know, but it doesn't change the fact that I feel as if we're just waiting."

"You worry that the dragons will not wait for us."

Fes sighed. "That's the concern."

There had been something about the creature that troubled him. It was an agitation, and he understood that agitation. Fes had felt something similar before and recognized a desire to do more. How could he not when he shared it? He had experienced that same feeling, wanting to be able to do more, wanting there to be some way to fight, and as they waited for the Damhur to attack again, it felt as if they were just biding their time.

And the Damhur were not.

He knew within his core that the Damhur were preparing. Fes and the rest of the Deshazl didn't know nearly enough.

If they could find the Asharn, maybe they would be able to get help, but Arudis warned him that in order to reach the Asharn, they would have to go through Javoor, and doing so meant confronting the Damhur. If they survived *that,* there was no telling whether the Asharn would even help. They had only come to the empire because of the promise of dragons. Would they help for the same promise?

He sighed and reached the door, pulling it open.

"Where are you going?"

"To think."

"Don't work too hard," she said with a smile.

Fes stepped outside and looked around the village. It was late, the middle of the night, much like when he had last seen the dragon. The moon shone overhead, nearly full, gleaming with silver lights. He paused and stared at it for a long moment. A few stars twinkled in the sky alongside the moon, but not so many that he couldn't count them.

Jayell joined him, squeezing his hand.

"You don't have to come with me."

She shrugged. "I want to."

Fes stared up at the sky. "When I was a child, some of the others living on the streets claimed the stars were the ancient dragons, and that they had flown off to the sky, burning brightly only at night."

"If only that were true."

"If it were, there would be hundreds and thousands of dragons. I'm not sure we want quite *that* many."

Jayell laughed, and they fell into a comfortable silence as they weaved through the village. There was no one else awake, at least not within the village limits. Others marched along the outside perimeter, patrolling, but within the streets, there was silence. It was comfortable. Fes would never have believed that he would find comfort in a small village like this, but there was something tranquil about it. He had thought that he loved the size of Anuhr and that he was meant to be in a place like that, a place where there was any sort of conveniences to be found. The longer that he spent outside the city, the more he wondered whether that was true. He enjoyed Anuhr, but outside of the city, there was this sense of peace that he didn't have within it. There was quiet.

Anuhr was active at all times of day and night. People moved in and out, and taverns never really closed. That had helped when Fes worked for Azithan, tracking and collecting on his behalf. But he had forced Fes to live a different lifestyle than what he had now.

He sighed, taking a deep breath. Here at the edge of the forest, the air was cleaner and fresher. It was nearly fall, and soon the leaves on the trees within the forest would begin to change, and he had never spent an autumn outside of Anuhr.

Distantly, he could feel the dragons. They tugged on his awareness, a vague sense that drifted to him. Every so often, Fes pushed out with his Deshazl magic, wishing that the dragons would respond in kind. They shared a connection, but they never returned it to him.

That shouldn't trouble him, but it did. He should understand that the dragons owed him nothing. He might have helped save them, preventing the Damhur from abusing them, but that was about it. The only time he had *really* shared in their power had been when he was working against the Damhur. If it came down to it, would the dragon lend power again or would it hold it back?

As he walked along the edge of the village, a different sense came to him. It was the pulsing power of fire magic.

Fes glanced over at Jayell. She was never aware of fire magic when it was used, though he had learned that some fire mages developed the ability to detect it over time. It would be helpful if she had that.

"Someone is using their fire magic," he said.

"Where?"

He pointed outside the village and toward the south. "It is Azithan out there?" It would be awfully late for Azithan to be out working his spells, but he would often do strange things. Azithan was nothing if not peculiar.

"Azithan is sleeping."

"Are you sure?"

"Pretty sure. I left him after our session."

Fes frowned, turning his focus toward the south, where he had detected the spell. It was there, and every so often it bloomed against him.

He reached the edge of the village. Jayell grabbed his arm. "If there's a fire mage, we should get help."

He shook his head. "If it's a fire mage, they might be here for help. Jaken wanted more partners to ensure the empire was safe from the Damhur."

"Fire mages won't do that willingly. Besides, what if it's not one of ours?"

"We'll go and scout. Nothing more."

Jayell stared at him and then raised her hand, motioning for him to wait. She hurried off, disappearing back into the village, returning only a few minutes later. "I wanted to have supplies in case we needed them."

"What kind of supplies?"

"The kind of supplies that would allow me to defend your foolishness if it comes to it."

"We're just going out on a scouting mission."

She shrugged. "We've been through that before."

He laughed softly and stepped out of the village and onto the grassy plain surrounding it. They made quick time as he hurried toward the sense of the fire magic. Every so often, he would detect it again, power blooming against him, and when he did, he paused, searching to see if he could identify the nature of the spell. The more he was around a fire mage, the easier it was to know the intention behind their spell. He still didn't understand what that meant, but it was a useful talent to have.

As a precaution, he pulled on his Deshazl magic, pushing it around him into something like a barrier. Since his capture by the Damhur, his control over his Deshazl magic had increased dramatically. Always before, it had been something that had burned within him, and it still raged deep within him, but now he knew how to let it out slowly and carefully, with much more exact control than he had previously had. It was a useful magic that way.

Fes slowed as they topped a gentle rise. The moonlight made it light enough for them to see their way, and traveling by foot gave them the advantage of moving quietly. Had they taken horses, they would have thundered through the night and would have made far too much noise for a scouting mission.

On the other side of the rise, the sense of the fire magic bloomed again.

It wasn't close, though.

Fes had expected that they would have found it nearby, but it seemed to be moving away from them.

"That's odd," he said.

"What's odd?"

"The fire magic," he said.

Jayell smiled. "Now you think fire magic is odd?"

"That's not what's odd. It's the fact that it seems to be moving away from us."

"Will maybe it wasn't a fire mage coming to the village. There are other reasons for the fire mages to travel."

"I know there are, but we've been in this village for quite a while, and we haven't seen any fire mages. The fact that I am picking up one now is odd. If it's not

Azithan and it's not somebody who's with us, do you think they could be chasing the Damhur?"

Jayell shrugged. "We haven't had any sign of the Damhur, Fes."

"Other than what the dragon detected." He continued onward. As they went, Jayell kept pace, but she was slowing. He knew that he was traveling too fast for her, his Deshazl connection giving him greater speed and strength than she had, and he slowed, not wanting to get too far from her. He would rather have her with him, and would rather have her help, if there was anything that she could do.

If it came to one of the Damhur, having Jayell with him might be a benefit. She could offer some protection, though he had progressed beyond the need for much protection from the Calling.

"I… I don't know how much longer I can go," Jayell said.

They continued to chase the sense of the fire magic, and though it was growing closer, it was still out there, distant.

"We can go back," he said.

Jayell studied him. "I'll wait here. Why don't you range ahead and see what you can see, and I'll hold onto a spell so that you know where to find me when you're done."

Fes considered refusing the offer but knew he wouldn't. Curiosity had gotten the best of him, and now he wanted to know how much farther they would have to go. If there was someone out there with the ability to draw fire magic, and if they were going away from him, he needed to know if it was empire or Damhur.

"Be safe," he said.

"You don't think that I know that?"

"Just be ready with a defensive spell."

She smiled and waved him on.

Fes gave her a longing look before turning away and racing after the sense of the fire mage spell. Now that he was separated from Jayell, he could move even more quickly, and he detected the sense of the fire magic growing closer. It was near enough that he thought he could practically reach it.

He topped another rise. The landscape around here had been undulating gently, gradually climbing before descending again, and from here, he could see out a great distance. Everything sloped down toward the sea, and he realized that he had traveled much farther than he had thought.

Had he really forced Jayell to march that quickly or was it only after he had gone on his own that he had moved fast enough to come here? Fes often lost track of when he used his Deshazl magic but suspected that he had been drawing upon it during his run, even though he hadn't done so intentionally. If he listened, he imagined that he could hear the waves crashing in the distance, though that might only be his imagination.

Where was the fire mage?

He remained hidden, crouched on the hillside, looking out into the night. The moon had shifted, seeming to follow him, and cast a gentle band of silver light over everything. Fes took a deep breath, letting it out slowly. There was nothing. The sense of the fire magic that he had been tracking was gone, almost as if he had imagined it.

Fes knew that he hadn't imagined it, so where had it gone?

It had to be nearby.

As he waited, it surged again, this time more toward the north.

How had it gotten behind him? He had been tracking it throughout the night, following it toward the south, so it shouldn't have managed to move here. Fes started to turn before pausing. He focused on the sense of the fire magic and waited to detect it again. As he remained, he put everything that he could into sensing it.

When he felt it again, once more it came from the north, and even more distant than the last. There was some character to it that was different than before.

Could he have been following more than one fire mage?

Fes turned and started running. He focused on the

fire magic, racing through the night. As he ran, the fire magic bloomed again, and again he noticed a distinct difference from the characterization that it had been marked by before.

There was no question in his mind that this was something else.

He had made a mistake.

The fire magic had drawn him this way. It couldn't have been unintentional.

Fes paused after running for nearly an hour, listening for Jayell's magic. He was familiar with her fire magic signature and thought that he should be able to pick up on when she placed a spell. It was there. Faint but definitely out there.

Fes raced toward it.

Not only was it there, but the sense of her spell was somewhat weakened.

Was she growing tired from holding onto it?

He didn't know much about fire mages and their use of their magic, nothing more than how they drew power from the dragon relics, but he did know that their ability wasn't limitless. It was a strength much like Fes's own magic required strength. And much like his, the user of the fire magic could grow tired and could lose the ability to maintain a spell. From what he'd seen, Azithan might be the greatest fire mage within the empire, able to maintain a spell for far longer than others, but even he had limits. Everyone had limits.

Fes ran, focused only on the sense of Jayell and her magic. If nothing else, he wanted to reach her, wanting to make sure that he got to her in time. If there were other fire mages out there, he didn't know whether they were dangerous or not. He needed to get to Jayell before these others might.

A faint glowing in the distance drew him.

It came from a dragon pearl. Fes was sure of that, and he streaked toward it, unsheathing his sword as he ran, fearful that something might have happened to Jayell. When he found her, she was lying curled on the ground, dragon pearl resting in the middle of her body, glowing with a soft orange light. He touched her arm, and she jerked awake, looking up at him.

She smiled. "Did you find the fire mage?"

He took a moment to catch his breath. "You're okay."

"Of course I'm okay. I shouldn't have fallen asleep, but I figured out a way to hold onto a spell while I was sleeping so that you could find me." Jayell studied his face for a long moment. "What is it? Something troubles you."

"There was more than one fire mage out there."

"Are you certain?"

"I could feel them. It seemed as if I were drawn away. One after another pulsed against me, almost as if knowing that I could follow them."

And if they knew that he could follow them, it meant that they wanted him gone. But if they did, why? What did they think to accomplish by pulling Fes away from the village?

There were others within the village who were skilled fighters. It wasn't only that Fes could fight. As tired as he was, he hadn't been thinking clearly, though he should have been. Damhur drawing him away wouldn't care about engaging him, not if they knew what he had already done. No… there was another—more compelling —reason.

The dragons.

"We need to hurry," he said.

"Back to the village?"

He shook his head. "Back to the forest."

CHAPTER FOUR

It was nearly morning by the time they reached the trees. Jayell couldn't run nearly as fast as Fes, and he didn't want to leave her behind again. If there were other fire mages out there, she might recognize them, and he didn't know if he were overreacting or if he really had reason to worry.

"It's so quiet," she whispered.

"I don't think I've ever heard any other creatures inside the forest."

"There have to be some."

Fes looked around. In other forests that he'd visited, there were squirrels and wolves and other birds, but not in this one, at least not in the parts that he had visited. It was almost as if the dragons scared them away, and he understood that they would. Why would animals risk themselves against a creature like a dragon?

They hurried through the forest, sticking to a path that wound between the trees. Fes focused on his Deshazl connection, heading toward the heart of the woods, but there was no sense of anything drawing him there. Not as there had been when he first found the dragons.

When they reached the Deshazl city, faint streamers of sunlight shone down. Fes looked around at the simple buildings, pausing only a moment to marvel at their structure. This had been a place of his ancestors, a place where they had lived long ago, and it was a place where they had welcomed the dragons. There was history here, and eventually, Fes hoped to understand it, but as it was, there was no way to take the time, not with everything else that they had going on.

"Where are the dragons?" Jayell asked.

"I can't detect them."

"Is that unusual?"

"They can mask themselves from me. I don't know if they would have that ability to mask themselves from the Damhur or not."

Yet, it troubled him that the dragon had mentioned detecting a Calling, and now he couldn't find him. It worried him even more that there had been several fire mages traveling outside of the village, just beyond the forest. If they were fire mages of the empire, why keep moving that quickly? And if they were Damhur, then he was already too late.

Maybe they hadn't intended him to be the one to detect the fire magic.

It had come in the middle of the night, and with that kind of magic, there could be other reasons for it. What if their intention was not at all about Fes, but about someone else with the ability to track fire magic?

Maybe it was the Asharn?

If it was the Asharn, Fes needed to find them. Though he didn't necessarily agree with the tactics the Asharn had used, they were possibly the best equipped to help the empire deal with the threat of the Damhur.

Unless they tried to claim the dragons, too.

Fes was determined to protect the dragons, and he was willing to do whatever it took to do so, but the Asharn had a far greater understanding of the Deshazl ability than Fes. As much as he had learned about his connection to his Deshazl magic, they had known that power for their entire lives. They were far better connected to it than Fes.

"We still need to find where the dragons could have gone," he said.

"If they're still in the forest, they're safe."

"But are they going to *stay* safe?"

Jayell grabbed his hand. "I don't know that you can be responsible for ensuring their safety forever."

The Deshazl protect dragons. The dragons protect Deshazl.

That thought rolled through his head. It was one Jayell wouldn't understand. "Not forever. Only until we figure out how to prevent the Damhur from harming them."

"Fes—"

He turned away, making a slow circuit of the city. As he wandered, he pushed out with his Deshazl connection, searching for any sort of sense that might reflect upon him, giving him an idea that the dragons might be out there, that they might be able to connect to him, but it wasn't there.

Fes paused in the middle of the city, looking up at the sun. How long had he been after this? Worse, what if he was wrong?

"We need to return to the village," he said.

"Good. I think you need some rest."

"It's not rest. I need to find Arudis and see what she might have picked up on."

"Why are you so convinced that there's something you are missing?"

"I can't explain it. It's there, but there is a sense that I've overlooked something, and there's a sense of power that I've missed out on. I don't know how to explain it any different than that."

With fire mages involved, maybe it wasn't Arudis he needed to go find. It was Azithan.

They hurried through the forest, and as he went, he realized something that should've troubled him before. He had overlooked that fact, his urgency driving him through the forest and taking away his awareness of what was taking place around him.

The haze of the Dragon's Breath was missing.

Fes skidded to a stop.

"What is it?" Jayell asked.

Fes looked around. The bases of the trees were visible in a way they had not been any time he'd been here before. He stared, scarcely able to breathe.

"The trees."

"What about the trees?"

"I can see them."

Jayell looked around, frowning. "So? Sometimes when the dragons retreat deeper into the heart of the forest, you can see the trees."

Maybe that was all it was, and the dragons had retreated, possibly fearing a Calling. If that were the case, would he be able to find them were it necessary?

He needed to find Azithan.

Fes hurried through the forest, and as they ran, he caught sight of its edge. From there, he could see the village, and he broke into a run. In the morning light, there was activity moving throughout the village.

He found Sarah. "Do you know where Arudis is?" he asked her.

She glanced from Fes to Jayell before shaking her head. "I haven't seen her. We were going to train in the forest."

Would it be safe for them to do so? He didn't know if there was any danger in going into the forest but feared that there might be. If the dragons were missing, then whatever had Called them away might still pose a threat to the Deshazl.

"It might be best for you to train in the village," he said.

Sarah stared at him for a moment before nodding. Fes was thankful that she didn't argue, but he had enough credibility with the other Deshazl that most would do as he suggested.

Fes grabbed Jayell and hurried through the village toward Arudis's home. When he found it, he knocked on the door, leaning back and waiting. It took a moment before the door opened. When it did, the face on the other side wasn't Arudis's. It was one of the other Deshazl, an older man by the name of Terrence.

"Is Arudis here?"

Terrence frowned. "I haven't seen her. Why?"

Fes swore under his breath and turned away. He ignored Terrence's questioning look and hurried through the village, looking for signs of Arudis.

"I'll see if I can find Azithan," Jayelle said.

Fes let her go and continued to make his way through

the village, feeling a rising fear that something had happened. He needed to know what it was. As he passed the different Deshazl, many of them training, he found nothing that he thought would explain what had happened. None of them seemed aware of what had occurred the night before. And maybe they weren't.

Detecting the use of fire mage magic wasn't something that all of the Deshazl seemed able to do. Fes suspected that they would be able to, especially as they came into their abilities, but most of them didn't have that great of a grasp of their magic. Arudis continued to work with them, training them, but they developed slowly—almost too slowly for him, especially if they were going to be of any use in stopping the Damhur.

At first, Fes had thought that he might be unique, but the more that he learned, the more he realized that the people of the empire, those who were descended from the Deshazl that were Called in these lands, just weren't as powerful as those who came from across the sea. His ability with his magic was greater simply because he was one of those descended from the original Deshazl.

When he reached the edge of the village and looked out, he saw nothing.

He should be at ease. The fact that there was nothing should be relaxing, but it made him more upset. Something was going on, and he was missing it.

Jayell joined him. "I couldn't find Azithan."

"I don't feel his magic here. Where do you think he's gone?"

"It's Azithan. You know that he could go anywhere."

Fes stared into the forest. "I know. After what we tracked last night, I'm troubled."

"Tell me what it was that you experienced again."

"There were the pulses of fire magic," Fes started. He thought back to what he had detected. When he had started following it, he should have known that it was unusual. He should have known that something was not quite right, especially in the way that the magic was moving away from him. None of the fire mages were powerful enough to disappear like that. Unless they were on horseback, though that wasn't impossible.

"I don't know what it was."

"They haven't brought fire mages against us other than the time they went to the temple," she said.

"The Damhur who Called me were all fire mages."

"Did you feel a Calling?"

He shook his head. There had been no sense of that. Always before, there had been.

"Maybe these were nothing more than fire mages from the empire."

"Don't you think that Azithan would have shared with you if there were fire mages of the temple coming through here?"

Jayell shook her head. "Azithan wouldn't necessarily

tell me. He probably views me as someone who is outside the connection to the temple."

Fes made another circuit of the village. As he went, nausea continued eating at his stomach. When he reached the southernmost point of the village, he paused. From here, there was a vaguely strange sense. The longer he focused on it, the more that it reminded him of a Calling.

Fes started forward.

"Fes?"

"Get horses," he said, continuing south.

As he walked, he began to increase his speed and started veering toward the east. He was tired from the night before, but he was determined to know whether he detected anything or whether it was merely his imagination. He wasn't sure whether this was a Calling or whether this was nothing more than his mind playing tricks on him. It could be just fatigue. He was tired, and with everything that they'd been through, it was possible that this was nothing, but he was afraid that perhaps the Damhur had discovered a new tactic.

It was possible that they avoided Calling to avoid alerting anyone of their presence. Or they had it focused so tightly on the dragons. The creatures had known something was off and had warned him. He should have known to trust that the dragons *had* detected something unusual.

Jayell joined him, holding the reins of one horse while riding the other, and he quickly jumped into the saddle, far more familiar with that now than he had ever been in his life. They galloped off, hurrying across the land. As they went, Fes unsheathed his sword, ready for the possibility of an attack. Next to him, Jayell built a fire mage spell and power bloomed from her, filling the space between them. It was something like a shield, and it pressed out from her, radiating away. She could hold it, and hopefully, she was strong enough if an attack came.

The more they rode, the more certain Fes was that he detected a Calling.

He stared out into the distance, focusing on his Deshazl connection. Just the two of them wouldn't be enough, not if they faced a serious threat, but he didn't dare bring any more Deshazl with him. If there were Damhur and they were strong enough to detect from a distance and strong enough to attack the dragons, they would pose a danger to any of the Deshazl.

In the distance, he saw them.

At first, he thought it was his imagination, but the farther they rode, the more that sense of the Calling built. It was almost a relief when he saw the Damhur in the distance.

"How many do you think are there?" Jayell asked.

"Not as many as I thought," Fes said. As he stared, he tried to make sense of what he saw. Barely a dozen in total, they were dressed in the distinctive clothing of the Damhur. That surprised him. He would've expected them to take a better effort to conceal themselves, but maybe they weren't concerned about being seen.

"What do you think we should do?"

Fes didn't know. If it were only a few of the Damhur, he thought he could withstand the effect of a Calling, but with a dozen—and any number of them capable of performing the Calling—he didn't know if it was safe to attempt to approach or not. It was possible that they would be able to push that Calling upon him.

There was no sign of the dragons. And the Calling that he detected wouldn't be powerful enough to work on a dragon, let alone both of them, but where had they gone?

"I think we should watch them," Fes said.

"We should send word to the others," she said.

"And tell them what? That a dozen Damhur have been sighted?"

"Yes. We can get the army. Jaken has promised—"

"I don't know what that will change," Fes said. "The army won't be able to defend against the magic of the Deshazl or the Damhur, and any Deshazl we have won't be able to face the Damhur."

"You don't give them enough credit."

"I've seen what happens when they face them," Fes said.

"You've seen what happened before, but they're training. They're learning. Everything that you told them and taught them, they're taking to heart."

"They still aren't strong enough. I'm not sure any of us are strong enough to handle this many Damhur."

"And yet you would still risk yourself."

"Better risking myself than risking others."

"You aren't going to be able to save all the Deshazl," she said. "Eventually, they're going to have to fight. There are plenty of the Deshazl who are willing to fight. They're able to do so. Your resisting that, your keeping them from that, does nothing. It diminishes them."

"I'm not diminishing them. I'm trying to protect them. I've already saved them once. I don't want to lose them."

"By not allowing them to fight?"

Fes sighed. "Let's follow for now."

Jayell frowned at him, and he thought she might argue, but she didn't. They climbed out of their saddles and found a nearby tree to tie the horses to. From here, they could stay on foot. Fes continued to hold his Deshazl connection, creating a shield around himself, insulating himself from the effect of the Calling. Jayell pushed out on her fire magic, and Fes worried that doing so would reveal her presence. If there were any of the Damhur Deshazl with them, they might know that she was holding onto a fire mage spell.

"We need to be careful," he said.

"I'm not going to release my magic," she said.

Fes smiled. "I wouldn't ask that of you. All I'm saying is that I think we need to be careful."

She eased back on her connection to her spell, and the barrier that she had formed began to retreat, becoming narrower. If nothing else, it would be more difficult for the Deshazl to detect. Even up close, Fes wasn't as able to recognize the nature of the spell.

They followed the Damhur, moving across the land. They were heading south, but not with any particular speed.

"It's almost as if they aren't concerned about being detected," Fes said.

"Maybe they aren't."

"Do you think they have others coming?"

"Think about the other times we've come across the Damhur. They haven't feared the power of the empire."

"They haven't until recently. They've been defeated."

"What if they don't know it?" Jayell asked.

It was a reasonable thought. These others might not know that he and the Deshazl had defeated Elsanelle. And if they didn't know, they would have no reason to fear traveling openly throughout the empire, but those other bands of Damhur had wagons and other preparations for any Deshazl they might encounter. Where were those supplies?

They continued to watch the Damhur. As they traveled, Fes began to feel uncertain. Why would they be here? There had to be some reason for them to have appeared, and it had to be more than simply not realizing the attack was over.

There was a sense of a Calling, a subtle sense, but it was definitely there. The longer that he focused, the more that he listened for it, the more confident he was.

The Calling couldn't be for dragons—a calling that weak wouldn't be effective against them. There were no signs of Deshazl—unless they were trying to draw other Deshazl out. If they were, the Damhur weren't prepared for them. They had no wagons—not as they would need to draw the Deshazl out.

"We're missing something," he said.

"What do you think we're missing?"

"I don't know, but it bothers me that they continue to perform a Calling."

Fes continued to follow the Damhur as they made their way south. They traveled for hours, and Fes never slowed, both unwilling and unable to do so. If he did, he would put them in danger of losing the Damhur.

"What if they're leaving?" Jayell asked.

Given the direction the Damhur traveled, it was possible that they were leaving, but why? If he went with the assumption that the Damhur didn't realize that Elsanelle and her people had been defeated, it was strange that they would depart, especially without completing whatever task they had.

Unless they had already completed that task.

It was possible that the Damhur had done what they had intended, but what was it?

"Fes," Jayell whispered.

He looked over and realized that another grouping of Damhur approached.

How had he missed them?

This one was larger—*much* larger than the last. There had to be several hundred Damhur in all. Among them were many more Deshazl, and Fes could tell even from a distance that they were following their Calling, controlled by the Damhur so that they obeyed. Not all of them were. Some were others of the Damhur, both men and women who were dressed in the traditional Damhur garb. They also made no effort to conceal themselves, almost as if unconcerned about the fact that they traveled through here.

"Why so many?" he whispered. "*How* so many?"

"Maybe they're beginning the attack."

That didn't fit with what he knew of the Damhur. They had no qualms about pressing into the heart of the empire. "Why wouldn't they return toward Anuhr and bring their attack there?"

Jayell shook her head. "We need to head back and warn the empire."

That might be what troubled Fes more than anything. He and Jayell shouldn't need to warn the empire of an impending attack. They should have patrols that defended the empire. There should be an army that protected the empire.

What had happened to the army? What about patrols?

As he stared down at the Damhur, he saw captured soldiers.

How many had been caught? How many more had been lost?

"What are you doing?" Jayell asked, grabbing his arm and pulling him back.

Fes realized that he had been creeping forward without really meaning to. He crouched back down, lowering himself so that he could observe.

"That's where the patrols have gone," he said, motioning toward the distant soldiers.

"The Damhur?"

Fes pointed toward the center of the caravan. "I would guess that nearly half are empire soldiers."

"How is it that they were able to capture that many empire soldiers?"

"Probably a combination of the Damhur, fire magic, and the Deshazl."

When he had been Called, controlled by them, he had been forced to use his Deshazl connection on behalf of the Damhur. If they did the same with the Deshazl that they brought with them, it wouldn't surprise him to learn that they had easily defeated the empire soldiers.

"If only the soldiers had fire mages with them," Fes said.

"There was a time when the fire mages went on patrol," Jayell said, getting low to the ground as she stayed near him. "It's one of the things that I learned when I was still in the temple. You hear stories about the earliest days of the fire mages, and they share how those fire mages served almost like soldiers, patrolling with the regular troops. Together, they swept through the empire." She looked over at him. "Most within the temple were thankful that they didn't have to patrol like the fire mages of old. When I was there, no one wanted to be a soldier. Everyone wanted to use their connection to the fire magic for—"

"Power," Fes said.

"It's more than power," she said. "It was about a connection to the dragons."

Fes shifted, turning his gaze so that he could stare down toward the Damhur. The fire mages were about more than merely their connection to the dragons. If that were all there was, they wouldn't pursue using their abilities quite like they did.

Still… Fes was thankful for them and everything that they did. If they didn't pursue that connection, the empire would have fallen, and though there would still be dragons in the world, they would have been controlled. Called. They needed the fire mages. Without them, there wouldn't be nearly enough strength to counter the attack.

Fes watched, debating what they should do. From here, it would take the better part of a day to return to the others. Yet there were too many for Fes and Jayell to manage on their own. They couldn't remain, and they couldn't pursue an attack. They needed to get word to Jaken and the Dragon Guard. Hopefully, they could reach the Damhur before they caused more trouble.

"What would you have us do," she asked.

As Fes started to answer, he felt power begin to build, and he frowned, staring down at the Damhur. "There's power building."

"What kind of power?"

He could only stare. "Fire mage magic."

CHAPTER FIVE

Power from the spell continued to build. Fes stared, unable to take his eyes off the caravan down below. It spread through a narrow valley running through the hillside. Small shrubs grew in places, and occasionally, there were trees, but not often. The caravan didn't make much noise, which surprised him.

There was something he didn't quite see, and though he could feel the power building, he couldn't tell where it was coming from. The sense was different than what he'd experienced before and reminded him of the power that he'd trailed after during the night. He didn't want to get caught in between the fire mages and the Damhur.

"Do you think that's what you detected last night?"

Fes hadn't thought that was what it was, but maybe it

had been. Perhaps all he had picked up on was the fire mages making their way toward the Damhur. "Maybe."

But the fire mages wouldn't be here to end a threat. They weren't fighters, not anymore. If they were here, there had to be some other reason for it. It was even possible that the fire mages didn't know about the Damhur.

"We have to find them."

"We don't want to get in the middle of this."

"What if we're not getting in the middle of anything?" He focused on what he detected of the fire magic. It was nearby, but not so close as to be readying for an attack. There was a power within it, the kind of power that Fes rarely felt from fire mages. Azithan had access to that kind of power, but he was one of the few fire mages who did.

Something wasn't right.

"Come with me," he said, guiding Jayell away from the Damhur.

"Fes—"

He paused. "Is there a fire mage temple near us?"

She frowned. "There's only one temple in the empire."

"Is there any other place that the fire mages might use as a collection of power?"

She shook her head. "I don't know. I haven't been a part of the temple in so long that..." Jayell started to frown. "There might be a place. I remember hearing about a storage site."

"A storage site?"

"The fire mages keep places throughout the empire where they store dragon relics. Not all of them are kept in the temple, though the most powerful are."

"Why would they have places like that scattered throughout the empire?"

"There are too many relics for them to all be stored effectively."

Could that be what he was picking up on? He hadn't known about a storage facility, but it was possible that was all he detected, and if that was what it was, maybe this wasn't an attack.

At least, it wasn't an attack the fire mages would be ready for.

He turned his attention back toward the Damhur. The faint sense of the Calling was there, though it wasn't very strong. It didn't need to be, not with what he detected. If the Calling weren't trying to draw Deshazl out, it would only be to control those they already had with them.

If the Damhur were readying to attack, he needed to warn the fire mages.

Fes began to run toward the sense of the fire magic.

Jayell chased him, struggling to keep up, but he didn't wait. If this were what he suspected, she would understand.

Up ahead, he caught sight of a cluster of buildings.

A small village. That was where he detected the sense of the fire mage magic.

More than that, it reminded him of a dragon bunker.

There had been other dragon relics in the last bunker he'd been in. Enough to make it valuable.

Fes paused, waiting for Jayell to catch up.

She leaned forward, her hands braced on her thighs, panting. When she managed to catch her breath, her gaze settled on the distant form of the village.

"Do all the dragon bunkers contain relics?" he asked.

She frowned. "What?"

He tipped his head in a nod toward the village. "That's a dragon bunker from the ancient war. I've been in others, and several of them have contained relics. Do all of them?"

"Fes, I don't know."

There was no denying that was what he detected. The power built from within the village, and it was enormous. A barrier pushed out against him, and it was potent, almost forcing him back.

With this kind of spell, he imagined that the fire mages were prepared for anything. It was the kind of spell he didn't want to interrupt, not knowing how that might affect the fire mages and not certain whether it was even possible to do so. As far as he knew, his ability to carve through spells had limits. Without others like him, other Deshazl with dragonglass weapons and the ability to cut through a spell, there wouldn't be any way to carve through what he detected.

"I can't go through here," he said.

"Then the barrier is safe," she said.

Fes turned and looked back toward the south. He had assumed the Damhur were planning to depart, but maybe that wasn't it at all. Perhaps they were heading *toward* here. The Deshazl with them would be able to detect the fire mage magic, and it would act almost like a beacon, dragging them forward. The fire mages within had to know.

"It's not safe. Not with as many Deshazl as are coming." He looked over at Jayell. "Can you pass through?"

"I'm not sure. If they've placed it with enough strength, it's possible that I won't be able to." Jayell stared at him for a moment and then took a dragon pearl from her pocket. Since she had begun working with Azithan, there had been no shortage of dragon pearls. This was a rather large one, much larger than some of the pearls Fes had seen when they first started traveling together, and the power she was able to draw through it was considerable. As it pressed out from her, a ring of magic that flowed outward, she took a step forward.

The barrier held its place and prevented her from moving.

Jayell pulled on more power from the dragon pearl until the entire pearl began to glow with a yellowish light. As it did, Fes could make out the striations within the pearl that matched striations found in dragon bones. With the dragons' return, he hadn't managed to determine what those striations indicated, only that they were distinctive and found on all true dragon relics.

Heat bloomed off Jayell.

She took another step and began to slip into the barrier.

"It's not easy," she said.

"You have to keep pushing," Fes said.

"They have designed this well. It is meant to keep all things out."

That made sense, especially as the Damhur had both fire mages and Deshazl, and with a powerful enough spell, they should be able to prevent both from reaching them, but Fes hadn't expected to encounter anything like that outside of the temple. The fact that they had something this powerful here surprised him.

"Why would they have such magic here?"

"I don't know."

The fire mage magic continued to build, and Fes let it swirl around him. As it did, he frowned, recognizing something within it that he had felt only one other time before.

"No..."

He took a step behind Jayell and reached the barrier. As he did, he pushed, no longer concerned about pressing through it. The barrier was in place, but it was also a mistake. Could they not see what they were doing?

"What are you doing?" Jayell asked.

"They are trying to raise a dragon," Fes said.

"Are you sure?"

"I'm certain. I can feel the spell they're using. It's the same one used when the Damhur raised a dragon."

"They wouldn't attempt it."

Fes looked over at her, frowning deeply. "Are you sure? I might not know the fire mages as well as you, but I have a hard time believing that they *wouldn't* attempt it."

And he should have expected it before now. The rumor of a dragon's return would have been more than enough to draw attention from the fire mages and considering their desire for power, and how that desire had changed over the years, Fes should have planned for this.

The emperor should have planned for this. Azithan should have planned for this.

Unless Azithan *had* planned for this.

Could there be a reason that the spell was as potent as he detected?

Azithan was possibly the most powerful fire mage that he knew, and raising a dragon required considerable strength. Now that he'd seen them—and seen the emperor's response to them—he would be most likely to try and replicate what the Damhur had done.

Fes unsheathed his sword, prepared to cut through the spell.

Jayell raised her hand, halting his movement. "Are you sure that you want to do that? You're the one who wants to see the dragons returned."

"I want to see the dragons return, but not like this. Not when they could possibly be used."

"What if they know the Damhur approach? What if they are trying to prevent an attack?"

If they had known, Azithan should have said something to him.

No. Fes didn't think they knew.

Which made this all the more troubling.

If Azithan were going to attempt to resurrect the dragons, why wouldn't he have involved Fes? He knew about Fes's connection to the dragons, and he knew the way that Fes felt.

He nodded to Jayell and slashed through the spell.

For a moment, Fes wasn't sure whether it would part, but slowly his attack on it began to succeed. He pressed through the spell, cutting past the fire magic. He wasn't sure how much of it was because of his strength and how much was because Jayell also tried to push through it.

He continued forward, pushing more and more of his

Deshazl magic into what he was doing, and as he did, the spell began to fade, retreating. Then it collapsed.

Fes let out a breath and went racing forward.

"How angry do you think they'll be?" Jayell asked.

"If it's Azithan, I suspect he'll be quite angry."

"Because you interrupted his spell?"

"Because he would view it as wasting the dragon magic."

A considerable amount of magic had been used, enough that he suspected dozens of relics had been involved, but Fes couldn't have sat back and done nothing. He needed to intervene, especially as the spell posed a risk.

Power began to build again, this time a little different. Fes ignored it, hurrying toward the village, and then paused. It was a village much like the one where the Deshazl now headquartered, and within it, he could feel the effect of the fire mage magic.

As he suspected, it came from beneath him.

Fes waited. If he were right, the fire mages would come from below ground, curious and concerned about what had happened.

He didn't have to wait for very long. He could feel the magic building, coming closer and closer. He remained, holding his Deshazl connection away from him, creating a shield around himself. Jayell paused near him.

"Be ready," he said.

"For what?"

"For anything."

As the power exploded upon him, Fes pushed back.

There was one particular aspect of the spell that he recognized. He started toward it and reached the building at the same time that the door opened.

He came face to face with Azithan.

"Fezarn. Do you understand what you—"

Fes turned and pointed. "Do *you* understand what you're doing? The Damhur are nearly here."

Azithan frowned. "The Damhur?"

Fes nodded. "There are several hundred not far from us. You would attempt to raise a dragon so close to them?"

"We didn't know the Damhur were there." He glanced over his shoulder. "But even knowing that, having… Wait. How did you know?"

"I recognize the spell."

"What do you mean that you recognized it?"

"There is a signature to each spell. This one has a particular strength that's required, and I recognized it." A different thought came to him. "And I'm probably not the only one who did."

Azithan cocked his head. "You think the Damhur will have recognized a spell from such a great distance?"

"Not the Damhur. The Deshazl they control. If they're strong enough—and given everything that I know about them, I suspect I'm not unique and that they are strong enough—they will have detected the nature of your spell."

Another idea came to him, but it would be even more dangerous. Could the fire mages have *drawn* the Damhur?

"You would have to have had the necessary components to resurrect the dragons," Fes said.

Azithan stared at him. "We have always had the necessary components. We have not understood the requirements. That had been lost to us."

"How could it have been lost?"

"I don't know. Not all is recalled from the war. Somehow, it seems the Damhur managed to recall the steps involved in raising the dragon."

"We need to be ready for an attack," Fes said.

"If they know the fire mages are here, they would be unlikely to attack."

"Only if you believe the fire mages intimidate them. I was there when they attacked the temple," he said. "I saw their willingness to confront the temple filled with fire mages. They don't strike me as particularly concerned by the threat posed by fire mages."

"Fezarn, we have centuries of experience."

"As do they. From what I saw, the magic they were able to use exceeds that of the empire's fire mages. The only thing that would be different would be..."

Fes frowned. Maybe that was why they had come this way. Could it be the Damhur wanted more than just the dragon? Could they be after the empire's dragon relics? If they had them, they would be even more powerful—and possibly find it easier to attack.

"You need to move the relics away from here," he said.

"Fezarn. We have nearly a dozen fire mages. Each of them is second degree or higher."

That should impress Fes, but with the number of Deshazl that he had seen, he wondered how much a dozen high-ranking fire mages even mattered. It was possible that they wouldn't make a difference at all.

"Trust me, Azithan. We need to move your fire mages —and these relics—away from here before the Damhur reach it. If you don't, I suspect you'll only make them stronger."

Azithan studied Fes, but then he nodded. "I will do as you suggest. You have proven yourself to the empire."

He turned away, but as he did, a different sensation exploded.

A Calling.

The Calling was powerful, and it washed over Fes, sweeping through him with so much strength that he struggled to resist.

"Oh, no."

Jayell took his hand. "What is it?"

"They have begun their Calling."

"What do you mean begun?"

The Calling continued to build, pushing on Fes. As he

felt it, he realized that it wasn't directed at him. A Calling with this much power could have only one purpose.

"We need to get moving," he said.

"Why?"

Azithan appeared from a hidden doorway and stared at Fes. "They are moving the relics away. We have them secured, and anything of significant value is taken with the fastest rider. Is that satisfactory?"

"It will have to be," Fes said. He turned toward the sense of the Calling. "We have a different problem, Azithan."

"What problem is that?"

"The Damhur have changed their focus."

"Changed it to what?"

"The dragon had said they were feeling the effect of a Calling. I wasn't aware of it when they were, and that troubled me. Having spent time with the Damhur, I thought that I should have been more attuned to the effect of their Calling, and the fact that I wasn't able to pick up on it bothered me, but now I feel it. It's a Calling that is stronger than even the ones Elsanelle had used."

"What kind of Calling is it?"

"One that's directed at the dragons."

CHAPTER SIX

Fes stood at the edge of the village, staring into the distance. The Damhur hadn't made an appearance, but it wouldn't be long before they did. He could feel the Calling nearing, but more than that, he could feel the pressure from their magic as it came closer. Soon that magic would wash over them, and when it did, he didn't know that he would be able to oppose it.

"We should go," Jayell said.

"I can't."

"You can't do anything to help the dragons if you're captured."

"I can't do anything to help the dragons if I'm not here, either."

"We have to be prepared for the possibility that they might succeed," she said.

Fes clenched his jaw, hating that she was right. He couldn't stay here, not if he intended to get everyone to safety. Could he somehow oppose the effect of the Calling? Not without knowing where the dragons were. If he had the dragons with him, maybe he would be strong enough, but so far, there hadn't been a genuinely natural connection other than when they had faced Elsanelle. It was possible that link wasn't enough against as many Damhur as he detected.

"I need to attack," he said softly.

"Fes, you can't do anything. Not against so many Damhur."

He looked back at Azithan. "Will the fire mages stay and fight?"

"They will do what they can, but few fire mages are skilled in battle."

"They defended the temple."

"Because that was the temple. You saw how quickly it fell."

Fes squeezed his eyes shut. For all the fire mages claimed themselves capable of doing, they weren't the warriors they once had been. "They might have no choice."

Azithan shook his head sadly. "That might not be enough."

He turned, and Fes didn't stop him. He disappeared

behind a line of buildings, and another fire mage spell bloomed into existence and began to retreat.

"We should go with them," Jayell said.

"You go. I'm going to stay here."

"Even if it means that you're captured again?"

"If I'm captured, at least I would have fought on their behalf."

"There isn't anything that you can do from here. The only thing you can do is get captured and die."

He let out a frustrated sigh. He wasn't about to lose the dragons to the Damhur, not after everything they'd gone through, but if he were lost to the Damhur, and if he were Called, he wouldn't be able to help the dragons at all.

"We need to get help," he said.

"What about the Dragon Guard?"

"We have to do as much as we can. You go, join Azithan, and convince him to send help."

"You aren't going to come?"

"I'm not going to attack them, if that's what you're concerned about."

"A little, but I'm more concerned they'll draw you away. It's happened before."

"This Calling isn't for me. They're using it on the dragons."

"Then return to the forest with me. The dragons

aren't here. You can do more there than you can here. Do what you've said and help the dragons escape it."

It was what he *should* do. The dragons weren't here, though he wasn't sure they were still in the forest. As far as he knew, the dragons weren't anywhere he could find them. If they wanted to hide, they'd be able to do so—which he should want for them. And he did.

Leaving was safest. Without having any other way of knowing where to find the dragons, he could use his connection to the first one to be raised and see if he could track them. Get there before the Damhur.

A soft roar built, echoing across the land, and Fes shivered.

When it came again, he turned his gaze to the sky. "It might already be too late." Turning to Jayell, he said, "Go!"

She hesitated before turning and racing away. She disappeared within the village, and from there, Fes turned his attention back to the sense of the Calling.

Its steady march had slowed.

The Damhur must have heard the dragon, and on hearing the dragon, they must have known that their Calling was effective.

Fes stayed in the shadows of one of the small buildings. The sun shone overhead, nearly midday, a time when the dragons once had flown freely in his visions, a time when they should be allowed to hunt, but now they had to fear. Rage built within him as it often did when he thought about what had been done to the dragons and the way that they had been used.

As he stood watching, waiting, the Damhur line came into view.

The dragon roared again, though it was distant.

Fight it!

He didn't know if the dragon could even hear him, though there *had* been a connection between them, however faint.

The Calling continued.

It was a mistake waiting here. He shouldn't have remained hiding near the village. As soon as the Damhur saw the village, they would come toward it. He should have waited outside it, but he had wanted to be close to the dragons when they neared, wanting to be able to do something—anything—to help them.

There was no sign of them. Just the Damhur.

Fes ducked into the building Azithan had come out of and searched through it until he found a second door. He pulled it open, hurrying down a series of stairs.

From here, he could wait. He could still feel the effect of the Calling, but he was better able to resist it.

As he reached the bottom of the stair, sound above him told him that he had very nearly been caught. He hurried along the hallway. All dragon bunkers were similar. They had interconnected tunnels, and if needed, he could race between the buildings.

He waited, half expecting an attack to come down the stairs after him, but there was none. He was left alone.

The Calling remained, continuing to build. There was no other sense of the dragons—nothing that would tell him they were coming.

Could they have fought the Calling?

The Damhur hadn't come down, and the sense of the Calling didn't increase. Did they think Deshazl were here? More likely, they feared the fire mages were here. And maybe that made them pause, made them more cautious with their attack then they would be otherwise.

Fes stood, hiding, and finally, the effect of the Calling began to fade, retreating, and he reached the stairs, heading back up, and paused at the door. At that door, he listened, waiting for an effect of the Calling, but it never came.

They weren't there.

He wouldn't have expected the Damhur to have left without the dragon.

Fes started up the stairs carefully, listening for any sense of a Calling, worried that he might be overlooking something, and as he went, he began to feel a faint sensation.

Almost too late, he realized a Calling was near.

He hesitated.

The door opened above him and he lunged forward.

A Deshazl greeted him by letting his power explode.

Fes shifted to the side, letting the Deshazl magic slip over him. As it did, he jammed his sword forward, catching the person in the gut.

As their blood sprayed over him, Fes moved on, hurrying up the stairs. This was foolishness, and he knew it, but he had been discovered. He should have waited, staying hidden in the bunker, but now that he was exposed, he needed to ensure that they didn't realize who he was.

Two other Deshazl were at the door.

Fes darted forward and slammed his sword into the first one, spinning with an explosion of Deshazl magic out from himself and sending it into the next attacker. They blocked, and he ignored them, driving his sword back and down, carving into them.

Fes dragged them away from the door, so the Damhur didn't know what he had done. He paused at the doorway, looking out into the village. There was movement along the streets, but not so much as to discover him.

He waited.

The effect of the Calling continued, but it wasn't as prominent as it had been. Once again, the impact of the Calling was retreating. It was moving away from him, almost as if…

Fes stepped out of the building and into the light. He

looked up and heard the roar of the dragon at the same time.

That would be the only reason the Calling would be heading away from him.

They had succeeded.

A pair of Damhur Deshazl appeared, and Fes roared, anger surging through him. He hacked through the two Deshazl before they had a chance to react. He stormed through the village, cutting down anyone in his path.

It still wasn't enough.

The Calling was out there. It pulled the dragons.

He reached the edge of the village. The Damhur were there, but not so close that he could reach them. And their Calling dragged on him, far too compelling to ignore.

He raced forward, unmindful of the threat to himself.

Heat exploded near him.

Fire magic.

Fes carved through the spell, using his connection to the Deshazl to sever it. He pushed against the effect of the Calling, ignoring it, knowing that if he couldn't, if he couldn't reach the Damhur in time, they would take the dragons and they would be lost to the empire, and worse than that, they would be used *against* the empire.

A shadow flickered across the ground, and Fes looked up to see one of the dragons gliding toward him.

The female dragon.

She had maroon scales and matched the colors of the empire, and she should have been safe, protected by the empire, but instead, she was Called by the Damhur. All the time that he had wanted to see them flying freely, this wasn't how he imagined it.

"No!"

She ignored him.

That wasn't entirely true. A burst of flame erupted from her nose, and she roared again, continuing her flight just above the surface of the ground.

Where was the blue-scaled dragon?

He wouldn't lose both of them.

Fes raced forward. In the distance, he could see the Damhur.

A line of Damhur stood watching the dragon.

Not watching. Calling.

They were the ones responsible for what was happening.

He needed to get to them, but even as he did, even as he started to run, his body betrayed him. Attempts to take a step failed, and he froze in place.

The Calling was not for him, but the Damhur seemed to know he was there.

Fes pulled on his rage, letting that power surge through him, but it didn't come. He couldn't move, and any attempt to do so failed.

He shook with the effort of it.

He wasn't going to lose the dragons like this. He couldn't.

But he needed to be able to move to reach the dragon.

The sound of activity near him drew his attention, but with his body failing to respond, Fes couldn't do anything.

He could only stare, watching as the Damhur Called to the dragons.

There came another roar, and the blue-scaled dragon appeared.

"Fight it!"

He doubted the dragon could hear him, and even if he could, the sheer number of Damhur attempting the Calling was too much. They were not able to withstand the power. There was nothing that could be done to stop them.

"Work with me! The Deshazl protect dragons! The dragons protect the Deshazl!"

There was no response.

"What is this?"

Fes couldn't even turn to see who approached and where the voice came from, but he recognized the accented inflection of one of the Damhur Deshazl. Power built from the Deshazl. A broad-shouldered man loomed in front of him. He had dark hair and eyes that reminded Fes of his own. He carried a curved dragonglass sword, its style different than the one Fes held.

"Are you the one they have been looking for?"

Fes took a deep breath. "I will cut you—"

The man backhanded Fes, sending him staggering off to the side. He righted himself, but that was all he could do. His body didn't respond otherwise.

"You will do nothing. You are an animal that must be trained."

"Like you?" Fes asked.

The man chuckled. "I'm not afraid to admit that I needed to be trained."

How could the Deshazl feel that way?

"They can't have the dragon."

"They are animals that must be trained. Like you."

Fes shook his head. "No. They are noble—"

Another blow struck him, sending him staggering the other way. Rage built within him, but there was nothing he could do about it. He was helpless when confronted with the Calling.

"Where are the others?"

"Others?"

"The Trivent sent an emissary. The others will have been corralled."

Fes chuckled, allowing himself that bit of victory. "The others have been lost. Your Trivent was killed."

"That is not possible."

"I killed her myself. Elsanelle is—"

The man smashed Fes another time, and like the

others, he staggered, barely able to stand. It didn't matter. He didn't care if the blow sent him staggering. All he cared about was angering this man so much that he lost control. And he had already seen that the man would lose control. It was in his eyes.

"You will not speak of the Trivent."

"She is gone. I can speak of her however I want."

He raised his hand to strike again, but the blow never came.

Fes frowned.

A blast lifted him from the ground, and he went flying, crashing nearby. Another blast came, this one equally powerful, but the Deshazl seemed to unravel the spell.

Hands grabbed him, and Fes wanted to fight and resist, but he couldn't. He was dragged away.

"Stop fighting, Fezarn."

"Azithan?"

"I couldn't leave you to this."

"They can cut through your spell."

"Perhaps, but they can't cut through Jaken."

Fes was turned and could see Jaken fighting with the Deshazl. He was outnumbered, but Jaken was incredibly skilled, and he carved through them, leaving them dying. He nodded to Azithan, and they retreated, dragging Fes with him.

"No!"

"We can't remain here, Fezarn."

"They have the dragons."

"They do, but they also have us outnumbered. Besides, they are retreating."

As he said it, Fes realized that Azithan was right. The sense of the Calling was retreating, heading toward the south—and the sea. If they managed to reach the sea, the dragons would be gone, and there would be nothing that he could do to save them. Reaching them would require heading to Javoor, and the emperor had already made it clear that he would not support such a mission.

"We can't leave them," he said. "If they take the dragons—"

"They *will* take them, and we will prepare."

Fes blinked away tears. They streamed down his face, and it seemed as if there was nothing he could do. His body still didn't react to his will, the effect of the Calling lingering. At one point, Azithan found horses and threw him into the saddle and dragged him away.

It wasn't until they were quite a distance away before Fes's control over his own body began to return. At that point, it was too late.

They had abandoned the dragons.

By the time they reached the village, anger filled Fes, but it was a useless sort of rage. There was nothing that he could do about it.

When he climbed from the saddle, Jayell greeted him. "There is nothing that you could have done."

"I would have tried."

"And you would have died," Azithan said. "They are too powerful for you. You succumb too easily to their Calling."

"I still would have tried."

"Even if it meant your life?" Azithan asked.

He glanced at Jaken. There were a few Dragon Guard soldiers who had joined the village, but not as many as there should have been. Had there been more, what would they have been able to do? Would they even have managed to rescue the dragons?

It was possible that they wouldn't have.

Despite his best efforts, the dragons had been lost.

And now there was nothing that he could do to help them.

"The emperor needs to—"

Jaken shook his head. "The emperor wants us to prepare and be ready for an attack. We will gather our troops, and we will secure our cities."

"Which means that he won't send anyone to Javoor."

"What would you have them do, exactly?" Azithan asked. "If they were to go, do you think there is really anything that could have been done that would have made a difference?"

"I don't know."

Jayell took his hand and guided him away. "You need to take a break before you do something foolish."

"Such as what?"

"Such as throwing yourself against a force that you don't understand. They have power that you can't counter."

She was right, but maybe there was help that would be able to ensure their safety.

"What if I didn't have to go after the dragons alone?"

"How would you go after them?"

"We need help. And it's time to see what Arudis can tell us about the Asharn."

CHAPTER SEVEN

"What were you thinking?" Fes asked Azithan as they made their way back to the village. The hillside rolled past, but he didn't bother to spend much time looking. Every so often, he found himself looking back, toward the distant shore, thinking that he might catch a glimpse of the dragons again. Each time the wind kicked up, he thought it came from the fluttering of the dragon's wings, but then it past without sign of the dragons.

There was nothing.

The fire mage kept his gaze focused straight ahead as they rode. There were a few other fire mages with them, but not nearly as many as he would've expected. A dozen Dragon Guard, but no more, rode alongside. Trees dotted the landscape, nothing like found in the forest and did nothing to block the sunlight burning in his eyes.

"I was thinking that we would prepare for the Damhur."

"By raising a dragon."

Azithan swung his gaze to him. "The dragons are powerful, Fezarn. We need to leverage that strength against a foe like this."

"You did this now rather than waiting until we had a better understanding? We barely knew what we needed to be doing with the dragons that had been raised."

"And now we won't know, will we?" Azithan said.

"You blame me?"

"I blame your stubbornness with the dragons. You refuse to bring them to the capital, determined to keep them with the Deshazl—"

"Because the Deshazl protect the dragons."

"Only they didn't."

Fes couldn't even argue with Azithan. He let the fire mage, along with Jaken and the other Dragon Guard, ride ahead. He lagged behind, with only Jayell for company, but he said nothing. It didn't make sense that the fire mages would have come all the way out here to attempt to raise a dragon unless they had intended to use it somehow against the Damhur. Given the way Azithan had been acting, he might not know what it was.

And Azithan had been right. He hadn't protected the

dragons. Maybe the fire mages would have been a better choice.

Exhaustion had overwhelmed Fes by the time they reached the village. He stood on the ridge with the village in the distance and turned away, making his way toward the forest. Darkness began to fall, dusk sending shadows drifting over everything, and he trudged forward, step after step, the trees looming in the distance almost as a taunt.

"Fes?" Jayell called after him.

He ignored her as he continued to make his way toward the trees. There had been silence on the journey back, though throughout that silence and during the entirety of the journey, Fes couldn't help but feel the sense of the Calling upon the dragons. Did that come from his connection to them? He wasn't entirely sure if that was the explanation or not. He only really had a connection to one of the dragons, not to both. The female dragon had seemed much more tied to those within the empire, and not so much to Fes.

"Fes?" Jayell called after him again.

"You can go back," he said.

"Where are you going?"

"I'm going to the forest."

She reached him, grabbing his arm and forcing him to stop. "They're not there. We saw them Called."

"I know they're not there. I'm still going. I can't help

but feel like there's something there." Since the dragons' capture, there had remained a sense drawing on him. He wasn't able to explain it other than that the dragons needed him.

"Why?"

Fes looked away. How could he explain to her that he felt responsible? The Deshazl protected the dragons, and the dragons were meant to protect the Deshazl. He had let down his side of the bargain. This after feeling so confident in his ability to protect them, to defend them, to provide some way of ensuring their safety and thinking that he would be able to prevent them from being Called, and yet despite that, he still had failed.

When he reached the edge of the trees, he realized Jayell was still with him. Azithan and Jaken had returned to the village, and he didn't mind going on his own. How could he when he wanted to be alone? At this point, he felt as if he needed to be alone.

They would stop the Damhur, and he was determined to find allies, thinking that he could go into Toulen and see if any of their warriors would help. As he had helped them, he at least hoped that there would be a willingness on their part to work with him, but there was no guarantee. Worse, he wasn't sure if they had enough in the way of numbers.

Already, he knew that they didn't have the numbers necessary to defeat them with the Deshazl. If the emperor was unwilling to send his troops, where else would they recruit help?

He trudged along the path, the Dragon's Breath absence a reminder of his failure. There was no sense of power within the forest, nothing that he had felt when he'd traveled through here before. All that was here was an emptiness. When he reached the heart of the forest, the ancient Deshazl city, he paused, looking around. This was where the dragons should be. They used this as their home, the place where they remained safe, and this was where they should have been protected by the Deshazl. By him. Only he had failed.

"Why did you come here?"

The voice came from the darkness between a pair of buildings nearby, and Fes stared, realizing that Arudis was there. He hadn't even known that anyone else was.

"Why did you come here?"

"I felt the Calling," she whispered.

"I saw the Calling," Fes said. "There wasn't anything that I could do, and I tried, Arudis, I did as much as I could, but there wasn't anything that I could do to prevent the Calling. They took the dragons."

"That was always a risk, Fezarn."

"I promised to protect them. I failed them."

"The Deshazl have failed the dragons before."

"This time was supposed to be different."

"How did you think this would be different? The

Damhur have had centuries to prepare for this. They were ready for the return of the dragons in a way that the Deshazl are not."

"I was just hoping..." What?

Fes didn't really know what he had been hoping, only that he had wanted to protect the dragons so that he could see them flying freely once again.

"We have to go get them."

"I don't disagree with that."

"Do you think the Asharn will help?"

"Fezarn—"

"Will they help?"

Arudis approached slowly, watching him. She looked weary, and he wondered if she had resisted the Calling on the dragons as much as he had attempted to. With her ability to detect a Calling, and with her Deshazl strength, it was possible that she had done just as much as he had. "You don't really understand the Asharn. I don't think that you can, as you have spent very little time in Javoor, but trust me when I tell you that they are unlikely to be of much assistance in this case."

"They came here before."

"They came to take the dragons. When you proved that the dragons weren't unsafe, they retreated. They had no interest in being here and no interest in opposing the Damhur so openly. They fear them."

There was something to her words that troubled him. "You resent the Asharn."

"I resent the fact that they could have fought but did not. I resent the fact that they left the dragons to face the fate that they did, allowing the Damhur to attack."

"What can you tell me about the Asharn?"

After the attack on the capital, he hadn't really known anything about the Asharn other than they were far more capable with their Deshazl abilities than he was with his. They might even be more capable than the Damhur Deshazl, able to utilize their capabilities in such a way that allowed them to overpower some of the most potent fire mages of the empire. They had managed to overwhelm Azithan.

"They once were captive, much like your family. They managed to escape, and because of that, they have disappeared."

"Do they try to help others disappear?"

"When it fits their goals, which it doesn't always."

"Defeating the Damhur would fit their goals, Arudis."

"You think that it would, but who is to say what fits the goals of the Asharn? Even if you were able to reach them, to cross the entirety of Javoor, you wouldn't be able to convince enough of the Asharn to assist in making it worthwhile."

"We need to stop them. We need to rescue the dragons."

"They are lost, Fezarn." Arudis turned her focus toward the heart of the ancient Deshazl city.

Fes stared, likely feeling the same as Arudis, possibly thinking the same, too. Even when the dragons had been here, they hadn't been free. Living within the forest, hiding, wasn't what the dragons deserved. They were meant for more—so much more. They deserved the freedom he had seen in his visions, the freedom that involved them soaring overhead, once again unencumbered by the threat of danger.

And now, because he had failed them, they were captive.

"They're going to use the dragons against us. They're going to use the dragons to attack the Asharn, and they will use them to attack the empire. If only they recognized the need to work together, to fight, to destroy the Damhur, we would have the allies we need."

"They won't bring the dragons after the Asharn first."

"How do you know?"

"Though the Asharn have hidden, they have nearly as much experience as the Damhur at understanding and knowing about their abilities. It's different with the empire. Though the fire mages are here, they aren't the kind of power the Damhur fear."

"Don't tell Azithan that."

"If your fire mage friend were to have been paying attention, he would have known that already. There's no reason for the Damhur to fear them. They've already proven that they can overpower anything that the empire's fire mages can accomplish."

Fes couldn't even argue with that. It was the same thing that he had been saying to Azithan, and yet Azithan remained steadfast in his belief that the fire mages would be able to manage an attack by the Damhur.

"If we can't count on the Asharn, we still need to find allies," Fes said. He glanced at Jayell. "Which means that we go to Toulen as I was initially planning."

"What is in Toulen?" Arudis asked.

"A type of magic that they have not likely seen before."

"You might be surprised. The Damhur have prepared for this time for centuries. They have been plotting, planning the return of the dragon so that they could conquer."

"Why?"

"Because they view this land as theirs. They believe that they have been kept from something that they were meant to possess."

"We have to destroy them," Fes whispered.

"Fes!" Jayell said.

He glanced over at her, shaking his head. "I don't know that we have any other option. We need to destroy them, to end the threat, and if we don't, the dragons will never be free."

"The dragons will never be free," Arudis said.

"But they will be. Once we stop the Damhur—"

"Do you believe that the Damhur are the only powers in the world that seek to control the dragons?"

"Who else in the world could threaten us?"

"The world is much larger than you or I can know, Fezarn. Perhaps the dragons would know otherwise, and if we were able to sit alongside them as our people once did, we might be granted that understanding, but it is not to be."

She breathed out and disappeared among the buildings, fading into shadows.

Fes watched her go before turning to Jayell. "I had thought that we would be able to ask the Asharn to assist us. Maybe they still can."

"If Arudis doesn't believe that they will be of much help, I'm not sure that they can be counted upon for something of urgency like this."

"They came after the dragons once before." That had been the only reason the Asharn had come to the empire. If they were willing to come after the dragons once, couldn't they be compelled to do so again? "Maybe I'm wrong in thinking that Toulen is the logical next step. Maybe I do need to head across the sea, to see if there's any way that we can convince the Asharn to assist us."

"How do you plan on getting there?"

"The empire has ships."

"By the time you make the crossing, the dragons will be—"

"Trained," Fes whispered. The same way that the Deshazl were trained. The same way that they had once intended to train him. And if the effect of the Calling on the dragons was the same as it was on him, there wouldn't be any way for them to resist it. They might want to, and if he were closer, it was possible that he would be able to detect them opposing the effect of the Calling, but so far, he hadn't recognized anything. There was no sense of the dragons. Not that he had much of one before their Calling. Even when they had been in the forest, his sense of them had been vague and faint.

"Why don't we go and talk to Azithan," Jayell suggested.

Fes allowed himself to be guided, and as they wandered through the forest, his mind raced, working through all of the various possibilities. The empire had fire mages, but with the Deshazl, the Damhur would be able to cut through that magic. If they reached the Asharn—something that wasn't a given—then it was a matter of trying to convince them to work with them, and if that failed, he would have wasted a journey. What they needed instead was an ally who would provide an element of surprise, much the way that he had intended when he first planned. That meant going to Toulen.

The Damhur wouldn't expect the totems. They

couldn't. If they knew of that sort of magic, wouldn't they have attempted to use it by now? The fact that Fes hadn't seen anything like that from the Damhur suggested that they weren't aware of it. He had seen how effective that power could be against fire mages, and magic like that wouldn't be dependent upon avoiding someone able to Call him.

By the time they reached the edge of the forest, he had come to a decision. They headed into the village, and he noted the faces of the Deshazl. Most wore dejected looks, so he tried to keep a positive expression, not wanting them to think that he was defeated, but he wasn't sure how effective he was at managing that.

"Look at all of them," he whispered to Jayell. "They all seem to know what happened to the dragons."

"They would have seen them flying," she said.

"I wish that I would have had more time to watch that."

"You will. We'll save them."

He smiled at her. He appreciated the confidence that she exuded, though he wasn't sure it was quite fitting. Jayell had never felt the effect of the Calling, had never known that utter hopelessness of her body betraying her, the inability to move, to fight back, only her mind free—and that only as much as the Damhur wanted them to be. When he had faced Elsanelle, she had wanted him to know exactly what he was doing.

That had been the worst of it.

Would they treat the dragons the same way?

He had to hope that the dragons wouldn't be used quite so brutally and that there wouldn't be such a personal vengeance against them, not the way there had been with Fes, but it was possible that the Damhur would be angry at the fact that they had been forced across the sea to capture the dragons.

Near the edge of the village, he found Azithan and Jaken. They had their horses saddled, and he watched for a moment.

"Where are you going?" Fes asked.

Azithan paused. Power radiated from him, a constant draw of fire magic. "We are returning to the capital, Fezarn. It would be beneficial if you would accompany us."

"Why?"

"We have already had this discussion. You could serve the emperor, and you would provide much value to him."

"I intend to go after the dragons."

"There is nothing to go after, Fezarn. They have been Called, and now is the time for the empire to marshal its forces."

"By marshaling its forces, you intend to go to Javoor and face the Damhur?"

"We need to protect the empire," Jaken said.

"Saving the dragons will do that. Arudis said that they

will most likely train the dragons and then bring them to attack the empire."

"She can't know that," Jaken said.

"She is from Javoor. She knows."

Jaken glared at him before turning away. Why such anger?

"Azithan, think about it. They don't fear the empire. They've already brought their people over here and have openly attacked. We haven't had to fight the same way the Asharn have. They won't bring the dragons against the Asharn. They will bring them against us, reduce the empire to nothing more than debris, and then they will go after the Asharn."

Fes could almost see it in his mind. Two dragons would give them more than enough strength to overwhelm the defenses of the empire, and with that power, they could soar from above, diving with flames blasting from their nostrils, leveling entire cities. During the ancient war, the Deshazl had worked with the empire, helping protect the dragons, but even that was not possible now. Where were the Deshazl?

Fes's gaze drifted to the encampment behind him, the village filled with as many Deshazl as the empire had gathered in one place. Few, if any of them, really understood the extent of their powers. Even Fes couldn't make that claim. Arudis might be able to argue that she fully understood her magic, but her abilities paled in comparison to the Asharn.

What they needed to do was provide a reason for the Asharn to help.

"What do you propose, Fezarn?"

"We need to go to Toulen."

"Toulen will not help the empire. Those wounds are far too fresh."

"If we can convince them of the danger, we might be able to find the ally that we need. Besides, there's someone there who should be able to help."

"Why is it that you are convinced this person would be able to help us?"

"Because I saved her. I helped her people. I prevented the loss of something they considered sacred."

Azithan glanced at Jaken. "It might not work."

"It can't hurt, can it?"

"My father won't be pleased," Jaken said.

"If you and Azithan agree, I doubt the emperor will have anything to say about it."

"You'd be surprised," Jaken said. "He has been unhappy that we have spent as much time as we have out here. The reason that he has allowed it was because he believed that we would potentially benefit from working with the dragons, possibly training them."

"Training?" Fes asked, arching a brow.

"Not like that," Azithan said, stepping forward.

Fes shook his head. "What other choice do we have? To defeat the Damhur, we need allies. More than that, we need something that will surprise them."

"Why will Toulen surprise them?" Azithan asked, watching Fes.

"I'm not sure that you would believe if I told you. If you agree, I will make sure that you see it and have every opportunity to fully understand what it is and what it means."

"Fezarn—"

Fes shook his head. "I won't betray their secret if you don't go."

"Even if it would compromise the empire?"

"First off, I don't think that it would compromise the empire, and second, I've already told you that I don't necessarily serve the empire."

"What do you serve, then?" Jaken asked.

It was such a simple question, and it was one that he would have been able to answer easily had he been asked only a year ago. At that time, he would have answered that he served himself. Jobs were taken based on how much money they would earn him, and little other reason. Now he still cared about money, though he wasn't sure where he would even spend it, but he cared more about the connection that he'd made. There were the Deshazl, people that he felt an obligation toward, but it was more than that.

The dragons protect the Deshazl, and the Deshazl protect the dragons.

"I serve the dragons."

Azithan studied him for a long moment, and in that time, Fes wondered if he would refuse to go with him. If he did, Fes intended to go off on his own, though he would much rather have the empire's blessing. Jaken continued to watch, saying nothing, as if waiting for Azithan to speak.

Finally, the fire mage said, "It appears that we are to head to Toulen, then."

Fes glanced over at Jayell and noticed that she wore a troubled expression. He didn't give himself the opportunity to wonder why that would be. There were preparations to make and a journey to undertake. Reaching Toulen wouldn't take that long, but they needed to go as quickly as possible.

The dragons needed him.

CHAPTER EIGHT

They were a unique party. A pair of fire mages and two Deshazl, all of them traveling across the empire, and strangely, Fes found them to be comforting. Every so often, he would glance over at Jayell, looking to see if she would meet his eyes, but she never did. She kept her gaze fixed on Azithan, mostly because he continued to teach her, demonstrating various spells as they traveled, and she didn't want to miss a single one.

Jaken wore the colors of the empire, the maroon and gold, and carried two dragonglass swords strapped to his side. His back was stiff and straight, and he sat upon the horse in a way that showed his comfort and familiarity with traveling this way. He had been mostly silent, willing to accompany them, but not much more. Fes had been surprised when Jaken had agreed to come, but after what happened with the dragons, that shouldn't have surprised him.

Everyone wanted to stop the Damhur. It was why the emperor had been willing to allow this trip in the first place. Without allies, they wouldn't be enough. Even with Toulen, they still might not be enough. The only other possibility was going to Asharn, but would they even help? He had no idea how to even reach Asharn.

"Would you like to practice resisting the Calling?" Fes asked.

It wasn't that he felt that he was some sort of expert, but he did have experience that Jaken lacked, and with Azithan along with them, there was the possibility that they could practice, though Azithan was not nearly as skilled at Calling as the Damhur.

Jaken merely shook his head. "There is no need."

Fes sighed. He wanted to engage Jaken, trying to get him to be a more substantial part of what they were doing, knowing that for him to recognize the necessity of what it was they did, he would have to be a part of it. So far, Fes wasn't sure that he had succeeded.

"No need because we haven't crossed the sea?"

Jaken looked over at him. "You really intend to do that?"

Fes shrugged. What choice was there but to follow the Damhur back across the sea?

Strangely, it might be something of a return home.

Now that he knew the truth of his heritage, and now that he understood why his parents had been traveling, there was a part of him that wanted to know what they had escaped from. Even understanding the dangers, he still thought that he needed to know. He felt as if he owed them that.

"When we get the help we need, I intend to make the crossing."

"And then what?" Jaken asked.

Fes noticed that Azithan and Jayell were watching them. They had been working on a spell, using one of the several dozen dragon pearls they carried with them, and had halted long enough to watch Fes and Jaken.

"I don't know. I think that I'll figure that out when we get there."

"That's no sort of plan," Jaken said. "What you intend to do involves traveling to a foreign land, where you know nothing about the people or the customs, and doing what? Do you think that you can end the war that has been raging there for the last few centuries?"

"It's been longer than centuries," Fes said softly. As far as he knew, the war had been raging for over a thousand years, a battle between the Damhur who sought to control the dragons and the Deshazl and the Asharn, people who shared the same heritage as Fes. They might not be Deshazl, not anymore, but there was still something about the Asharn that made them similar.

Now that the Damhur had claimed the two dragons, there might not be any way of stopping them completely, but he had to try.

"I'm here to make sure that you don't end up dead."

"I didn't realize that I matter that much to the empire."

Jaken frowned at him. "You didn't realize? You have a connection to one of the two known remaining dragons. How would you not have known that you are important to the empire?"

Fes stared into the distance. The massive river that spread between the empire and Toulen raged in front of them, there in the distance. It had been months since he'd been there, months since he had helped rescue Indra from Elizabeth and her attack, and months since he had begun to understand the way she used the golem and the totems that she crafted, filling them with power from her dragon blessing.

That was the reason he came.

Jaken might not believe in the power of the dragon blessing, but Fes did. He had seen it firsthand, and he recognized just how potent that magic could be. To stop the Damhur, they needed something unexpected. To save the dragons, they needed allies. The dragon blessing—and the totems the people of Toulen could craft—might be able to help with both. A surprise attack like that might turn the tide and allow them to rescue the dragons.

An army of totems, all fighting on their behalf, might be exactly what they needed.

They reached the bridge crossing into Toulen. The river served as a barrier between the empire and Toulen, and there were only a few places that were safe to cross. Jaken had guided them, leading them toward the southerly bridge, one of the most accessible points to reach from the capital, and Fes looked out at the bridge. From this vantage, the stone archway sweeping up and over the water had a majestic appearance. A dozen guards stood on the empire's shore, blocking access. Even without Jaken and Azithan, Fes wouldn't have worried about crossing. Jayell would have been able to get them access, and she would have been able to use magic to subdue the guards long enough for them to cross. With Jaken, they essentially had the empire's permission.

After they were over, reaching the Toulen lands, Fes glanced over at him. "Does it ever bother you that you can't reveal who you are?"

"There's no need for me to reveal who I am, not yet. If my father falls..."

"If your father falls, who will know that you are his son?"

Jaken nodded at Azithan before saying to Fes. "He knows."

"What happens if he falls, too?"

Jaken cocked his brow. "Do you intend to eliminate both of us on this journey?"

Fes shrugged. "If that's what it will take for me to rule." When Jaken frowned, Fes chuckled. "It's more a concern for the succession planning for the empire."

"You don't need to fear, Fezarn," Azithan said. "The line of succession is well documented. In the event that the emperor passes, it will be unsealed, and all will know that Jaken is his son."

Fes studied Azithan for a moment, saying nothing. What would happen if both Jaken and the emperor fell? Who would lead the empire then?

In the thousand years of the empire's existence, it had passed down through the generations, staying within the emperor's family. In all that time, there had been no concern for succession, especially once the empire had stabilized and once war no longer pressed upon them. With what they planned—at least, what Fes planned—there was a very real possibility that war would return to the empire.

Then again, it already had. Not only had the Damhur come to the empire, Calling Deshazl, thinking to enslave them as they marched toward the fire mage temple to resurrect a long lost fire mage, but the Asharn had come, attacking in the palace. They hadn't known the reason for the attack, but that didn't change the fact that the

Deshazl weren't necessarily safe in the empire, not as they once had believed themselves to be.

They continued riding, and the landscape around them began to change, the lush grasslands of the empire sweeping out and becoming the flat expanse of the plains of Toulen. Fes had never visited Toulen from this direction, and coming at it from the south surprised him with how beautiful the scenery was. Farther north, the lands of Toulen changed, more wild and dry, the arid lands not nearly as welcoming as those of the empire.

Would he have felt that way had he lived here his entire life?

He only viewed the empire as welcoming because it was all he knew. Had he been raised in Javoor, forced to serve the Damhur, would he have felt that to be his home? Or would he have been like Arudis, always wanting to escape, knowing that there was something else—something more?

He hoped that he would be more like Arudis, but Fes wasn't sure. It was possible that he wouldn't, and even though he thought himself stronger—and certainly strong enough to resist—what if he wasn't?

Azithan raised a hand, pointing in the distance.

"What is it?" Jaken asked.

Fes stared. He had sharp eyesight—he always had. He suspected it came from his Deshazl heritage, though he wasn't entirely certain whether that was the case or not.

As he stared, he saw two people standing watch in the distance.

"Are you certain this is what you want to do?" Azithan asked Fes.

"We need their help. If we intend to take on the Damhur and find a way of stopping the attacks, we will need allies."

"And you would have them for allies simply because they can't be Called?" Jaken asked.

Fes smiled. "Something like that."

He started forward, galloping toward the two figures standing watch in the distance. He had been somewhat surprised that there were no soldiers on the other side of the bridge leading to Toulen, though they had long been at peace with the empire. There would be no reason for them to fear the empire, no reason to keep a watch.

As he rode, he realized something was not quite right. He raised a hand, slowing their approach.

"What is it?" Jayell asked.

Fes stared, and it took a moment before he realized what it was about the figures that unsettled him. They weren't men at all.

"Totems," Fes said.

Azithan pressed his lips together into a tight frown, staring into the distance. Power from a fire mage spell built off him and swept away, leading toward the distant totems. His jaw clenched for a moment. "Why would they have totems of that size here?"

Azithan had never seen the totems working quite the same way as Fes had, and he had no experience with knowing that the totems exerted a certain type of power, power that was not easily replicated by the rest of the empire, even by fire mages. It was possible that they wouldn't be able to pass through here, not if the totems chose to resist them. He would need to find whoever had the dragon blessing and controlled them.

"We need to be careful," Fes said.

"They are sculptures," Azithan said. "The people of Toulen have always believed in the power of their sculptures, using them as a way to connect to their gods."

Fes shook his head. "These are more than sculptures."

He glanced at Jayell. Should they veer off? It might be safer to take a different approach, but if they did, he wasn't confident where they would go. From what Jaken had said, this was the easiest way to reach the nearest Toulen city, and from here, he could find Indra and ask for her assistance. Besides, the presence of these two massive totems gave him hope that perhaps she was closer than he had realized. If they were here, he had to hope that perhaps she was responsible for their creation.

"Be on alert," Fes said.

Azithan frowned at him. "On alert for what?"

Fes shook his head. "Just be on alert."

They continued riding, but they moved more carefully, and Fes stayed in the lead. He reached deep within him, drawing upon the Deshazl power, pushing it out and around him into something like a barrier. It wasn't all that long ago that he could scarcely believe that he was Deshazl and had the potential to reach for more power than he ever considered possible. In that time since discovering his connection, he had not only learned how to use that magic, he had begun to master it.

The totems loomed nearer.

They were massive, easily nearly twice as tall as Fes, and they towered over them. Both had strange features, blunted and rough, and Fes knew that was significant, though he didn't quite understand why. A sense of power emanated from them. Fes never had a similar sense with the totems before, though the ones that he had been exposed to had always been much smaller. These were on a different scale altogether.

"Do you think that she made these?" Jayell whispered.

"It's hard for me to tell."

"But their faces," she said, nodding at them.

"What is it about their faces?" Azithan asked.

"Look at them."

Fes studied the faces of the totems, giving them his full attention. Why would Jayell have remarked on that?

"They look like—" Azithan began.

"Him," Jaken said.

Fes blinked, and he realized that what Jaken said was true. The two totems *did* look something like him, if rough and somewhat obliquely.

There was no question. If they resembled him, then it meant that Indra had been responsible for their creation. But why sculpt them to look like him?

Fes knew very little about totems other than the fact that there was power stored within them, power that came from the person who created them. He didn't understand the way that power was unleashed and didn't know how she managed to free them, to allow the totems to move on their own, though he suspected that the magic was similar to what he had, if only because of the proximity to the empire.

Fes remained cautious, worried that if he moved too closely, the totems might attack. Even though they shared a passing resemblance to him, that didn't mean they wouldn't view him as a threat. And maybe Indra had carved them in such a way because she regarded *him* as a threat. He knew their secrets and he had more than a little experience with Toulen, so it was possible that she had done so in a way that would allow her to protect those secrets, trying to keep them from Fes.

"Go on," Jayell said.

"I'm nervous," he said.

"What if she meant them as a way to allow you to pass?"

Fes stared, uncertain. “And if that’s not the case?”

“What are you worried about?” Azithan asked, looking from Jayell to Fes. “They are sculptures, nothing more.”

As he said it, the nearest totem started to tremble. Legs split off from either side, the stone seeming to part, and arms withdrew from the center portion. Within the totem’s hands, a pair of makeshift stone daggers appeared.

There was no question that was intended to represent Fes.

Azithan pulsed out with a fire mage spell, and Fes lunged forward, unsheathing his sword in a fluid movement, slashing through the spell, trying to unravel it before it had a chance to strike the totem.

“No!”

Azithan glanced back at him. “Fes?”

He turned away from Azithan, looking at the nearest totem, watching him. “We mean you no harm,” he said, holding his hands up. He didn’t know whether the totem would even understand him, but on the off chance that it did, Fes wanted to ensure that the totems didn’t attack. Even with Azithan and Jayell, the odds of surviving an attack from these massive stone totems would be small.

The other totem began to tremble and, much like the first, arms and legs separated from the stone, and it stood before them, blocking their movement.

In the other totem's hands was a long, curved blade.

"I would seek passage to your mistress," Fes said.

The totems stopped moving. They didn't seem as if they were going to attack, which gave Fes a moment to relax.

"Maybe they will—"

He didn't have a chance to finish.

The first totem started toward them, sweeping the stone daggers down.

Fes reacted, slamming up a Deshazl magic barrier and pushing outward with it. The totem was thrown back.

The totem with the sword turned toward him, and Fes attempted to explode against him, but either his magic was weaker, or the totem had prepared for the possibility of Fes attacking. The magic reached the totem and slipped around it, practically harmless.

"Why are they attacking?" Azithan asked.

"I don't know."

"*How* are they attacking?"

"That's a long story. We have to settle them if we can."

Azithan pulled a dragon pearl from his pocket. It glowed a bright orange and yellow, and power pulsed from it.

"Don't try to harm them. Just try to restrict them from following us," Fes said.

"Don't *harm* them?" Azithan asked, frowning at him.

"If they're controlled by the person I think, you can't harm them. They could be useful."

"*This* is why we came here?" Azithan asked.

Fes looked at the two massive totems, still amazed by the sheer enormity of them. "Not necessarily these, but this type of magic."

"We will have to talk about you keeping secrets from me when this is over," Azithan said.

Fes laughed bitterly. "I think we have both kept secrets from each other, Azithan."

The fire mage pressed out with his spell and Fes traced the effect, watching how he wrapped it around the nearest totem. The massive figure stopped moving but struggled against the magical bindings Azithan placed.

As he watched, Jayell did much the same, holding the other totem in place. "We should go," she said.

"Are you certain this is safe?" Azithan asked. There was a strain in his voice and tension at the corners of his eyes. How much was it taking from him to hold this? How long would he be able to maintain his connection to it? If they rode off, circling around the totems, there was a possibility that the totems would chase them, and Fes had already seen how quickly stone totems could move, fast enough that it might be more than they could outrun.

"We just have to reach Indra," Fes said.

He looked over and saw that Jaken had unsheathed his sword, but he stared at the totems almost helplessly. It was a feeling Fes completely understood. Facing a totem like this with his sword was useless. Fes had tried attacking a golem with his dragonglass sword, and it had been the only thing his sword had failed against.

"We should hurry," Azithan said. "I don't know how long I can maintain this."

Fes turned his horse, and they quickly rode around the totems, circling to the path behind them. They kicked their horses to a gallop and raced ahead, hurrying into Toulen. They hadn't ridden for long when Fes heard Azithan let out a breath in a sigh. Somehow, Jayell managed to last a little longer, but not much.

"Now we will have to see how well we can outrun them," Azithan said.

The ground began to tremble, shaking with each step of the totems. It shook, a thunderous sound, and vibrated deep within Fes.

They wouldn't have much time at all.

He glanced back and wished that he hadn't. The totems chased them, much closer than they should be.

When he turned his gaze back in front of him, he pulled the reins of his horse, stopping them suddenly.

"What is it?" Jayell asked.

Fes nodded. Another pair of totems approached in the distance.

They were trapped between them.

CHAPTER NINE

"I know you want to speak to your friend, but perhaps we need to head north," Azithan said.

Fes glanced to the north, squinting despite the gray sky. The dark swath of green that was the forest stretched in the distance, though not near enough for them to reach safety. Even if they did, he didn't think that the totems would be hindered by the presence of trees.

"I don't know that it matters," he said.

"What do you want us to do?" Jayell asked.

His heart hammered and he tried to reach for his Deshazl magic, but even if he were able to reach it, it wouldn't do much good, not against the power that radiated from these totems.

The other possibility meant submitting to them, but

would they allow them to submit, especially now that they had already attacked?

"I'm sorry," Fes said. "Maybe we should have—"

One of the totems jumped, landing in front of them.

Fes blinked as he looked up at the totem, noticing that like the other two, this one resembled him, however distantly.

Once again, he wondered why Indra would use his likeness to carve the totems.

The totem quietly stood, blocking their way. It didn't attack, and for that, Fes was thankful. If it had attacked, he wasn't sure there was anything that he or the others would have been able to do to counter it.

When the other totem approached from the west, it stopped next to the first. Much like the other, it had a face that reminded Fes of his own, though the features were a little sharper than the other two. This totem carried no weapons and stood with empty hands in front of it. Fes didn't think that mattered. Even empty-handed, the totem would be dangerous and would pose a risk to them, especially if they were to try to attack.

And then the two pursuers joined them. They were trapped between them, the four totems making a circle around them, holding the four of them inside.

"Well, this is an interesting predicament," Azithan said with a dark laugh.

"Why is it that you seem amused?" Fes asked.

Azithan surveyed the totems. “Here I am, surrounded by four stone Fezarns, my magic useless against them. A part of me thinks this should have happened long ago.”

“Mage?” Jaken said.

“If they intended to harm us, they would’ve done so already,” Azithan said. “These totems are incredibly powerful. That much I can feel, even if I can’t deduce anything more about them. And if they don’t mean us any harm, then they have captured us for a reason.” He glanced over at Fes. “I suspect that reason is tied to you, Fezarn.”

Fes looked up at the ring of totems. They stood motionless, but each time the horses shifted position, the totems seemed ready to move. Fes wasn’t sure why he felt that way, but he felt it deep within himself. The totems were prepared to block him from going anywhere.

As Azithan said, they were trapped.

And if they were trapped, it meant that Indra—or whoever intended to hold them—would be here soon. Fes had to believe that it was Indra, especially since they bore his likeness.

“How long do you think we need to wait?” Jayell asked.

“As long as it takes,” Azithan said.

They sat on their horses, all of them staring out at the totems, saying nothing. Long moments passed, and the totems didn’t move and made no attempt to attack, which let Fes settle into a sort of relaxed tension. He was able to study the totems, and he marveled at the detail on them. They were different than the other totems that Indra had made. Fes still wondered why she had chosen his likeness. Knowing her as he did—which, admittedly, wasn't all that well—he would have expected her to make something else that would be more powerful, similar to the totems of hers that he still carried. Those had been useful—and powerful.

The sun began to set, and all the while, they remained stuck in the middle, unable to go anywhere. Fes remained seated on the horse, shifting from side to side, trying to find a comfortable position. As he did, he continued to study the totems but saw nothing else about them that would help him understand *why* Indra would have carved them.

Azithan reached into the saddlebags of his horse and pulled out a strip of jerky that he began to chew on. The longer that they were here, the more relaxed Azithan had become, and now seemed almost amused rather than worried. Every so often, he turned, looking at the other totems, before turning his attention to the next, and then the next. What was the fire mage learning from them?

As dusk grew thick, something changed.

The totems no longer took on the appearance of a man and seemed little more than a sculpture again.

"Did you see that?" Jayell asked.

Fes nodded.

"What does it mean?"

"I suspect it means that she's close."

At least, he hoped that Indra was close and that the sudden change to the totems meant that she had come to find out why the totems had circled him.

They didn't have to wait too much longer, as a line of riders approached. Fes shifted his horse so that he could see out and count the people approaching. There were only a half dozen or so, certainly not enough to worry about, but then, with the totems, the numbers were much more tilted in favor of the people of Toulen. He couldn't see any sign of Indra, which made him uncomfortable. If she was responsible for the totems, then he wanted her present so that they could be freed.

"I don't see her," Jayell said.

Fes shook his head. "I don't either."

"What if it's not her?"

Fes frowned. How could it not be her who had made these totems?

"It's her. It has to be," he said.

As the riders approached, Fes stared. A spell built, radiating from Azithan, but not going beyond the ring of totems. He held it at the ready, practically prepared to assault the Toulen riders, but if he did, Fes suspected the totems would attack. So far, they had been lucky that the totems had not, but how long would that luck remain?

"Who dares to come to our lands from the empire?" a voice called out. It was a deep voice, and not familiar.

Azithan shifted and opened his mouth as if he were to answer, but Fes set his hand on his arm. "Let me speak."

Azithan frowned at him. He regarded Fes for a moment before nodding.

"I am Fezarn. I have—"

As he said his name, the totems shifted. It happened fast—almost as fast as the blink of an eye—and when they did, they created an opening, one that was large enough for his horse to go through. Something warned Fes that he was not the person intended to travel through the line of totems.

One of the Toulen riders approached.

With a wave of her hand, the totems moved back into place. "Indra?" Fes whispered.

She looked nothing like the young girl he had met during his travels. This was a young woman coming into her own. She was dressed in traditional brightly colored Toulen attire, and her hair was braided, hanging down to the middle of her back, reminding him somewhat of the Damhur. There was a hard edge to her eyes that had never been there before.

"Fes? Why have you come?" She looked at the others with him, her gaze settling on Azithan and then on Jaken before looking at Jayell and Fes. "And traveling with men of the empire."

"For help," Fes said.

She cocked her head to the side, studying him. "What kind of help?"

"The kind of help that I suspect only the people of Toulen would be able to offer." He looked up at the totems, his gaze sweeping around them before settling back onto Indra.

"Fes, I don't think that is anything we can help you with."

"You don't even know what I'm asking."

Indra glanced at the totems before looking back at Fes. "I suspect you're asking to use my dragon blessing."

Fes studied Indra for a long moment. It had been a long time since he'd seen her, almost too long, and he had begun to think that perhaps his experience with her had been imagined. Maybe it had been one-sided. From the moment he'd met her, there had been a desire to protect her. Then again, Fes struggled with that, feeling as if he needed to protect people who didn't really need his protection. That came from losing his parents at such a young age combined with a need to protect his brother—and failing.

That girl he had wanted to protect was gone. In her place was a commanding young woman, someone who had grown accustomed to leading, and why wouldn't she? Indra was gifted with the dragon blessing, and she had already demonstrated how powerful she was with that ability. While Fes didn't know how many others in the Toulen lands could animate totems, he suspected that Indra and her ability were, if not unique, at least potent, perhaps more than others.

And she accused him of wanting to use her dragon blessing.

It wasn't that he wanted to use it so much as he thought that he needed allies, and the kind of power that Indra had access to was something that the Damhur wouldn't expect. In that case, maybe he didn't need to use her dragon blessing.

"Fine. I do want to use it, but it's not for the reason that you think."

Indra cocked her head to the side, watching him for a moment. "And what reason is that?"

Fes smiled. "You accused me of coming here with members of the empire, and I have, but not for the reason that you believe."

"They are fire mages," Indra said.

"And I'm Deshazl."

Indra frowned as he said that, crossing her arms over her chest. "Do you finally understand what that means, Fezarn?"

Her words were accented, and she said his name in a way that rolled off her tongue, a familiarity to it. Had she known the meaning behind his name all along? He didn't think that she had, but given the way she spoke his name, he had to wonder if perhaps she had. And if she had, why wouldn't she have told him?

Maybe because there wasn't anything to tell him. He shared a name with an ancient dragon, and because of that, he was… what?

It meant nothing, other than the fact that his parents had known the names of dragons and had chosen to name him after one. How many children of the Damhur Deshazl were similarly named?

The way that she watched him told Fes that she understood more about the Deshazl than he had expected.

Indra had always been precocious, and her connection to her magic had been something that Fes didn't completely understand. They were useful skills, and he had not ever met anyone quite like her, but had she learned more about the Deshazl since meeting him?

"I have met someone who helped me understand who I am," Fes said.

Indra took stock of him. "When you came to us, my father recognized the power within you. Are you aware of that?"

Fes smiled. When he had come upon them while traveling, it had been chance, little more than that. He had hoped for a night of safety, and staying with Indra and her father had granted him that. Somehow, they had seen something about him, though they had never really explained it. That evening, he had sat with Indra, watching as she carved her totems, somehow knowing that there was more to the totems than what she let on. Even now, Fes wasn't sure how he knew that, only that he did.

"I think your father wanted me to help you."

"My father wanted to help himself," Indra said.

"We don't know that," Fes said.

Indra smiled. "Don't we? I've told you why we came to the empire. Had we not, and had my father not had me create the golem, would it have been necessary for you to pursue me across the entirety of the empire?"

"Had I not, I wouldn't have met Jayell. I doubt I would've learned about my true connection to the Deshazl. I doubt that I ever would have seen a dragon."

Jayell gasped. He should have warned her that he might have to reveal that secret, but if nothing else, that was the way he was going to draw Indra into this. She would need to know what he had seen and would need to understand why he thought it necessary to come here. A dragon was reason to do so. It was certainly reason enough to risk the totems, regardless of how much he knew about how powerful they were.

"A dragon?"

Fes nodded slowly. "The dragons have returned."

Indra glanced at the others with him before her gaze settled back on Fes. "The empire has dragons?"

"The empire doesn't *have* them. Dragons are free, as they always were. The empire never attacked the dragons; that was a story told to prevent others from attacking. They were allies."

"Fes—"

"I know that it's difficult to believe, but I've experienced enough that I believe it. The dragons worked with the empire, and they willingly allowed their bones to be used by the fire mages." He glanced from Indra to the space beyond her, trying to count how many of the Toulen warriors she had along with her. Enough that she was safe. Enough that even if anything happened to her while she was within the ring of the totems, it would be difficult, if not impossible, for the rest of them to escape.

"That sounds crazy," Indra said.

Fes laughed. "I know how it sounds, but I also know the truth. It burns within me." He raised his hands and pressed them out, pulsing a hint of power through himself and pushing it gently upon Indra. It wasn't enough to do any harm, just enough to draw attention and to indicate to her that he had some control over his abilities.

Her eyes widened slightly. "Could you really understand your abilities?"

Fes smiled and nodded.

Indra looked at him, turned to the others, and then stepped back out from between the totems.

"Indra?"

"Fes… I'm afraid that what you said is dangerous."

"I know it's dangerous. I know about the Damhur. I know about the Asharn. They've attacked. There is so much that we need to talk about, and so much that I need your help with."

He didn't know whether she was aware of the Damhur or Asharn, but the sudden change in her demeanor troubled him. How much had the people of Toulen remembered? Could it be that they had never forgotten about the old attacks? And if they hadn't, did that mean that Indra knew what those titles meant, too?

"I'm sorry."

"Sorry for what?" Fes asked.

Indra turned away and climbed atop her horse, turning the line of Toulen warriors away from them. As they rode off, Fes could only stare after her, wondering what had just happened.

"Fes?"

He pulled his attention away from watching the band disappear and looked over at Jayell. "What is it?"

"Look," she said.

The totems had begun to move closer.

CHAPTER TEN

Fes pushed off with his connection to the Deshazl magic, surging against the totems. Had they wanted to destroy him and the others, they could have done so easily, and the fact that they didn't attack told him that there was something he was missing. What was it? It wasn't merely that Indra had chosen not to attack, though that was at least a part of it. Why had she ridden off?

Something had changed when he had told her what he'd known.

Could the Damhur already have reached Toulen? If they had, then it was fear that had forced her hand. Knowing Indra, she wasn't afraid of much, if anything.

Why else would she have turned away? Why else would she have acted the way that she had?

"What do you suggest that we do?" Fes asked Azithan.

The fire mage studied the totems. "I've been considering them since they first placed themselves around us. It seems as if they are autonomous, yet I think they remain controlled by someone."

"And I thought they were controlled by Indra," Fes said.

"You don't anymore?" Azithan asked.

Fes shrugged. "I don't know what to think. She left us before this attack, so I'm not sure if there's a reason behind that or if she has been turned by the Damhur."

"And if she has been turned?" Azithan asked.

Fes already knew the answer to that. If she had been turned by the Damhur, then he owed it to her to do whatever he could to offer his help, didn't he? Indra was his friend, and because of her, he had been through so much. He had promised to save her, to do as much as he could to protect her. What would it say about him if he abandoned that promise now, after everything that they'd been through together?

"I have to follow her," Fes said.

"Fes—" Jayell started.

He shook his head. "I know that you don't want me to and that you'll think that I'm foolish to try, but I owe it to her. She's my friend, and if she's doing this, then there has to be a reason."

"What if the reason is that they view you as a threat?" she asked.

"I don't think Indra sees me as a threat, which means that there's someone else here who does."

The idea of facing off with another powerful Damhur troubled him, but now that they had the dragons, he had expected them to have returned over the sea. If not… he didn't know what to make of it, other than he couldn't leave Toulen like this.

If it were one of the Trivent again, he had barely survived the last time. There was a key to protecting himself during a Calling, but it required a strength he didn't have alone. Without the dragons, Fes might not be able to withstand another.

And with Jaken traveling along with him, Fes was certain it was more than what the head of the Dragon Guard could withstand. He still needed training, and though he was close to beginning to understand his Deshazl abilities, there were gaps in his knowledge, and the largest of them was his ability to resist a Calling. During the travel from the Deshazl camp, he and Azithan had been working, trying to train him so that he could ignore the effect of the Calling, adding to what Arudis had taught him, but Azithan didn't have nearly the power or seductive quality that the women of the Damhur did. Their ability to perform a Calling was far more exquisite than anything that Azithan could attempt. Without having the opportunity to experience that—and resist it—how could he know what he might need to do?

He turned his attention to the nearest of the totems. Somehow, he had to find a way free, and though he didn't know what that might involve, it would require that he somehow stop the totems.

Would he have to destroy them to do so?

He didn't like the idea of destroying them. Not only because they resembled him, but because these totems could be used to defend against the Damhur. Wasn't that reason enough?

It might not even be possible to destroy them, regardless of his desire to do so. They had resisted magic so far, and Fes wouldn't be surprised if anything he threw their way would be overpowered.

Was there a way to steal the power within them?

The Deshazl magic was connected to the Asharn. What if Toulen magic was somehow connected to the Damhur? It was something he hadn't considered before, but now that he did, he wondered if that could be the case.

The totems were getting closer.

He would have to make some move, and if he didn't, he ran the risk of the totems entirely encroaching upon him.

He had to admit that the magic had some similarities.

The totems were controlled in much the same way as the Deshazl were controlled.

That couldn't be it, could it?

The more that Fes thought about it, the more he began to wonder whether or not it might be possible. It made a particular sort of sense, and if they were connected, then he might even be able to understand why Indra had reacted the way that she had.

Was there anything that he could use of his ability to disrupt the Calling that might help him stop the totems?

"If you're going to do anything, Fezarn, I think you should do it soon."

Fes nodded and started thinking about his connection to the Deshazl magic. The totems didn't have magic, but there had to be something about them that allowed them to be controlled in the same way as Fes or the dragons. There had to be something in the way that Indra had poured herself into the totems.

And maybe now wasn't the time to think about that. Now was more the time to figure out how to escape.

"Focus on the ground," he told Azithan.

"The ground?"

"Sink them."

Azithan smiled slightly. He pulled a dragon pearl out of his pocket and began to work his spell, power building from it causing the pearl to start to glow orange and red, colors that seemed to correspond to Azithan's affinity for the dragons. The spell built and the ground started to steam. As it did, the nearest to totems began to sink.

Fes jerked his head around to see Jayell doing something similar. Her magic wasn't nearly as tightly controlled as what Azithan was able to do, but she did have the same amount of power, and she caused the ground to shift, confining the totems.

They squeezed together, trapped between the totems.

"Hurry!" he said.

Azithan shot him a hard look but said nothing.

The power from their fire magic spells built and built, growing increasingly powerful as they focused on the ground rather than the totems, and with each passing moment, the totems sank even deeper into the ground.

And then they stopped moving.

Fes shook. He half expected the totems to reach out, to stab him with the makeshift daggers, but none of them did. It was almost as if sinking into the ground had changed something about them, turning them back into little more than stone.

"A clever idea and one I should have thought of." Azithan calmly placed the dragon pearl back into his pocket and nodded to Jayell, who did the same thing.

Fes studied the totems and then motioned for them to follow as they squeezed between the widest section. As close as the totems had begun to force them, there wasn't much room, and they scraped over the stone. As they did,

Fes had a concern that the totems might awaken again, and if they did, they would grab at him, pulling him back, but it didn't happen.

When they were outside the ring of totems, Fes stood staring at them. Could he have been right?

It made little difference. It wasn't as if there was anything that he could do to counter that magic, especially if it were focused on the totems rather than on him. If he was right, it meant that perhaps Indra would be able to Call to him.

Did she know that?

And if she did, was that the reason she had forced him away?

"There's that look again," Jayell said.

"What look is that?"

"The look on your face. You have this unsettled expression. What is it?"

Fes stared at the totems. "I... I worry that there's more to the totems and the magic of the people of Toulen then what I believed."

Azithan frowned. "And what is it that you worry about?"

"I worry that perhaps Toulen people and the Damhur are connected in much the same way as the Deshazl and the Asharn."

Azithan's eyes widened slightly. "It would be possible.

If they were here before, it makes sense that they would have left others behind."

"Except we aren't at war with Toulen," Jaken said.

Fes shook his head. "At least not that we know of."

That wasn't necessarily fair of him, but it was possible that the people of Toulen were hiding something from the empire. They had a presumptive peace, and the two nations had always worked together, but what would happen if that changed? What would happen if the people of Toulen used the dragon blessing, and others like Indra, against the empire?

Fes didn't think that they would, but then again, he wasn't from Toulen, and he didn't know whether or not that would happen.

"We need to find her again."

"The last time she came across us, she did that," Azithan said, nodding to the ring of totems. "Are you certain that you want to experience it again?"

Fes studied fire mage. "We need allies, Azithan. If we're going to rescue the dragons, we need someone with power. Besides, she's my friend. Had she wanted to harm me, she would have."

"You say that, but I wonder if it's true. Yes, she could have harmed you had she wanted to, but at the same time, she made it very clear that she doesn't want you to follow her."

"Which is even more reason for me to do so. If she's in trouble, I need to offer whatever protection I can."

As they started off, Jayell grabbed his sleeve. "I don't like this."

Fes shook his head. "I don't like it either. I don't know what choice we have."

"We can go back to the capital, and we can gather troops and go after the dragons—if you still intend to do that. That's how you can prepare."

"The Damhur expect us to attack. And if they don't now, they soon will. We need to surprise them."

"I'm not sure that this is a way of surprising anyone," she said.

Fes smiled. "She doesn't mean us any harm. You were there when we helped her. She owes us."

"She owes us, but do the people of Toulen owe us?"

Fes didn't know. And that bothered him.

CHAPTER ELEVEN

They had been riding for the better part of two days across the Toulen lands. Throughout the ride, he continued to feel the steady pulling sense that seemed to come from the dragons, but he didn't think he should be able to detect them from Toulen, not if the dragons were in Javoor. Unless the Damhur hadn't dragged them off. If that were the case, then maybe there would be a way to help them. There seemed an urgency to what he felt, but strangely, it didn't seem to be coming from where he expected it. Instead, it appeared to be from the direction of the capital.

In that time, they had encountered several other totems, and each time they had, they circled wide around them, not wanting to draw attention. Could their presence mean that they were close to keeping up with Indra?

Or was it merely that the totems represented a way of defending the people of Toulen? The last time Fes had been here, he didn't remember such totems, but that didn't mean that they hadn't been present. He had barely gone inland, forced to try to find some way of getting help, and had only reached one clan, not nearly as many as he would need to encounter to know whether or not there were totems scattered throughout the country.

The sheer number of totems gave him hope that they would be able to use them to help in the attack on the Damhur. With weapons like that, they would be able to rescue the dragons, maybe free more of the captive Deshazl. They could stop the war before it even started.

There had been no sign of Indra.

For that matter, there had been no sign of any of the other people of Toulen. They traveled empty roads, making their way generally westerly.

Near the end of the second day, Azithan motioned for them to halt near a stream. They all climbed out of the saddle, taking long drinks. When he'd had enough, Fes wiped his arm across his mouth, looking out over the Toulen landscape. "It's much larger than I had imagined," he said.

Azithan smiled. "It is large, though I would suspect that it's not nearly as large as the empire."

"Suspect? You don't know?"

"The people of Toulen have not had open borders.

They allow the empire to cross the bridges, and we have sent people into their lands, but we have rarely spent much time in them." Azithan looked around, his mouth curling into a smile. "And perhaps I understand now."

"You didn't know that they had power over the totems?"

"Did you?"

"Not until recently."

"It is an interesting ability, and your comparison to the Damhur intrigues me."

"Because you wonder if you can Call to a totem?"

Azithan's eyes narrowed, and he patted his pocket. "My ability to Call is minimal, weak compared to what we have experienced. I should think that you would know that."

"I know it, but it's still more than others have."

"We each have our own abilities," Azithan said.

Fes studied him. For Azithan to have those abilities meant that he was of a particular descent, though from what Fes had seen, there wasn't anything distinctive about the people of Toulen or the Damhur that fit Azithan's appearance.

Fes reached into his pocket and pulled out the metal totem that Tracen had given him. He kept it with him, little more than a trinket that represented luck, a reminder of his friend. It wasn't all that heavy, especially as it was made of swirls of metal, and he'd carried it long enough that it felt strange not having with him. In some ways, it had replaced his second dagger. Fes held the totem out, staring at it. "When these became popular in the empire, I thought it was because the people recognized something impressive about them."

Azithan motion toward it. "May I?"

Fes nodded. "Of course."

He lifted the totem, holding it in the palm of his hand. He focused, and there came a faint stirring from deep within Fes, almost a sense that he could recognize what was being done to the totem. It resembled a Calling, only it wasn't the same.

Nothing changed for the totem.

"Are you trying to use it?" Fes asked.

"If they are related, I thought that I might…" Azithan smiled and set the totem back on Fes's hand. "Perhaps there is nothing to it. Perhaps I can't use this."

"Maybe not yet. The more you work with it, you might be able to understand how to do so."

"You give me far too much credit, Fezarn."

"I give you the credit that you deserve."

"Deserve. That would be an interesting way of phrasing it. I'm not so sure that I deserve anything. I am a fire mage, and I serve the empire. That is the credit that I deserve. That is the credit I want."

"I wasn't trying to take that from you," Fes said.

Azithan smiled tightly. "I know that you were not,

Fezarn. It's only that…" Azithan looked out over the Toulen horizon, his gaze sweeping over the rolling plains. His eyes softened and wrinkles formed at the corners of them. "Much has changed for me. The power that I understood has shifted beneath me. Perhaps that power will always remain there, but it is different than what I understood." He smiled at Fes. "Then again, I suspect you understand that all too well."

Fes nodded. It was something that he understood. He had grown over the last few months, and during that time, he had changed. The person he was had shifted beneath him, leaving him not only uncertain of himself but unsure about what he was meant to do and not knowing the depths of his power.

He was Deshazl, which meant that he had a connection to the dragons, but what did that connection mean?

The dragons protect Deshazl. The Deshazl protect the dragons.

How could he protect them from the power of the Damhur? Was there anything that could be done? Not if they didn't get help.

More than that, it was possible that the people of the empire didn't *want* to resist an attack by the Damhur. The places where they had attacked had turned over quickly, allowing themselves to be consumed by the Damhur influence, falling to them. If that were the case, what would happen if they reached the capital? How many people would side with the Damhur? How many would view the dragons as something to be controlled?

Fewer would have sided with them had they known the truth. Knowing about the dragons and the empire's role in preserving them might have changed things, but now it was too late. As far as most knew, the empire had exterminated the dragons, causing their downfall.

That lie might be the end of them.

"I worry about what happens if we fail," Fes said softly, breaking the silence that had fallen between them.

"That is a mark of a leader," Azithan said.

"I've never wanted to lead anything. My job is to—"

Azithan shook his head, chuckling. "Your job? Fezarn, your job was to collect for me. You served on behalf of the empire through me, but even that was never your job. You were always your own man, and I doubt that anything I could have ever done would've changed that. Not that I would've tried. Doing so would have demeaned you."

"But you knew I was Deshazl."

"I didn't know, but I certainly suspected."

"How?"

"There are certain telltale signs. The Deshazl have an affinity for dragon relics. You've always had a nose for them, sniffing out where to find the relics, which made you valuable when I still was trying to get a handle on how best to use you."

"That was all I was to you? Someone you could use?"

"I paid you well," Azithan said.

Fes stared. Azithan *had* paid him well, but he had also tested him, and had made no effort to disguise the fact that were Fes to cease being useful, Azithan would cease using him.

"Did you intend for me to reach the dragon heart?"

It was a question that he'd long wondered. At the time, Fes thought he'd gotten the best of Azithan, thinking that he had somehow pulled one over on him, but since then, and since learning that the dragon heart had been brought to the fire mage temple, he wondered whether or not that was even true. Could Azithan have known all along what Fes had done? Could he have somehow manipulated things for him to have done it?

"I find that it's best to be prepared for all possibilities," Azithan said.

"So you didn't know what I would do?"

Power radiated off Azithan as he held onto a spell. "You are unpredictable. Perhaps that's why I'm drawn to you, Fezarn. I don't know quite what you will decide. You have power, yet you are reluctant to use it. You can lead, yet you try to avoid leading. When I sent you off, I didn't know whether you would return the dragon heart to me, or whether you would keep it for yourself. Either way, I was prepared. There were only so many places where you could unload a dragon heart, and I made sure that I had influence at each of them."

"And when I left it with the rebellion?"

"I'll admit that surprised me," Azithan said. "Thankfully I was prepared even there."

"How did you manage to bring the dragon heart to the fire mage temple?"

"Do you think that I have so few connections? I wouldn't be nearly as beneficial to the emperor if I weren't connected."

From the comment, Fes knew that Azithan had no intention of sharing what he had done or how he had done it. And maybe it was best that he didn't know. Perhaps the mystery was better for him to have; it was better to be left with the belief that he was somehow responsible for bringing the dragon back to life. Were it not for him, and were it not for the fact that the dragon heart had made it to the fire mage temple, the dragon would not have been resurrected. And were it not for Fes, had he not opposed the Damhur, the dragon would not have been freed. He should take pride in that, and part of him did. And another part of him felt as if he had not yet done enough. Now that the dragon had been claimed by the Damhur, there was so much more that needed doing.

"What should I do now?" Fes asked.

Azithan only smiled at him. "I think that you are beyond me telling you what you should do. As I said, you are unpredictable. That unpredictability is what makes you dangerous to the Damhur. And it's because of that gift of yours that you may help the empire survive this attack."

Fes met his gaze, thinking through what he had said. He wanted to help the empire survive, and more than that, he wanted to be able to no longer worry about another attack, able to have time where a threat of the Damhur didn't unsettle the dragons. Would there ever come a time like that?

More than anything, he wanted to protect the dragons in a way that they hadn't been when they had last flown freely.

It amazed him that so much seemed bound up in events of the past.

They got back on their horses and continued riding, Fes leading them as they crossed the Toulen lands. The longer they traveled, the more Fes began to wonder whether he was making the right choice. Could this be a mistake? Should he have returned to the capital and to the empire? Regardless of what Arudis had told him about the Asharn, maybe they were the allies they needed.

Jaken remained solemn throughout the ride. Fes began to watch him, wondering if there was something more to his quiet that he needed to know or if it was only the fact that they were in these lands and he felt so out of place. With Jaken, it was difficult to identify. He was accustomed to leading, accustomed to having the Dragon Guard follow him. This took him out of his comfort, but then, perhaps everything that had been happening lately had taken Jaken away from what he considered comfortable.

"How much longer would you have us ride?" Jayell asked.

It had been hours since the last totem, and in that time, they'd lost sight of anybody from Toulen, making him wonder whether he was even taking the right path anymore. The deeper they went into the Toulen lands, the more danger they were under.

"We can camp for the night," Fes said.

"That wasn't the question."

"I know wasn't the question, but I don't know how much farther we need to go. We can't save the dragons alone. We can't even face the Damhur alone." He turned to look at her. "I came to Toulen thinking to get help, to see if we could partner with them and those with the dragon blessing. With as many totems as we've seen, *this* is how we can stop the Damhur."

As they started to settle for the night, making camp, Azithan placed a dragon pearl on the ground and created a spell, power pulsing out from it and sweeping around.

"What happens if they bring the dragons to attack the empire?" she asked softly.

"I'll be there before then."

"And if you don't know?"

It was possible that he wouldn't know. The Damhur could Call the dragons, force them to attack, and retreat. Fes wouldn't even necessarily know.

"That's why we're here," he said.

"How long will you have us continue to look?"

"I don't know."

"We could return. Use the fire mages."

"The Damhur Deshazl would disrupt anything they can do."

"Or the Dragon Guard," she said, indicating Jaken.

"The Damhur Deshazl are as skilled."

"You really are stubborn, Fes."

"I don't have any other choice. It's how I stayed alive on the streets for as long as I did." He watched Azithan for long moments. "What's he doing?"

"He's trying to create a protection," she said.

Fes couldn't detect the effect of the protection, but knowing Azithan, there would probably be some hidden part to it. Was it merely a barrier? He focused on the power coming off the spell and wasn't able to pick up on any sense of a barrier, not the way that he could when Azithan had made others.

"What kind of protection is it?"

Azithan turned toward him. "It is one that will give me an alert. I doubt that I can do much more than that in these lands. We've already seen that my other barriers have been ineffective. This way, I can exert less energy and have a greater effect. If nothing else, it would be beneficial for us to be alerted long before anyone comes upon us."

"How big of an area are you able to stretch?"

Azithan turned to him, smiling. "At least a mile."

Fes blinked. He hadn't expected anything nearly that extensive, and the fact that Azithan could reach out for that far was impressive. He glanced at Jayell, who nodded.

"He's not focusing on anything other than detecting someone else moving."

"Will it pick up on the totems?"

"That's where I feel I have been the most clever," Azithan said. "The totems are a different challenge. They aren't alive, so detecting their movements required me to key into what I could sense of movement over the ground. They are heavy enough that I should be able to pick up on anything passing through here." He smiled at him. "We are as safe as I can make us, Fezarn."

If only Fes had a little better handle on his Deshazl magic, maybe there would be something that he could do. Even if he could, the Deshazl magic was different than the fire mage magic. They were connected, both using the power of the dragons, but in different ways.

As they settled near a campfire that Jaken had started,

he looked over at Azithan. The older fire mage had taken a seat, pulling his cloak around him. He left a dragon pearl resting on his lap. Fes marveled at that. There was a time when he thought dragon pearls were incredibly rare, but in the time that he'd learned about himself, he had discovered that the fire mages had countless dragon pearls. He didn't even know what they were. Unlike the bones, the pearls weren't a part of a living dragon.

"What happens if the dragon relics dry up?" Fes asked.

Azithan looked at him over the fire. His eyes danced with the flames, and there was a particular heat to his expression. "You aren't the first person who has asked that question. What we know of the earliest fire mages tell us that they weren't completely powerless, even without the relics."

"Have you tried to understand what power that is?"

"We have tried, Fezarn. It's difficult, especially as we only identify someone who has the potential to be a fire mage after they have connected to one of the relics." Azithan smiled widely. "Besides, from what we understand, the dragons did not live forever. Even when they flew freely, they were like any other creature—mortal."

"The dragons might be mortal, but how long do they live?"

"Another good question. There are stories of ancient dragons that lived for hundreds of years. And then they simply choose to pass on."

"They *chose* to pass on?"

"It is much like the connection that the empire has to the dragons. When the Damhur attacked, the dragons chose to leave this world. The made their way to the dragon plains, and in doing so, they passed on from this world. It was as if they didn't want others to use them unless they so chose."

It was difficult for Fes to imagine what had happened during that time. Something had caused the dragons to head north and settle in the dragon plains, where they had all perished. Why had they chosen that place? And why had they gone in such a way that it made it difficult for the empire to gain access to those artifacts? If not for the Deshazl, they wouldn't have been able to acquire them.

"Why didn't the people of that time defeat the Damhur for good?" Jaken asked. He continued to stare at the fire, the haunted look in his eyes. It had been there ever since confronting the totems. Jaken was a strong man and had years of experience leading others, but when it came to dealing with this kind of magic, he seemed to struggle. Fes suspected he could be powerful if he could reach his Deshazl connection, but so far, Jaken had not managed to do so. The magic was there, but Jaken hadn't been able to tap into it. "If the fire mages had access to those relics, why wouldn't they have taken them and chased the Damhur?"

Azithan stared at the fire. "I don't know. If they knew that the Damhur remaining free posed a challenge to the dragons' return, and if they knew exactly what they were dealing with, why wouldn't they have wanted to defeat them?" He looked up, meeting Fes's eyes. "There are things that we don't know; perhaps we never will know. All we can do is take what we've learned and move on, accepting our new reality."

"The Damhur never accepted anything. That's why they're still a threat," Fes said. And the Deshazl of that time never managed to succeed in offering the protection the dragons wanted—and needed.

Could he change that now or did he need to accept this new reality, one where the dragons had been reborn but were now under the control of the Damhur?

CHAPTER TWELVE

About midday the following day, they came across a trail.

It wasn't guarded by totems and was a narrow trail that wound alongside a stream, giving them access to water as they traveled, but the hardpacked surface was different than what they had been crossing over the last few days. Fes hesitated, looking in either direction, wondering if perhaps they should follow the trail or whether they should turn off.

"This appears to take us deeper into Toulen," Azithan said. He rested his hand on the ground and power built from him, seeping into the ground for a moment before he stood. "There were travelers through here recently. I'm unable to tell how many, but it was within the last day or so."

"Then we should follow," Fes said.

"I am supportive of your desire to try to find allies to defeat the Damhur, Fezarn, but I question the single-mindedness that you approach this with. What happens if we reach the people of Toulen and they refuse to assist? We have already seen that your friend is reluctant to aid you in quite the same way you expected. What happens if, when you reach her again, she refuses you once more? What happens if she sends her totems after you?"

"I don't believe that she will."

"You've already seen it. There is no need for you to believe it."

There was something about the attack that had troubled him and had wondered if Indra had done it for a reason that he still didn't fully understand. Maybe she worried that someone had been watching. If that were the case, then maybe Indra was in danger.

"We need to know whether the people of Toulen have any ability to Call. If they are somehow connected to the Damhur, then we need to know that, also."

Azithan tapped the ground without looking up. "And if we lose our way?"

Fes looked at them. "There's only four of us. The empire can go on without the four of us."

"You have the emperor's son. You have one of the most powerful fire mages living, if I do say so myself. You have a fire mage who may one day exceed me. And you have perhaps the most powerful living Deshazl in the empire. I would say that the empire would lose quite a bit if the four of us are lost."

Fes glanced at Jayell. "Did you hear that? He said that you may one day exceed his ability."

"Fes. Now isn't the time."

He took a deep breath as he turned his attention up to the sky. There was nothing there. Turning back meant abandoning the dragons. Was he ready to do that? "Let's just follow it a little bit longer, and when we see where they've gone, we can make a decision at that time. If anything happens, we know how to escape."

Azithan nodded, and they continued riding, following the trail as it meandered along the stream. A trail of smoke drifted into the sky somewhere in the distance. It was possible that the pale smoke represented a village, and considering how far they'd come into Toulen, time that they had traveled without seeing anyone else, Fes wondered if that wasn't what they had finally come upon.

Jayell joined him, and they stared out into the distance, looking to see whether there was sign of any movement, but he saw nothing that indicated anything.

"I don't know what that is," Fes said.

"You don't have to know what it is," she said her hand to the ground. A fire mage spell built, the power coursing from her increasing in intensity, spilling free. It happened quickly— much more rapidly than she had managed before—and Fes realized that she was gaining in confidence and skill. What she was capable of doing now was much more than she had been when they first had come together, and some of that skill had come from her time training in the temple, but some of it came from continuing to work with Azithan, using his knowledge to help further her own.

When Fes had first met her, she had followed the Priests of the Flame, and in doing so, she had seemed more fulfilled. Ever since learning about the dragons, she had followed a different path, coming to follow Fes. He still wasn't sure whether that was better for her or not. Maybe it would've been better for Jayell to have remained in the temple, continuing to learn how to master her fire magic, or perhaps it would've been better for her to have stayed with the priests.

She looked up at him. "I can detect nearly one hundred people," she said softly.

Azithan joined them, and his gaze swept out over the horizon. Power surged away from him, and Fes wondered which artifact he chose to use to power his spell. "I concur. You are growing more skilled."

Jayell flushed slightly before standing. "That's more than we encountered before."

Azithan turned back, looking in the direction from which they had come. "I grow increasingly troubled about this."

"We need allies," Fes said.

"Yes, Fezarn, we need allies, but I am uncertain that the strategy we employ is the most effective one to find them. Considering what we have seen from the people of Toulen, perhaps this isn't the best way to go about it."

"You would have us return to the empire?"

"I would have us consider it," Azithan said.

If they turned back, the help they needed to rescue the dragons would be gone. Then again, it might be that they never would have been offered that help. Regardless of whether Toulen shared abilities with the Damhur, they had to protect themselves. Would they even be willing to help the empire?

Would they be willing to help the dragons?

Yet… He still struggled with the idea that Indra wouldn't help him. "I'm willing to go on my own," Fes said.

Azithan stared at him. "I won't allow that."

"This is about more than the empire," Fes said.

"I am all too aware what this has to do with," Azithan said. "You are the one who convinced me that this had to do with more than the empire, that it had to do with the dragons and their safety, and it had to do with ending a centuries-old war. We can't do that if the people who understand what is at stake disappear."

"And we can't do it if we don't help those who are willing to fight alongside us," Fes said.

"And if they *aren't* willing to fight alongside us?" Jaken asked. He waved off Azithan and came to stand in front of Fes. Jaken was a large man, nearly ten years older and much more muscular. He had decades of experience leading men, time spent fighting as a soldier on behalf of the Dragon Guard and the empire. That experience had intimidated Fes when he first met Jaken, and perhaps it still did, but he understood there was more to the man than how he appeared. Jaken might be large and imposing, but he wanted to serve the empire. There wasn't much more to it than that. "What if they've already sided with the Damhur?"

"The people of Toulen have been at peace with the empire."

"But they have not always," Azithan said. "There has been no fighting for many years, but that has not always been what we've known. It could be that the people of Toulen see what the empire has and want it for themselves."

Fes smiled. "I don't think it's quite that easy."

"There's nothing easy about maintaining peace between two powerful nations."

"Powerful?" Fes asked, arching a brow, his gaze sweeping around all of Toulen. From here, there was nothing more than empty plains. In the time that they had traveled, they had come across nothing.

"Yes, powerful. There was a time when the people of

the empire and those of Toulen battled for supremacy over these lands. Borders shifted over time, eventually settling on the river as a mutually agreed-upon separation. It made it easier, a natural divide, though perhaps not quite as natural as it would appear. Have you not considered the fact that these lands resemble more of the empire?"

"I haven't seen anything of Toulen to know."

"Which is my point," Azithan said. "The Toulen lands around you all once belonged to the empire."

That was news to him. "The empire lost land? I thought that they continued to push, spreading throughout the entire continent, gaining strength and spreading their influence."

"That is the story that the empire would have the people know."

"Another story. Sort of like how the dragons are a threat to the empire."

Azithan tipped his head, nodding slightly. "Much the same. It is better for us to spread the story that we offered control of these lands to Toulen rather than for people to know that we weren't able to maintain them. But there was a time long ago when these lands were a part of the empire. If you look closely, you can see evidence of that."

"I haven't seen evidence of anything. The lands are empty. There's nothing here."

Azithan smiled. "If you believe these lands are empty, then you haven't been paying attention." He turned, sweeping his gaze around them before finally looking back at Fes. "I had wondered whether we were making a mistake when we came to Toulen and thought that perhaps you had insight that you were unable—or unwilling—to share. The longer that we have been here, the more certain I am that this is a mistake. The capital needs to prepare for the possibility of an attack now that the Damhur have the dragons."

"How would you have them prepare?"

Azithan glanced at Jaken before turning back to him. "Do you really believe that all in the empire serve so blindly? Think about yourself, Fezarn. What were your feelings toward the empire for the majority of your life?"

Azithan was right. For the majority of Fes's life, he had viewed the empire as more of a nuisance than anything else. It was a presence, but nothing more than that. There was power to the empire, but it was a nebulous and distant sort of power. The more that he had learned about the empire, the more that he had learned about his role and that of the Deshazl, the more he had begun to see them as something else, something more.

But there would be others like himself. There had to be others who didn't view the empire in a positive light and wanted nothing more than to remove the threat of the empire. Once the Damhur returned—and Fes suspected they would, especially if it meant they could claim the dragon relics—the empire needed to be ready.

It all came back to needing allies.

Azithan might not believe in what Fes wanted, and he might not believe in the need to go to the people of Toulen, but Fes did. He understood that to survive the next Damhur attack—even if they failed to rescue the dragons—they would need to work together, coordinating with all the strength the empire could bring to bear. Whether that required them using a people who had long ago been enemies, wasn't that worthwhile?

As he stared at Azithan, he wondered if he would even be able to convince the fire mage of that. Seeing the look on Jayell's face, he knew that she sided with Azithan. There was sadness in her eyes, and he nodded. He wasn't going to be the one to cause her heartbreak.

"Let's camp for the night, and then we can head back in the morning."

Azithan nodded. "It's probably for the best, Fezarn. When we reach the capital, I am certain the emperor would be willing to integrate you into the defenses. You have already shown your worth to him, and now that you have..."

Fes stopped listening. Instead, he was paying attention to the distant trail of smoke that came from far in the Toulen lands. Somewhere over there, Indra might be waiting. Then again, there might be hundreds of Toulen warriors, far more than they could confront on their own, and more of a risk than he was willing to take. Especially if it put empire resources in danger.

As he settled into camp for the night, he sat quietly, somber, staring out into the darkness. The others might not understand, but Fes still believed that there was more to the people of Toulen, and somehow, they would need to turn to them, and he would need to find help, whether that came from Indra and her totems or whether it came from someplace else, he didn't yet know.

CHAPTER THIRTEEN

When night had fallen in full, Fes crept away from the camp. He left his horse, abandoning the creature, knowing that he could move nearly as quickly and quietly on foot. The others slept, curled around the fire, content in the belief that Fes was standing guard.

How could he stand guard when he needed answers?

He hadn't lied to them about his desire to have them return to the empire. Azithan was right in that they needed to return. If anything happened to him, he couldn't drag them deeper into some ancient disagreement with the people of Toulen. If the empire lost the son of the emperor and two powerful fire mages, Fes didn't want to be responsible for it, not with the possibility of a coming war with the Damhur.

But if they lost Fes? He might be of value to the empire, but there were others who had the same ability as he, others who could use the Deshazl magic, the same as Fes could. He wasn't unique, and because he wasn't unique, it was safer for him to see what he could discover.

Besides, sneaking away at night gave him another advantage.

He could move silently, and he could use the darkness to shroud himself. His Deshazl abilities gave him enhanced eyesight, and he didn't need nearly as much light to see clearly, but it was more than that. If he could see what the Toulen people were doing, he might be able to find Indra, and if he could do that, then perhaps he could pull her aside, figure out what was taking place, and then maybe they could get some answers.

All of it depended on his ability to reach her.

The more that he thought about Indra, the more confident he was that she had been unable to speak freely. Was that because she was with others? Or was that about the totems? Fes had believed that she had carved them in his likeness, but what if it had been someone else? What if the totems hadn't been made by Indra at all but rather by another of the Toulen people? Her ability to carve was much more significant than he'd seen on those totems, so he had to wonder if perhaps she *hadn't* made them.

If that were the case, then he had even more questions.

Fes reached the Toulen campsite a short while later.

As Jayell had suggested, there were at least a hundred, though probably many more Toulen warriors camped for the night. From here, he could see several campfires, smoke drifting into the darkness before disappearing into the night. Occasional movements, flickers of shadow that he tracked, told him that they had left sentries. They moved quietly, though not so quietly that Fes couldn't follow them.

The way they patrolled told him that they didn't think it was likely they would be attacked. Why should they worry about that, especially here in the Toulen lands, a place where they should have been completely safe?

Fes waited for one such patrol to pass and crept forward, keeping an eye out not only for Toulen warriors but also for totems. He wasn't sure what ability the totems had for detecting when someone else was there. It was possible that they wouldn't be able to discover Fes, needing whoever controlled them to be alerted to his presence, but then again, it was equally as possible that they had some way of detecting him moving through here on their own. If that were the case, then the moment he revealed himself to a totem, he would be in danger.

The worst part about it was that the totems could be any size.

The ones Indra had carved had been small, at least initially. They had been nothing like the totems he had come across at the edge of Toulen. What if she left small totems surrounding her?

It was a chance he would have to take. If there were other totems, Fes would have a better chance of evading them. They might be indestructible, the same as the golem, but smaller wouldn't necessarily mean slower. It would more likely mean that they weren't nearly as strong, however.

Fes crawled forward, staying low in the grasses. The hills swept down below him, leading to a valley where they had camped. Most of the warriors had set up in clusters, though there were several central tents, and that was where Fes thought he needed to head. If Indra were here, it would make sense that she would be in one of the central locations and that she would be surrounded by other warriors. With her dragon blessing, she was valuable to the people of Toulen.

How was he going to sneak through?

As he watched, very few of the warriors moved. Most of them were probably sleeping. Others sat near the campfires murmuring. There were a few who looked as if they worked on carvings, making Fes suspect that they were trying to craft more totems, the same way that Indra had carved the totems when he had been with her. He had to avoid those people.

He could deal with warriors. He didn't want to fight his way through the camp, but if it came to it, he liked his chances against another armed soldier. Not only did he have increasing skill with the sword, but his Deshazl magic gave him an edge, and he had been well rested—certainly well rested enough that he could use his magic without worrying about whether he had enough stores of strength to continue to do it.

The only thing he really had to fear was the people who could control the totems. If they managed to reach him first…

He entered the edge of the campsite.

From here, it was a straight shot toward the tents near the center of the camp, and he weaved his way through them. Starting slowly and being very careful not to make any noises, he crawled between rows of sleeping soldiers. At one point, he came close enough that he could practically feel one man as he rolled over and he narrowly avoided a stray arm striking him.

Fes control his breathing, crawling forward.

Every so often, he would pause and look around, making sure that he wasn't missing any patrols or random people managing to wake up and leave the fire, heading to their sleeping place for the night. So far, there had been none.

When he reached the first tent, his heart hammered in his chest. It was loud enough that he was confident it would be heard by whoever might be inside, but he pushed back the fear surging through him, ignoring it, crawling around until he found the opening. He had considered cutting through the fabric, but that would only reveal that someone had been there. This way, he had half a mind to believe that he could pass in and then back out unnoticed.

Inside, the tent was spacious.

A pallet with blankets rested in the center, and a small form slept on top of the blankets. Fes crawled forward, thinking that it might be Indra, but it was too small to be her. Surrounding the bed were four small sculptures.

Totems.

So far, they hadn't stirred, but Fes suspected that if he managed to get too close to them, they would awaken and protect whoever it was that slept on the bed.

This wasn't where he needed to be. Even if he could reach the person sleeping on the bed, he didn't like the odds of his success in getting to them. And he didn't want to attack a strange child. What he wanted was to find Indra, and though she might have totems surrounding her much like the child did, he thought that she would render them inactive, if only to allow him a chance to have a conversation with her.

If she didn't, then everything that he had attempted so far would be a failure.

Outside the tent, Fes turned to the next. There were

five tents at the center of the camp, and now that he had checked one, he knew that he was on the right path. Whether or not Indra would be in the next was a different matter.

Fes reached it one, pulling back the fabric as he snuck inside.

It was much like the last. A pallet rested in the middle of the tent, blankets were strewn haphazardly across the top. Someone lay motionless, dark hair spilling off to one side.

They were too tall to be Indra.

As before, totems surrounded the bed. These were small, much like the last, and they wouldn't be much of a threat in this size. Any larger and he knew what kind of damage they could do. He had seen how even a small totem had managed to defend him against the golem.

Fes ducked back out of the tent.

There was movement near one edge of the campsite, so Fes remained motionless, waiting. He couldn't tell what was happening but did hear raised voices.

Moments passed before the commotion eased and the Toulen warriors disappeared. Fes breathed out and crawled into the next tent.

As he pulled this one open, he wondered whether or not he would even be successful. Was it going to be just like the last one, leaving him with no chance of finding what he needed?

A pallet rested on the floor, and blankets were neatly pulled up, and no one slept on top of it. His breath caught.

A figure sat off to the side, their back to him. Three totems surrounded the person, forming an arc around them. At first, the person didn't seem to recognize that he was in the room, remaining hunched over whatever it was they were working on, but after a moment of Fes sitting there, saying nothing, unable to decide whether he should back out of the tent or continue in, the person sitting there stiffened.

Fes pulled on his Deshazl connection, ready for whatever he might need, pulling it from deep within himself. It was powerful magic, stirred from deep inside him, and his time spent with the Damhur had taught him how to hold that connection, to reach for it in a way that he had never known before and focus it. He could use it cautiously, and did so now, creating something of a protective shield around himself. It was much like what the fire mages used, and if nothing else, it would deflect power that might be thrown his way.

The three totems stirred to life.

They knew he was here.

If he backed out now, he could run through the camp and disappear into the darkness, but he wouldn't know whether this was Indra. Given the size of the person, he didn't think that it was. And because whoever this was had hunched over in the corner, it was doubtful that she would have been hiding here, though surrounding herself with totems was something she would do.

The three totems started toward him.

Fes pushed against them, using his Deshazl magic to hold them in place. He shifted that connection, turning it to focus on the ground beneath the tent, wanting to soften it, but rather than diminishing it the way that the fire mages had managed, Fes only exploded it.

The sound was loud—too loud in the confines of the tent.

The figure spun around.

"Fes?"

Fes breathed out but didn't release his connection to the Deshazl magic. "Indra. Could you ask your totems to ease back?"

His gaze swept around them. They were now triple the size and were coming straight toward him. In his position, they would be at his face in no time, and he would either have to defend himself against them, or he would have to try and escape. Considering how quickly they were increasing in size, Fes didn't know whether he would even be able to escape from them in time.

With a wave of her hand, the totems stopped moving.

"What are you doing here?" Indra asked. Her gaze swept past him, looking to see if anyone else was with him. "Where are the others?"

Fes shook his head. "The others didn't come."

"You left them behind?"

"They intended to return to the empire. They felt as if Toulen isn't safe."

"It isn't safe."

Fes frowned, pulling himself entirely into the tent and securing the fabric in front of him. He pushed out behind him with his Deshazl magic and surrounded the entirety of the inside of the tent. Indra cocked her head, frowning as she did. Was she aware of the magic he used? That surprised him if it were true, but then, he was aware of fire mages using their magic, so it seemed only fair that others would be aware of him using his connection to magic.

"What happened? What's this about? I thought that we could come to you and get help."

Indra looked around. Her gaze drifted to the opening to the tent behind him before spinning and looking the other way.

"I think it's safe," Fes said.

Indra smiled sadly. "Safe? There is nothing safe, not anymore."

"What happened?" Fes asked.

Indra sighed. The totems wobbled back to her, shrinking back in size, and she lifted one up, holding it in her lap. "I thought that returning here would mean that my people would welcome me."

"They didn't welcome you?"

She shook her head. "They welcomed me, but they also wanted to use me. You know what it's like when your people want to use you?"

Fes grunted. "I know what it's like to be used by others."

Indra studied his face, and a deep frown furrowed her brow. "It looks like you do. What happened?"

Fes shook his head. "It doesn't matter." That wasn't quite right. What happened was the entire reason that he had come. He needed her help because what happened was what had motivated him to risk himself breaking into her campsite. If it didn't matter, why would he have done those things?

No… It very much mattered.

"The empire has been attacked."

She stared at him, saying nothing.

The lack of surprise on her face spoke volumes. "You knew."

Indra nodded. "We have known."

"Have known?"

Indra sighed. "If you want to blame me, you can, but I had nothing to do with it."

"You had nothing to do with what?"

"What has happened to your empire."

"Did you know that the Deshazl can be controlled?" He leaned toward her, trying to keep the heat from his voice. When he had met Indra and her father, he had trusted them, and he still thought that he could trust Indra. "Did you know that there were people across the sea who can Call the Deshazl, and they use that ability to force them to serve them? Did you know that it's those same people once thought to control the dragons, using those creatures to attack?"

Indra stared at him. Gone was the strength that he had seen when she had appeared with the others by the totems. There was an indecisiveness to her, an uncertainty that he remembered from the last time he had seen her. She was a child, even still. She might be a powerful child, her dragon blessing giving her the ability to do things that very few people could do, but she was a child nonetheless.

"You did know this."

"My people call it the dragon blessing."

"I thought the dragon blessing meant that you were able to animate your totems."

She smiled sadly. "The totems are but a part of it. They are considered practice, especially as the dragons have not been seen in centuries. We have remained vigilant, prepared for the next coming, ready for another attack."

"How have you kept this from the empire?"

"We haven't kept anything from the empire."

"But you have. The empire doesn't know that the

people of Toulen are descendants of the Damhur." Unless they weren't. What if the Damhur were descendants of the people of Toulen?

Could that be it? Could he have it backward? Fes didn't know, but either way, it made little difference. At this point, the fact that both were willing and interested in using the dragons was what mattered.

"Are *you* responsible for the attack on the empire?"

She shook her head. "We haven't attacked. My people have been comfortable in these lands, and we haven't wanted to attack, but we have heard word that an attack was coming. We were advised to be ready."

After everything—all of his belief that coming here would give him an element of surprise against the Damhur—he would fail.

Again.

There would be no protecting the dragons.

Azithan was right. It *was* time to return to Anuhr and prepare. They needed to be ready for when the Damhur attacked.

Fes laughed darkly.

"What is it?"

He shook his head. "I came here thinking to ask for the people of Toulen to help. I came looking for allies, but instead, I found more of the same."

"You don't understand, Fes."

"Don't I? You would control me. What is there not to understand?"

"I would never control you."

"No? And what of those totems that were carved in my likeness?"

She said nothing.

There was tension in the corner of her eyes. She shifted as she sat, cradling the totem, and Fes's gaze drifted down to it. Unlike the other totems that had attacked him, this one did not resemble him. The one that she held was more like the others he'd seen from her, made with exquisite detail and not resembling any individual person.

"You didn't make them."

Indra shook her head. "Why would I make a totem in your likeness? Doing so devalues you. I have to pour something of myself into the making of each totem, and when I do, it allows me to control them. I've never wanted to control you."

"Your father seemed to think that I had some talent."

"My father recognized that you were connected to the Deshazl, and he recognized that there was power within you."

"Power. That's why he wanted me to protect you. He knew that if it came down to it, you would be able to use me."

When she didn't answer, Fes knew that was right.

Had he been controlled all along? Here he had thought that Indra and her father had been allies, friends, but that didn't appear to be the case at all. Indra had intended to use him if it came down to it. It was possible that she still might try to use him, regardless of what he would do.

And Fes would fight. He didn't want to fight with Indra, but he wouldn't allow anyone to control him, even a friend… or someone he thought was a friend.

What was she now?

Maybe that was a question he would never have an answer to. She certainly couldn't be a friend if she intended to use him, but Fes had a hard time viewing Indra as an enemy. She was still the young girl who he had seen and gone after, thinking to rescue.

Fes had thought that he knew so much and thought that he was acting on behalf of the right side, but all along, he had been misled and misused.

"You should go," she said.

"And if I go, what's to stop you from coming after me?" There was hurt in her eyes, but Fes knew it was a valid question. If he left, if he turned away now, would she come after him?

If she did, what would he do?

He still didn't want to fight Indra—or the people of Toulen—but they might not give him a choice. "How many people are dragon blessed within Toulen?"

"I don't know."

"You have some idea."

She nodded. "The clan leaders are."

"And that's how you maintain power."

"That's how about we maintain our safety."

"The empire hasn't been your enemy for a long time."

"Just because the empire is no longer our enemy doesn't mean that we don't need to prepare for the possibility that they will one day become our enemy."

Fes shook his head. Azithan had been right.

"I'll just be going. I'm sorry that I thought that our friendship meant something to you."

"It *did* mean something to me. Does. If it didn't, you would have been captured back there."

"And now?" Fes asked.

"I don't intend to capture you, if that's what you're asking."

"I don't know what you might do," Fes said.

"Return to the empire. Prepare for whatever might be coming."

Fes sighed. "The empire protected these lands. From what I've learned, the empire partnered with the dragons. For as long as I lived, I believed that the empire destroyed the dragons, using their remains to power their magic, but I've learned a different truth, perhaps a better truth. The empire didn't destroy the dragons because they were dangerous. The empire worked with the dragons to defeat the Damhur—or Toulen or whatever you once were—because they were Called, controlled and used against the people to attempt to rule over them."

"That's not the truth as I know it."

"And the truth as I knew it wasn't the truth as it is," Fes said. He took a deep breath, debating whether he should admit the next, but maybe he could change something. "Dragons have returned, Indra, and they are not dangerous creatures. They fear for their safety. They are powerful, that much is true, but they aren't this mindless destructive force that some would have you believe."

"You only say that because you haven't seen the extent of their damage."

Fes sighed. "I say that because it is the truth."

He looked down at the totems that she held, an idea coming to him. It was one that he hated, especially seeing as how he had done everything he could to protect her from the moment that he'd met her, but it might be the only way that he would get her to understand.

What did it mean if he resorted to abducting her? Did it mean that he would be twisted, turned into someone—or something—else?

No. He couldn't do that. He couldn't take the same tactics that had been used upon him and use them against someone who was his friend.

Indra watched him, but finally, her gaze drifted down

to her totems, staring at them as if knowing what Fes had been thinking about.

"I won't report that you came here," she said. "But please don't attempt to come into Toulen again."

Fes released his Deshazl magic bubble, letting it out with a soft burst of power. As it retreated, he backed out, heading into the night, spinning to head back toward the distant camp, ready to return to the empire. There he would figure out how he would find the help he needed. Somehow they would have to rescue the dragons.

When he neared the edge of the Toulen camp, power from a Calling built.

CHAPTER FOURTEEN

Fes froze for a moment, listening to the effect of the Calling. It was indiscriminate, an unfocused sort of Calling that was designed to draw anyone with Deshazl abilities—and possibly totems.

Could that be why they had used it?

Were they trying to activate totems, or was there something else?

There was activity in the camp, so Fes crawled forward, staying low as he reached the edge of the campsite. So far, the Toulen warriors sleeping within the camp remained motionless, but he didn't doubt they would soon wake up, ready for the attack.

When he reached the edge of the camp, motion near the northern side of the camp caught his attention.

Toulen warriors rode out, heading away from the camp, looping… Back toward where he had left the others.

Had he made a mistake in leaving them alone?

He should have known better than to have just abandoned them, leaving them so close to the Toulen camp, but had he awoken any of them—Jayell in particular—he wouldn't have been able to sneak away, and he wouldn't have had the conversation with Indra that he'd had, and he wouldn't have known how far gone they were, and how unable they would be to offer assistance.

Fes raced into the night and nearly collided with a trio of Toulen warriors on patrol.

They appeared out of the darkness and lunged toward him.

"I don't want to harm you."

Two of the men unsheathed long, curved swords and surged toward him.

Fes drew upon his Deshazl connection and sent it out in a blast, splitting it so that it struck both men in the chest. They flew backward, leaving him with only one man to face.

Only… It wasn't a man.

A totem.

The totem was incredibly detailed and looked nothing like the totems that he had seen before. This one had been carved with such detail that it appeared to be no different than a man.

Was it the golem?

The golem had looked much like a man but had enough in distinctiveness that it made it less likely that he was, but this totem was even more detailed.

Maybe he wasn't a golem. Maybe he was something else. The level of detail suggested to Fes that this was made by Indra. Her ability was much more impressive than many of the others, something that her father had her hone in practice sessions that Fes had witnessed.

Fes held his hand up, not wanting to attack the totem. For that matter, he wasn't confident that he *could* attack the totem. His sword was useless against it, something that he had discovered when fighting the golem. He didn't know how effective the Deshazl magic would be against it, but it likely wouldn't be any more effective against it than his sword was.

The totem stared at him.

Fes tried moving around it, expecting to be stopped, but it didn't come after him.

It was Indra's doing, he was sure of that.

Fes raced off, leaving the totem and the fallen Toulen warriors behind. As he did, he finally reached his campsite, expecting to find the others.

They were gone.

He looked around, thinking that perhaps they might have realized that there was an attack on the way, but there was no sign of any of them. The campfire had been kicked out quickly, and the horses were missing.

Fes made a quick circuit of the campsite, looking for where they would have gone, and his heart sank when he realized the direction that they had taken.

They had gone *toward* the Toulen camp.

They had gone after him.

Fes let out a frustrated sigh and raced back. In the dark, it was difficult to follow any tracks, leaving him with nothing other than the trampling of the grass to follow.

That was enough.

Fes followed it, racing along the ground, surging his Deshazl magic into his steps without entirely meaning to.

And then he saw them.

Spells lit up the night.

Azithan.

He lunged forward, reaching them just as a spell erupted.

Azithan looked down from atop his horse, glaring at Fes. "Where did you go?"

"I needed to find out whether or not we could trust her."

"Fezarn, what you did was dangerous. You risk yourself unnecessarily, and—"

"And I wasn't willing to risk any of you for me to know. *I* needed to know. It was for my peace of mind."

Azithan turned his attention toward a dozen Toulen warriors riding toward them. Power exploded from him, slamming into the nearest three, sending them toppling from their horses. Jaken was there, knocking them down.

Where was Jayell?

"They came across us while we were sleeping," Azithan said.

"What do you mean they came across you?"

"When you abandoned us, they came across us. They grabbed Jayell and took her with them."

"Why did they grab Jayell?"

"Because Jaken and I managed to fight them off. Had we not, they would've taken all of us."

Fes swore under his breath and lunged forward, joining Jaken in the fight. If they had taken Jayell, he was no longer going to hold back.

Deshazl magic exploded from him as two Toulen warriors neared him. They were thrown from their saddles and Fes lunged forward, punching, his blow reinforced by his magic.

He spun, facing another pair of attackers, and pushed out with his magic, splitting it into three streams that slammed into their chests, throwing them from the saddle.

And then the attack was done.

Jaken turned him, the same rage that Azithan had shown clear in his eyes.

"I needed to know."

"You needed to know what? That your friend couldn't be trusted? Wasn't the attack when we first entered Toulen enough for you to know that?"

"I needed to know whether or not the attack had another meaning."

"And did you find it?" Jaken asked.

"They serve the Damhur. They knew that an attack was coming. And they… they can Call Deshazl, the same as the Damhur."

"Are you sure about that?"

Fes nodded. "The totems are their way of training. They use them to learn about how to Call the dragons. I suspect they do it because they don't have Deshazl to use."

Maybe there was more to it than that.

"While you were off testing to see whether or not she could be trusted, we were losing your friend."

"I'm going after her," Fes said.

"You don't even know where they took her," Jaken said.

"No, but I can feel where they took her," Azithan said, hopping off his horse and landing with a thud. Power circled around him. Feeling Azithan in the throes of his magic was an impressive thing. Azithan might even have enough power to withstand the attack from a Damhur fire mage.

Fes had to hope that he did. He had to hope that they found Jayell, because if she had the potential Azithan believed, they would need her.

"Where did they take her?" Fes asked.

Azithan pressed his hands against the ground. Power raced through it. It was heat and magic and a steady rumbling that rolled back toward them. When it was done, Azithan stood and nodded toward the campsite. "The center of that camp. There are more people than we thought, and if we're not careful, she will not be safe for long."

"It's more than just people in that camp that we have to worry about," Fes said.

"What else do you worry about?" Azithan asked.

"There are totems, and there is someone quite powerful at Calling."

Azithan's brow furrowed. "Then we must be ready."

"You intend for the three of us to take them on?"

"Unless you intend to leave her behind?"

Fes shook his head. "I'm not leaving without Jayell."

"I did not think that you would."

They started forward, and as they went, Fes began to pull on his Deshazl connection, preparing for the next battle. It wasn't until they reached the edge of the campsite that another one came. This was in more significant numbers than before.

When he had snuck into the camp, he had suspected

that there were a little over a hundred warriors there, and that fit with what Jayell had suspected, using her magic to detect the Toulen people. All of them seemed to be readying to attack.

A hundred versus three.

And not only a hundred, but whatever totems they would bring to bear upon them.

At least Azithan had some way of neutralizing the totems, whether or not that would be fully effective. Fes pushed out with his Deshazl connection, sending a powerful explosion out.

The first line collapsed.

Surprisingly, it was Jaken who followed up on what Fes did. The power that exploded from Jaken sent the next wave of attackers backward.

He leaped forward, his sword blazing as he cut through Toulen warriors.

Fes marveled for a moment too long.

And then he was surrounded.

Had it only been Toulen warriors, Fes thought that he might be able to withstand it, but two of them were totems.

They were easy to identify. Neither of the totems was nearly as well defined as the one that he'd seen out on patrol.

Fes focused his energy on their feet, exploding the ground. The totems fell into a sudden hole that he created. He knocked down the warriors but already began to feel his strength waning. Using his Deshazl magic this widely, attacking so violently with it, was almost more than he could manage. There wasn't much longer that he would be able to keep at it. And then he would be left with only his swordsmanship.

He was a decent swordsman, but that wasn't going to be enough to keep him safe. And it wasn't going to be enough to get Jayell to freedom.

He was going to have to fight, and he was going to have to work quickly.

He darted forward. Each attack came slowly, and he saved his Deshazl connection for the possibility of another totem appearing.

Around him, he felt the power of fire magic. It exploded, coming blast after blast, with enough force and energy that he knew it was Azithan throwing those spells. How much energy from artifacts was he using? What would happen if he ran out of power?

There were limits to Azithan, and Fes didn't want to encounter them.

He turned toward the tents in the center of the camp. If they had taken Jayell, then she would be there, though what else would he find? Fes wasn't interested in attacking Indra, and he didn't know who else was there and what control they had over their totems. If it came down to fighting, he would rather simply escape.

Azithan's anger might make that difficult. He was filled with power, and his fury at what had happened, the way that the Toulen people had attacked Jayell, might drive him to continue his violent attacks.

Fes needed to get in and then back out before anything else happened.

He reached the first tent.

As he did, he felt the stirring of a Calling.

It wasn't targeted at him.

Totems.

He reached for his Deshazl connection, prepared to use it, but saw no sign of the totems. Fes cut through the nearest tent and found the young boy lying inside, sitting on his bed. The four totems surrounding him began to shake, and Fes noticed that they were carved more in his likeness.

He wasn't about to fight himself, but he had seen how powerful those totems could be.

"Don't hurt me."

Fes shook his head. "I have no intention of hurting you. Indra is—was—my friend." At the mention of Indra's name, the boy's eyes widened. "I'm only looking for another friend of mine. She was captured by your people."

Almost too late, Fes felt movement behind him. He spun. A massive stone totem approached.

Fes focused on the totem's feet and sent an explosion

of Deshazl magic toward it. The ground exploded, sending the totem flying. That wasn't quite what he had intended, but that would work.

He raced out, hurrying to the next tent. He cut it open the same way he had with the boy's tent, and the inside found the older woman he'd seen before. Much like the boy, she sat in the middle of her pallet, though she was much older than the boy had been. Her totems had already sprung into action, surrounding the bed. They were beginning to grow in size.

Fes ducked back out, heading to Indra's tent.

They wouldn't have brought Jayell to Indra's tent, but she might be able to help him, though he wasn't sure that she would even do so.

When he cut into her tent, he found her standing, almost as if waiting for his appearance.

"Fes—"

Fes shook his head. "They took my friend. I intend to bring her with me. You didn't have to do this."

"You came to Toulen."

"I came for help. Not to attack." Her totems started to stir, growing taller. Fes turned his head to the side. "Really?"

Indra stared back at him. "You attacked me. They are only defending me."

"I haven't attacked you. All I've ever done is protect you."

He darted forward and grabbed the first of the totems. It started to writhe in his hand, and he pushed his hands together, squeezing with his Deshazl connection.

The totem exploded.

He heard Indra gasp.

Fes grabbed for the other totem nearest him and scooped it up. Much like the last, he pressed it between his hands, sending his Deshazl connection out from him, blasting the totem.

Now that he knew that he could do it, at least he had some way of defending himself. He didn't know whether it would work against a more massive totem, but against the smaller ones, he was hopeful that it would be effective.

"Don't make me do that to your last."

"What makes you think it's my last?"

"If you had others here with you, they would have surrounded you."

"Fes. You're making a mistake."

"Probably. And if you send the golem after me, I will have to destroy it, as well." He didn't know whether that was even possible, but the threat of it—and his recent display of power—was enough to elicit another gasp from her. Fes grabbed her and pulled her with him, dragging her out of the tent. "I was willing to leave. When you let me go, I was willing to disappear, to take my people back to the empire, but you weren't content with that."

"It wasn't my decision," she whispered.

"No? Considering how many totems of yours I've seen, I doubt that's true."

"Fes, you don't know what you're talking about."

"Probably not. But I do know that you have my friend, and you've seen what I'm willing to do when someone has my friend."

She looked up at him. "I didn't use you."

"No. I know that you didn't. I chose to help you." Fes hesitated as he turned to the next tent over. "I don't have a whole lot of friends. I never have. But those I do have are important to me. I will do anything in my power to protect them."

He cut open the tent. Inside, he found Jayell surrounded by three totems. They kept her trapped inside the tent.

She jerked over to see him. "Fes—"

As she pointed, Fes jerked around and saw a totem approaching him. He grabbed the totem, a strange twisted creature that came to his waist, and pressed his hands together on either side of the stone, pushing his Deshazl power through it. The stone exploded, and the totem collapsed.

He shoved Indra forward. "Release her."

"I'm not in control of these."

"You might not be, but I've seen how strong your dragon blessing is. Release her."

Indra tapped her hand on top of the nearest totem, and this time, Fes paid attention to what she did. There was a strange stirring, and power passed from her and into the totem. The stone writhed for a moment before falling still. She turned to the next and did the same thing. The last turned his attention to Fes and raced toward him.

Fes scooped it up and blasted it before it had a chance to attack him.

Jayell let out a shuddering breath. "I thought you had abandoned us."

"I came for answers," Fes said.

"From her?" Fes nodded. "How did you know I was here?"

"I returned. When you weren't there, I went after you."

She threw her arms around him, wrapping him in a hug, and then pushed off, slamming him in the chest with a hint of fire magic exploding against him. It hurt, but probably not as much as it had hurt her to realize that Fes had left her, however briefly. "Include me next time."

"I'm sorry." He looked around the tent. "Do you have your artifacts?"

"They didn't take them from me. They simply took me. I think… I think they were trying to distract us."

Fes frowned. "Why would they try to distract us?"

Indra shook her head and magic built from her, surrounding her in a protective shell. Fes turned to her.

"What's this about?"

"You don't understand. I was trying to warn you. I tried to send you away, but you kept coming."

"Indra?"

Another Calling came, this one more focused than the others he'd felt. There was power within it, and it reminded him of what he'd felt from Elsanelle.

She was the most powerful Damhur that he'd ever encountered, and her Calling had been more than merely seductive. It had overwhelmed any defense that he had against it. Even at the end, he had barely managed to overpower her ability. Doing so had required that he draw upon the power of the dragon. If a Calling like that were turned upon him here, would Fes have enough strength to resist?

He thought that his experience would grant him some defense, but it was possible that it wasn't enough. He hadn't expected to encounter a Calling here and wasn't prepared for the possibility that it would come and that he would be attacked, but perhaps he should have been.

"We need to get moving," Fes said.

He grabbed Indra, dragging her with him.

When he stepped out of the tent, he stopped short. A line of totems confronted him.

Behind the totems, he could feel Azithan battling with

the Toulen warriors. Blast after blast of fire magic exploded against the night. Occasionally, he would see flames shoot up from the attack, but not every time.

Where was Jaken?

If there was a Calling, Jaken was potentially in danger. He was improving in his ability to defend himself against a Calling, but the power Fes detected was much more than he would be able to withstand. It might be more than what Fes was able to endure.

"How do you intend for us to get past them?" Jayell asked.

Fes shook his head. That was a difficult question. He didn't know how to get past the line of totems. Already his connection to his Deshazl magic was waning, and he didn't think that he could blast his way through a dozen or more totems, especially fully formed ones. Attacking the smaller ones had required incredible strength, and it had required him to have his hands on either side of them, cracking the totem in between. Catching a totem from one side might not be enough.

"Just go," Indra said.

Fes glanced over at her. "You expect me to trust you?"

"I'm trying to help. I don't want anything to happen to you, Fezarn."

"It's too late."

"It's not too late. You could get away. I can prevent the totems from following, and I can make excuses for what happens, but I won't be able to do it for much longer. You have to go."

Fes glanced over at Jayell. She nodded, and he started toward the totems, dragging Indra with him.

"What are you doing?" she asked.

"I'm going, much like you said."

"You're going to force me to go with you?"

"That hadn't been my intention before you took Jayell."

"I didn't take her," Indra said.

"Who did?"

Indra's eyes widened, and she looked around, a Calling radiating from her, striking the totems. Fes could feel the warring effects of the two Callings and realized that she was trying to help, much as she had claimed.

What was she doing?

If she was trying to help him, if she did want to allow him an opportunity to escape, should he drag her with him? Fes didn't want to abduct her and had risked himself time and again to get her to safety, but that was before. Now he didn't know whether he could trust her not to come after him.

If he did take her with him, would it not incite the people of Toulen to come after her? They had come after her before, but that was a different time.

If he did this, it was possible that he might be restarting

the war with Toulen. The empire didn't need another war, not with what was coming from the Damhur, but then again, it was possible that even if he did nothing, if he left Indra behind, that war would come regardless. It was possible that there was nothing he could do to stop that.

As he debated, power exploding from Azithan near him, he felt something else.

Another Calling.

This was as powerful as the last, though it was different. It was directed toward him.

He ignored it, using what he'd learned from the Damhur to do so, but ignoring it required focus and took away his ability to use his Deshazl magic.

Did they know what they were doing?

Focusing on him in this way meant that they viewed him as a threat. And if they viewed him as a threat, then they knew who he was.

"How much have you told them about me?" Fes asked Indra.

"You don't have it quite right," she said.

"No? You haven't told the Damhur about me?"

Could that be why Elsanelle had known about him? He had believed that it came from what he'd done to help free the Deshazl, but maybe they had always known about him. Perhaps it hadn't mattered that he had released the Deshazl. Perhaps they would have always come after him, attacking because of who and what he was, because of his experience with Indra.

"Fes, if we're going to go, we need to do so soon."

Fes pushed Indra in front of him, forcing her forward.

As he did, the totems took a step toward him.

"Stop them from attacking," Fes said.

Indra looked over at him. "I've told you that you don't understand."

"What don't I understand?"

"I don't control them. He does." She pointed, and Fes turned his head to see someone he thought dead.

"Theole?"

CHAPTER FIFTEEN

Fes couldn't take his eyes off Theole. How long had it been since he'd seen the other man? He looked… Well. Certainly not dead, not as Fes had been led to believe. Theole had the same graying hair and dark eyes, though there was anger in them now that hadn't been there when he'd seen him last.

Why would they have convinced him that Theole was gone? What purpose would there have been in allowing Fes—or anyone else—to believe that?

Fes could think of one reason: the Damhur attack.

He glanced over at Indra. She stared at her father, her eyes blank. There was something here that Fes wasn't understanding, and he thought that he needed to get a better handle on it, but how? If Theole were involved, it would explain why Indra was unable—and unwilling—to help.

"What are you doing here?" he asked Theole.

Theole cocked his head, shifting his Calling so that the totems maneuvered in front of Fes. He was aware of the Calling in a way that he hadn't been the last time he'd been around Theole. He felt the pressure of the Calling, the way that it pushed out from the man, surging toward the totems. A part of the Calling rolled over Fes, but not nearly with as much power as what struck the totems.

"You are in Toulen. I would ask you the same thing."

"I came to look after your daughter."

"My daughter is perfectly safe."

Fes shook his head. "If she was safe, then why does she seem terrified?"

"My daughter had grown far too fond of you."

"Because you had me watch over her. What did you expect would happen?"

"I thought that she would gain an understanding of her abilities. Her dragon blessing allowed her the opportunity to Call to you."

Fes swallowed. Had Indra attempted to Call him before, he had little doubt that she would have been successful. He would have had no way of resisting. When he had traveled with Indra, he had very little understanding of his Deshazl abilities. As it was, he still didn't have much understanding.

"Maybe you raised her better than that."

The totems shifted, beginning to march toward him. They came slowly, moving at him steadily, and Fes tried to ignore their onward march, but the totems were enormous, and he could practically feel the power coming off them.

He swiped at the nearest totem with his sword, and the blade clattered off the stone harmlessly, sending sparks into the night.

"Jayell, is there anything that you can do?" he asked.

Jayell attempted a spell and shifted her attention to the ground, but the totems stepped over it.

She shook her head. "I… I don't think there is. It's almost as if they anticipated this."

"You won't be able to win," Indra said.

Fes glanced over at her. Surprisingly, she seemed upset by the possibility of something happening to him.

Could he have read it wrong? Could she still care about him?

"Help me, Indra," he said.

Indra looked beyond the line of totems. For a moment, he felt a fluttering of a Calling, but it wasn't nearly as powerful as what he felt emanating from Theole. Indra might want to try to help, but she didn't have enough strength with her Calling.

"There's nothing that I can do," she whispered.

Fes breathed out. "I don't want to hurt your father."

"I don't know that you can," Indra said.

The totems continued to march toward him. They moved steadily, a certain inevitability to each step that they took. When they reached him, what would they do? Would they harm him?

It wasn't so much himself that he worried about. It was more about Jayell. Indra was safe. Theole wouldn't harm his daughter, especially because she had a dragon blessing. But he would have no such qualms about harming Jayell, and because she was with Fes, he might be motivated to do so.

Fes stared at the totems, trying to draw upon his Deshazl magic, but it didn't come with as much strength as he wanted. There wasn't going to be any way for him to blast his way free of this.

There would have to be another way.

Arudis's warning to him came to mind. She had advised him that he wouldn't always be able to succeed with strength. There would have to be another strategy, but was there one that Fes could use? Was there some way that he could get free?

If there was, how?

He needed to buy time.

To do so meant delaying Theole, and it meant finding a way of distracting him long enough for Fes to figure out what it was that he could do to escape.

"What do you want?" he asked Theole.

"Want? I want what any clan leader wants. I want my people to be free. I want them to not fear for their safety."

"The empire hasn't attacked in Toulen in a long time."

"They might not have, but that doesn't mean that my people remain safe. It's much better for us to go on the offensive. Besides," he said with a smile, "now that the Damhur have made their move, the empire is in a precarious situation."

How much did the people of Toulen know about the Damhur attacks?

"You used me," he said.

"I used you no differently than you used me."

"I didn't use you."

"That night that you came to us, you weren't afraid of others on the road?"

"*You* were afraid of others on the road."

"I was afraid of the possibility of failing before my task was complete. You helped ensure that I succeeded. For that, I suppose I could thank you, but it wouldn't matter. Soon enough, you will be useful to me in a very different way."

Fes felt irritation building within himself. It started slowly, rising within him, growing with power. Theole would use him the same way that the Damhur intended to use him.

He would fight against it with every bit of his being.

"What about now? Don't you fear failing now?"

Theole grinned. "Fail? I'm close to my goal. I thought that I would have to risk bringing my people into the empire to capture you, but you come here. When I detected you crossing the river, I thought that I could draw you in, and you cooperated far more willingly than I had expected."

Fes glanced over at Indra. "Was this your plan?"

Indra stared at him, almost as if she didn't know how to answer or what to say.

"Don't blame her. Blame yourself."

"I blame you for your willingness to put your people at war."

"We've never not been at war."

"The empire and Toulen have been peaceful nations."

"You don't remember the past. None do."

"I've learned enough about the past to know that what you believe to be the truth is nothing other than lies."

"Lies about the dragons?" Theole smirked, and Fes could feel the movement of the totems. They took a step toward him, and soon they would be near enough to reach him. If he did nothing, they would be close enough to attack. "Yes. I know about the dragons."

"You don't understand anything. You've been used."

Theole glared at Fes. "I never expected that you would come here yourself. When I received reports of a Deshazl attacking the Damhur, I didn't think that it could have been you, but they spoke of a man with much power.

When I had encountered you before, I was fully aware that you had potential, and that given time, you would grow into your power. I'm pleased to know that I was right."

"You won't get to use my power or my potential."

"That, Fezarn, is where you're wrong."

A Calling shifted, sweeping off the totems and directed toward Fes.

It was a powerful Calling, and it rivaled what he'd detected when he had been suffering from Elsanelle, but it wasn't so powerful that he couldn't ignore it.

Fes focused on what the Calling was asking of him. There was a demand within it, a requirement that he set down his sword.

If he did that, he might be able to convince Theole that he had been Called, but a better option was taking the opportunity—and his freedom—to prevent Theole from harming the others with him.

"Fes?" Jayell asked.

Fes took a step forward. Theole watched him, a grim smile on his face.

In that time, Fes continued to pull on his Deshazl connection, focusing on that rather than on the effect of the Calling. He reached deeper within himself, thinking back to the connection to the dragon, wondering if there was some way that he could connect to the dragon even here, regardless of how the dragon had been stolen away from the empire. It seemed impossible to be able to do so, but if he could, maybe he would be able to overpower this Calling, and perhaps he would be able to escape Theole and get his friends to safety.

Knowing that Theole was involved in this plot was troubling. Even more disturbing was the fact that he didn't know the extent of the plot, and it was entirely possible that there were others in Toulen who might be involved. Perhaps even those in the empire.

How much had the Damhur infiltrated?

"You can't resist it," Theole said, watching Fes. "You are one of the Deshazl. An animal. You serve the Toulen people."

Fes gathered himself and then jumped.

The jump cleared the line of totems, and he landed behind Theole, his sword pressing up against his spine. "Release the Calling."

Theole stiffened.

"I have faced more than you. Release the Calling."

Theole shifted the effect of the Calling. No longer did it sweep over Fes, but now it was directed toward the totems.

Fes stabbed toward Theole, jabbing his sword into his spine.

Theole hesitated.

"I'm fully aware of what you do. Don't think to use the totems against me. I will know."

"How?"

"The Damhur thought to use me, but they failed. What makes you think that you would succeed where they failed? They have continued to use the Deshazl over the years, and it's time that ends. Deshazl aren't slaves to the Damhur. The Deshazl aren't animals," Fes spat. Heat rose within his words, and the power of the Deshazl filled him. "And you won't use us. You won't continue to use your daughter, poisoning her. She was—*is*—my friend."

Fes brought his sword up and slammed it into the back of Theole's head. The man crumpled.

He looked over at Indra. "If you think to use the totems on me, I— "

Indra shook her head. "I won't use them."

"What about the woman and the boy?"

"They won't either." Indra turned and faced someone Fes couldn't see. "Will you, Mother?"

The woman stepped out from the darkness of her tent and stared at Fes. "We never wanted to harm anyone."

"I have a hard time believing that. But you will be given the opportunity to prove yourself," Fes said.

He stepped up to the nearest totem and pressed his hands together on either side of it, then exploded power through it. He moved along the line, destroying each of the totems. If nothing else, he didn't want Theole to come around and have a weapon to use against him. Then again, Fes intended to take Theole with him, meaning to drag him out of Toulen. They would have answers, and whether or not Theole intended to answer, Fes would see that he came along.

He had come looking to see if they could use the totems and now he was destroying them. "Do you lead?" he asked the woman.

She shook her head. "Theole leads us."

"Theole doesn't lead any longer. Do you lead?"

She sighed. "I am not dragon blessed."

"Does that mean Indra leads?" Fes turned to her, meeting her eyes. She stared back at him, and there was a definite uncertainty within her gaze.

"Fes…"

"Someone has to lead. Someone has to tell your people that the attack is over. Someone has to make certain that there isn't another. The cooperation with the Damhur must end."

"I'm not sure that I can," she said.

"Because you fear what your father might do?"

"You don't understand. You don't know what he might do."

"I don't have to know what he might do. All I know is that he intended to use you in a war that needs to be over." Fes pointed to Theole, who lay motionless. "It *is* up to me that he won't harm anyone else. I will see that he answers for his crimes."

"He's not alone among the clan leaders who believes that way," Indra said.

"And we have to find some way to end this. We have to find some way to bring peace between the empire and Toulen." If he couldn't bring peace between the people of the empire and those of Toulen, what chance did he have of stopping the war between the Damhur and the empire? Or even more than that, with the Damhur and the Asharn? What chance did he have of preventing others from attempting to use the dragons?

Probably none, which was why this mattered.

"I will help," she said.

Fes sighed. He dragged Theole with him over to Azithan. Azithan looked out at Fes, a deep frown furrowing his brow. "Is it over?"

"He was the one responsible for the totems. I had wanted to use them to stop the Damhur, to rescue the dragons, but now they'll use that same power to attack the empire."

"Totems." Azithan looked up, turning his gaze back toward the empire.

"What is it?"

"There's just something that you said that troubles me," Azithan said.

"What is it?"

"You mentioned totems."

"That's what these are. That's what we've called them ever since we first encountered them."

"Yes, but I didn't make the connection before now."

"What connection?"

"The connection between these totems and the ones that have spread throughout the capital over the last year."

Fes thought about what Tracen had made, the totems that he had carved. He hadn't made the same connection either. And yet he should have. If the totems could be controlled, and if they could be Called, and if the people of Toulen opposed those of the empire, what would prevent them from using them against the empire?

"We need to get back," Fes said.

Power washed away from Azithan for a moment. "I worry that we are already too late."

CHAPTER SIXTEEN

The return ride to the empire went far too slowly. When they crossed the bridge leading back into the empire, Fes didn't feel anything other than a continued sense of urgency. The desire to help the dragons burned within him, but building along with it was a persistent fear that he might already be too late.

Fes stayed near Theole, choosing to watch over him as they rode, not wanting him to have an opportunity to speak to Indra without his presence. For his part, Theole generally remained silent. Every so often, he would glare at Fes, but his glare did nothing other than amuse Fes.

The rest of his family stayed back near Jaken. Indra offered to help if totems were used on Anuhr, though Fes wasn't sure they would be able to trust her anymore. Her mother and brother were withdrawn, barely looking up.

The rest of the Toulen warriors who had attacked had been incapacitated so that they couldn't chase them back into the empire. It helped that they had stolen their horses, bringing them with them so that Toulen couldn't attack. It allowed them to ride faster, changing horses every so often.

Crossing into the empire seemed to irritate Theole, and when they paused near a stream, Fes leaned over. "You won't be able to escape."

Theole glared at him. "I will get free of you."

"You made your mistake. I'm going to show your family the truth."

"My family knows the truth. I have hidden nothing from them. They understand their purpose, and once we return, you will find that there is very little that you can do to stop what's coming."

"I imagine they Damhur thought the same thing," Fes said. "I've already managed to defeat one of their Trivent." It was an empty boast, and he knew it. He might have defeated Elsanelle, but the Damhur had still succeeded.

He watched Theole as he said it. There was a little tension in the corners of his mouth. If nothing else, Fes hoped to have his attention.

"So you understand what that means," he said.

"We have not been separated from the Damhur nearly as much as the empire would like to believe."

"Then if I tell you I killed Elsanelle, what would you say?"

"I would say that I don't believe you."

Fes snorted. "You don't have to believe me. Elsanelle and her daughters are gone. They made a mistake of trying to Call me."

"No Deshazl could refuse their Calling."

"You believe what you must. I believe that others will learn what it takes to defeat the rest of the Damhur."

Theole shook his head. "You are more of a fool than I ever expected."

"Because I prevented an attack?"

"Because you have made the mistake of drawing the attention of the Trivent."

Fes left Theole sitting alone and joined Azithan.

The fire mage glanced over at him. "What do you intend to do with him?"

"I don't know."

He nodded to Jaken. "Keeping him alive only places us in danger. He has continued to try to Call Jaken."

Every time that he had, Fes had felt the effect, and he had forced Theole to abandon his Calling, but how long would he be able to do that? At some point, it was possible that Theole would overpower Jaken and use his connection to force a confrontation between Jaken and Fes. That had happened more than once before.

"You think it would be better if we simply executed him."

"After what he's done, I think that might be necessary."

"We still need answers, Azithan. Toulen has known about the Damhur. We need to know the extent of it. And his ability is minimal compared to the Damhur. I will keep an eye on him and will know when he tries to Call."

"There are others in Anuhr that might be susceptible to the Calling. You can't be around him all the time."

Fes couldn't, which meant that wasn't a workable plan. There was a place where it would be *quite* unlikely that he would have any influence. Would Azithan agree to it? "We could bring him somewhere that he can't harm others."

"You mean the fire mage temple."

Fes nodded. "We can't be that far from it."

Azithan glanced over at Jayell. She spoke quietly to Indra, leaning toward her and listening. In the days that they had traveled, time since they had left Toulen, Jayell had made an effort to spend time with Indra. Fes appreciated the fact that she took that time. They needed Indra, and without her, he wasn't sure that they would be able to stop the Toulen, with or without the Damhur.

"I don't like bringing people from Toulen toward the fire temple."

"The fire mages can keep them from attacking. And

the advantage there is that the fire mages aren't Deshazl, so they should be able to avoid the effect of the Calling."

"And if he manages to animate a totem?"

"They should be able to stop it."

"My magic was very nearly not enough against the totems. When I tried before, there was little that worked against it. The only thing that helped was acting against the ground. An attack within the temple could be devastating."

Fes nodded, watching Theole as he did. They needed something—anything—that might be more than what they had done so far. He didn't like the possibility that Theole would be executed—there was information that they could obtain from him that might be beneficial in the coming attack—but he also didn't like the possibility that he might cause difficulty for the empire.

"I'll defer to your judgment," he said Azithan.

Azithan chuckled. "*Now* you defer to my judgment? After all this time when you have not?"

"We're facing a threat that seems to be more than what I can understand."

"That's not true at all. You understand the threat quite well. Because of you, we have learned that Toulen is more of a danger to us than we ever understood."

"I don't want to be responsible for destroying her father."

"Ah. There it is. It's not so much a gentle heart as it is fear of upsetting your friend."

"Upsetting? This would be devastating."

"I understand and don't blame you for it, Fezarn. Who would want to be responsible for ending the life of his friend's father?" Power built from Azithan for a moment as it often did. "You've seen what the Damhur are willing to do against us. If the people of Toulen would do the same, we are in even more danger than we knew. We need to be able to defend ourselves, and we need to be prepared for the possibility that they might attack us in ways that we would not expect. We need to be ready."

Fes stared at Indra. "We do need to be prepared for that, but we can't become the thing that we're trying to defeat." He looked up at Azithan. "During the last war, the dragons willingly gave themselves up, removing themselves from the world so that they wouldn't—and couldn't—be used against the Deshazl or the empire. Is that the world we want to remain in? You've seen the dragons. You've seen how graceful and powerful they are. You've seen how they are very much a part of the world. And you have to have seen how they shouldn't be used."

Azithan waited a moment before answering. "I'll admit that I didn't know what to make of the dragons when you first showed them to me. Everything that I'd learned had convinced me that they were too dangerous to exist in the world. Maybe they are." He raised a hand when Fes started to object. "You have also shown me that they have uses."

"Uses? Don't sound like the Damhur. The dragons are intelligent creatures, at least as intelligent as you and I."

"But we don't know what their agenda might be," Azithan said.

"Their agenda was to allow themselves to die out from the world to not be used against it."

"So what would you have us do?"

"I already made my suggestion," he said to Azithan.

"Then the fire temple it is."

Azithan started to turn, but Fes reached for the sleeve of his robe, catching him. "All of that was for my benefit?"

Azithan smiled. "You have doubts about yourself, Fezarn. As competent as you have been, you continue to have them. I'm only trying to get you to recognize that when you have those doubts, you have to embrace your beliefs. As long as you are acting in a way that you believe to be good, you will not be wrong."

"And what if I make a mistake?"

"We all make mistakes, Fezarn. Think about how you helped him," he said, pointing to Theole. "The rebellion once held him, I believe."

"You knew about that?"

"There isn't much that happens in these lands that I don't know about," Azithan said.

"And was the rebellion working with the Damhur?"

Azithan shook his head. "It's possible. I just don't know. Had I known at the time, I would have changed some things."

"What sort of things?"

"I would have changed how much direction you were given," Azithan said. "When you first worked for me, you did so as little more than a collector. You gathered items that I felt were useful, bringing them to me, but doing so because you wanted money. There is nothing wrong with working for financial gain, but you have made different decisions over the last few months."

"You mean the Deshazl."

"I mean that you have stopped working on behalf of financial gain and you have started to do what you feel is right. There is much more power in those decisions."

Fes could only stare at Azithan. He *had* changed over the last few months, and it was change about which that he still wasn't sure how he felt. Yet every time that he helped the Deshazl, every time that he had done something that had rescued another person from the clutches of the Damhur, he had been pleased. As much money as he had made over the years, he couldn't help but feel as if these tasks had been even more meaningful.

And the more that he learned about Azithan, the more that he wondered how much he had influenced Fes.

"Did you intend for me to do this?"

"Do what?"

Fes waved his hand. "This. All of it."

"How could I have known what you would have done?"

"I don't know. You seem as if you have understood everything else. Why wouldn't you have been involved in that?"

"As I serve the empire, I searched to ensure that the necessary parts are in place. The more that I've learned about you, Fezarn, the more that I've come to believe that you are a necessary part. You *will* play a role, though I suspect that neither you nor I know what that role will be when this is all done. You have talent, and you are only now beginning to fully understand what talent you fully possess."

"But what if I don't want to only serve the empire?"

Azithan studied him. "You have said that before, and that is a choice you will have to make. Even if you don't, I suspect that the choices you make will ultimately serve the empire, perhaps not in the way that you intend them to."

"By protecting the dragons."

Azithan nodded. "That, and other things that you decide."

"Such as attempting to end the battle between the Damhur and the Asharn?"

"That is a very different thing, now isn't it?"

"It needs to happen," Fes said.

"I don't disagree. And yet, the reason that *you* feel that it needs to happen is very different than the reason *I* feel it needs to happen." Azithan glanced over at Jaken before looking back at Fes. "In your mind, the war between the Damhur and the Asharn needs to end because it impacts the Deshazl. You view yourself as one of them."

"I *am* one of them."

"You are descended from them, but the Deshazl have been gone for centuries, Fezarn. You are no more Deshazl than I am of Toulen."

Fes blinked. "You're from Toulen?"

"As I said, you're no more of the Deshazl than I am of Toulen. You come from their people, and you share their magic, but the Deshazl were more than simply a collection of people. They were a belief. They had ideals. They were a culture. All of that is gone. It has been gone for nearly a thousand years. Those who once were Deshazl have scattered, and they have integrated into the empire, becoming a part of it." Azithan shook his head. "And even that is not necessarily the same for you. From what I understand, you come from Javoor, dragged across the sea as a means of escaping a war you never were a part of. If nothing else, that should be your motivation. But that isn't the reason you want the war to be over."

Azithan turned to him. "I could care less what happens on a continent far from us. What I care about is when that war comes to our lands. I care when that battle stretches across the sea, dragged to our shores, and then deeper into our lands when the Asharn think to attack the temple, fearful that we have brought a dragon there. That is what I care about."

Fes smiled. "What happens if I choose to cross the sea to take the fight to the Damhur?"

"I won't be able to go with you, if that's what you're asking."

"Will you stop me?"

"Why would I stop you?"

"My going there will incite war."

"My dear Fezarn, war has already been instigated. You do nothing to incite it. When they first came to our lands, capturing our people, they instigated war. I think they didn't expect us to resist, or if they thought that we would, they didn't expect us to be able to do so successfully."

"Why won't you come with me?"

"I am needed here. The empire must remain intact, and the emperor—and his descendant—need my protection."

"I don't know that we can overthrow them without bringing forces to bear upon the Damhur. We need the fire mages. The Dragon Guard. Allies."

"That is where you will have to come up with a different strategy, Fezarn."

He sighed. After surviving Elsanelle's attack, he had

anticipated heading across the sea, thinking that he would bring the fight to the Damhur, but since then, he had begun to wonder whether he had enough help. The allies that he thought they might have had failed him. Now there weren't any allies, though that didn't mean they had no support, only that who he had suspected was not there.

He didn't think that taking the Deshazl was safe. If he attempted to bring an army of Deshazl across to the Damhur, there wasn't anything that would prevent them from attacking and destroying them, controlling them with a Calling.

They would need to find a way to be more powerful, but how?

He watched Azithan, but the fire mage gave him no indication that he would offer any advice.

As they rode, the rolling plains of the empire flowing past, Fes thought about what he would do and what needed to be done. Azithan was right. Fes's reasons for doing what he would were much different than what Azithan intended. Fes wanted to protect the dragons, but was that going to be possible?

The dragons were the key. He had wanted to find allies—and they would be, but only if he rescued them first.

"What is it?" Jayell asked.

Fes breathed out. "I wanted to go to Toulen because I

wanted allies in the attack, but what if the allies that we have aren't at all what I thought?"

"What allies do you think we have?"

Fes nodded to Azithan, who rode in front of him. He kept Theole near him and power built from him, a spell held continuously, either a barrier or some other type of protection designed to prevent Theole from harming him. "Azithan mentioned that we have different reasons for doing what we do, but he wants me to serve the empire."

"And you don't?"

"When we went to Toulen, I did so thinking that we could ask for their help, and now that we know they aren't able—or willing—to help, I begin to wonder whether what I intended was even feasible."

"Why?"

"All we'd be doing is repeating the mistakes of the past. Think about what happened a thousand years ago. The people of Javoor came to what is now the empire, and they controlled the dragons, forcing them to attack on their behalf, and because of that, the empire was forced to fight the dragons, putting down those they had to, and the rest willingly gave themselves up, becoming weapons for the empire to push back the Damhur."

"What's your point?"

"Did the dragons and the Deshazl ever take the fight to Javoor?"

Jayell blinked, looking at Fes incredulously. "You can't be serious."

"I don't know if it's even possible," Fes said.

"The dragons are already there now."

"Right. And what if I rescue them? *They* become the allies we need."

"Even if you can rescue the dragons, all you're doing is giving the Damhur what they want."

"When I was helping the dragon resist the Calling, there was a connection between us. If I can understand that"—and maybe if there were enough Deshazl involved —"I think that I can continue to help the dragons oppose the effect of the Damhur."

"What if you're wrong?"

Fes breathed out heavily. The consequences of failure if he was wrong were enormous, but then, the dragons had already been Called. Doing nothing was worse.

More than anything, Fes felt deep within him that whatever else they did, they had to find some ending for this where the dragons were allowed to fly freely again.

To do so, they couldn't attack the empire.

"Maybe it's a mistake," Fes said.

"There are other options," Jayell told him. "Azithan might not want to send soldiers into Damhur, but the emperor knows the threat they pose. He was there. You have to trust that he recognizes the need to prevent another attack."

"You're right. I know that you're right, it's just… it's just that I worry about what might happen if this goes wrong."

Jayell reached across and patted him on the hand. "It's good that you worry. It means that you care, and because you care, you will do anything that you need to assure that the dragons are safe."

They continued riding, the day changing over to night. As they rode, Fes wondered how much longer they would travel. Eventually, they would need to take a break and camp for the night.

"I need to know about the totems," he said to Indra as they rode.

She looked to her father for a moment, her gaze lingering. "There's nothing much that I can tell you. You've seen the way the totems work."

"The person who creates the totem doesn't have to be the one to animate them?"

"No."

He thought of the totems Tracen had made, reaching into his pocket. He would have to destroy it, as much as it pained him. It might be a marker of his friend, but it was also a potential weapon that could be used against them.

Holding his hand in his pocket, he squeezed on the totem, sending a burst of his Deshazl magic into the totem until it deformed. Hopefully, that would keep it from changing.

"Why?" Fes asked.

"They are my people."

"The empire hasn't harmed you. Why start a war?" He watched Theole a moment. "That's what this is, you know. War. Is that what you want for your people?"

She didn't answer, and they rode for a while in silence.

"We aren't far from the temple," Azithan said.

A brisk wind gusted, swirling around him. He carried the fragrance of the grassy plains along with a hint of smoke. It was a pleasant odor, and it reminded Fes of a simple time. He'd never traveled outside of the city much before recently, and there should be no reason that he would find such aromas appealing, which made him think that the reason he did was because of his childhood. He didn't remember much of that time, only his escape and running, eventually reaching the capital, where he survived on the streets until he managed to make his own way.

And yes, the smell of smoke was serene, almost comforting.

"Be prepared," Azithan said suddenly, sitting up in his saddle stiffly.

Fes blinked, shaking away the effects of his memories. Was that a memory, or had Theole been seducing him with the Calling? The Calling that he'd used in the past had not been nearly that subtle, but what he'd just experienced reminded him of the type of Calling that he had felt when subjected to Elsanelle and her powers.

"What do you notice?" he asked.

"Something's off." Azithan reached into one of his saddlebags and pulled out a dragon pearl, holding it cupped in his palm. As he held it aloft, it began to glow, and a spell streaked away from him, heading out into the night. He focused for a long moment, and the spell returned. Strangely, Fes could feel it when it did and saw Azithan's entire demeanor change when it did.

"Oh, no."

"Azithan?"

The fire mage didn't need to answer. The answer came from the glowing on the horizon. As they continued forward, Fes realized the glowing came from the fire mage temple.

The temple burned.

CHAPTER SEVENTEEN

As they approached, Fes detected the heat coming off the temple. Not only was it burning, but it did so with incredible power. More than just the temple burned. The entirety of the city surrounding the temple was aflame.

How had they not seen it sooner? The city burned brightly, much of it long since destroyed, leaving nothing more than the remains of the sprawling complex that had once been there. What had happened to the people living in the city? That act of war might be enough to stir the emperor to action regardless of what had happened.

He watched Azithan. There was more than a look of anger on his face. There was sadness. When he looked over at Jayell, he saw the same sadness mirrored on her face.

"This is recent," Fes said.

"It appears to be," Azithan whispered.

A spell continued to build from him, swelling out and sweeping toward the temple. When Fes had been here before and confronted the Damhur, they hadn't managed to cause such destruction—and they had released the dragon.

"Why do this?" Fes asked.

"They wanted to weaken us," Azithan said.

"Weaken?" Theole looked from Fes to Azithan, grinning far more widely than Fes thought he should, especially considering how he was captured. Yet, he seemed almost giddy about the fact that the fire mage temple burned as it did. "It's more than about weakening the fire mages."

"Then what is it?" Fes asked.

"You'll have to find out."

They pulled their horses up to a stop, and Azithan stared at Theole. "If you are responsible for this—"

"How can I be responsible? You have me captured."

"If you know anything about this and do not share, you will know my wrath."

Theole chuckled. "Such strong words for someone who has seen their temple destroyed. The fire mages will no longer pose a threat to the Damhur."

"You wouldn't have been able to kill all of the fire mages," Azithan said.

"We don't need to kill the fire mages."

With the words, Fes realized the purpose of the attack on the temple.

It wasn't at all about destroying the fire mages.

"They came for the artifacts," he said.

Azithan looked over at Fes. Theole's smile told Fes that he was right.

"Like I said, they didn't need to destroy your fire mages. All they needed to do was take away the source of power. And now what are you? You are mages without any magic."

The look of anguish on Azithan's face was a torment to Fes. They had planned on having the fire mages for protection for the empire, and more than that, Fes had hoped that the fire mages might be able to assist him in spreading his attack to the Damhur. Without them, and without any access to their magic, what chance would they have of stopping the Damhur?

As far as he could tell, they might not have any chance of stopping the Damhur.

He stared at the destruction. The city around the temple was massive, and it would have been difficult to destroy it in such a way, even with hundreds of Damhur and their Called Deshazl. Had there been numbers like that, they would have seen them, wouldn't they?

The burned husk of the city could be caused by something else.

Would the Damhur have used the dragons already? Could they have been so trained?

"No…"

Jayell looked over at him, but he couldn't look back. If this was the dragons, then it was partly his fault for not protecting them. If he had, then the temple wouldn't have fallen.

Fes saw movement in the city.

"Azithan?"

He pointed, and Azithan followed his direction. Movement down in the remains of the city caught his attention.

They were soldiers, not villagers.

"We need to go learn what we can," Fes said.

Azithan pointed to Theole and his family. "They stay here."

"I can stay with them," he said.

"I think that with your Deshazl connection, you might be necessary," Azithan said.

"I can stay," Jaken said.

"You're a soldier, one of the Dragon Guard. If there is fighting to be done, you will be needed." Azithan looked over at Jayell. "I would ask that you hold them captive. If they try to run, do whatever you need to restrain them."

Jayell glanced at Fes before her gaze turned to the city and the temple in the distance. "Find out what you can."

He turned away before he betrayed what he feared.

He wasn't sure that the dragons were involved—and they might not be—but if they were, he couldn't tell them that. Even if they were, it wasn't the dragons' fault. It would be the Damhur who had Called them, but the fire mages might not understand that.

Fes unsheathed his sword, and Jaken followed. Together, they followed Azithan down into the city. He pulled on his Deshazl connection, surging it out into a shield, creating a barrier around him. Heat pressed upon him as he got closer to the city, with enough force that he was thankful for his Deshazl connection. He wasn't sure whether he would suffer without it, but at least with his Deshazl magic, he wasn't exposed to nearly as much power as he would've been otherwise.

"Where did he go?" Fes whispered.

A fire mage spell exploded from Azithan, crashing along the street. A distant shout echoed out, muted in the silence of the night.

"There," Azithan said, pointing.

Barely controlled rage hid within his voice. Fes had never seen Azithan quite this angry. He'd felt his power—he'd been around him when he had used it to free the emperor—but he had never seen the barely restrained rage within the fire mage before. It was enough to terrify anyone, and Fes was thankful that Azithan was on their side.

"He won't have been alone," Jaken said.

"I can't detect anything through the fire that raged here," Azithan said. "We'll have to search the streets."

"I don't know how long I can withstand the heat," Fes said.

"You are Deshazl."

Fes turned to Azithan, frowning. "What does that have to do with anything?"

"You are Deshazl. You don't need to fear the heat."

"I can burn like any man."

"Perhaps you can, but that doesn't mean that you need to fear the heat."

Fes tried to ignore it but was thankful that he had his protective barrier around him. If nothing else, that helped him ignore the swell of heat more than anything else. And it wasn't so much ignoring the heat as it was attempting to survive it.

They made their way along the street, Azithan leading them. He kept his hands pressed out in front of him, and whatever spell he used emitted enormous power, enough that if there were another Deshazl, they would be well aware of what Azithan did.

They turned a corner and were confronted by three soldiers.

Fes exploded his Deshazl magic at two of them while Azithan attacked the third.

Jaken stalked over to them, stabbing his sword into each of them.

"They don't look like Damhur," Fes said. None of them were dressed as he would've expected the Damhur to be dressed. When he had faced the Damhur, they had a particular style that didn't fit with the empire. It wasn't impossible to believe that the Damhur would have acquired clothing to fit into the empire, but they didn't look like anyone from the empire.

"I don't believe that they are," Azithan said.

Fes looked them over. He frowned for a moment until he began to understand. "This is the rebellion."

Azithan nodded slowly. "The rebellion, such as it was."

Jaken turned and faced Azithan. "The rebellion turned into this?"

"It's more than the rebellion," Azithan said.

Could he know that this had to be the dragons? Jaken looked as if he wanted to say something more, but he closed his mouth, biting back whatever he had thought about saying. Azithan didn't elaborate, so Fes didn't know if he knew.

They continued to weave through the street, and as they did, they came across another grouping of soldiers. Much like the last, it didn't take much to subdue them, and Jaken made short work of ending them.

It felt more like a slaughter than anything else.

They continued through the remains of the city. When they encountered another cluster of people, Fes darted forward and slammed his Deshazl magic into them, choosing to attack before the others had a chance to intervene. He didn't throw so much power at them that he would kill them. That wasn't his intention at all. Without knowing what they were after, he didn't want them dead. It was better for him—and them—to know what he might be missing.

As Jaken started to stab at the first fallen soldier, Fes blocked his sword, knocking it back. "No," Fes said.

Jaken looked up at him. "No? I am the commander of the Dragon Guard, and I am the next emperor. You would defy me?"

"I would prevent you from slaughtering them like this. They aren't any threat."

"Not now, but they will be."

"We don't know that," Fes said. "We can use them for answers, but not if we slaughter them."

"And what answers do we need?" Jaken asked, eyeing Fes for a moment before his gaze darted down to the people lying motionless. Two of them were younger and could barely be into their midteens. They might have fought on behalf of the rebellion, but he doubted that they truly understood the actions they took. "If they're following commands, what do you think they will tell you?"

Fes shook his head. It was possible that they wouldn't be able to provide any answers. And if so, it meant that they would have to imprison them, and depending on how many other soldiers they found wandering through the remains of the city, Fes wasn't sure that they had the necessary support to do so.

But these men had not put up much of a fight. Certainly not enough of a struggle to worry about them harming him. They might be members of the rebellion, but they weren't dangerous men.

"Think about it," Fes started. He looked around the city, noticing the overwhelming destruction. "The attack on the city is more than these men would have been capable of doing. They might have some talent, but do you really think they were responsible for destroying the fire mage temple?" Fes looked over at Azithan. "Do you really believe that your fire mages were overwhelmed by simple soldiers?"

Azithan stared at Fes for a moment before shaking his head. "No, I do not, Fezarn. This was more, as I suspect you have surmised."

"I have, but they're gone now."

"What is gone?" Jaken asked.

"The dragons," Azithan said, watching Fes. "That is what Fezarn suspects."

"They used the dragons here?"

"It fits," Fes said, closing his eyes, searching for any fire magic that he could, testing to see if he could detect fire magic or even a Calling. If there were Damhur somewhere, he had to find them. "But they're already gone."

"Why would they risk coming here with the dragons?"

"An attack like this would weaken the fire mages, and once they got in, it wouldn't be a big stretch for them to be able to grab the dragon relics the temple stored, and in doing so, it would strengthen the fire mages from Damhur."

Azithan wore a troubled expression as they continued through the streets, leaving behind the fallen rebellion teenagers, and Fes was thankful that they hadn't needed to argue more about doing so. He had worried that Jaken would continue to debate with him the benefits of leaving behind the injured, and thankfully, he had not.

As they headed closer to the temple, Fes heard more commotion.

He raised a hand, halting them. He focused on his fire magic, listening for any sign of any attacks, but none came. There were no spells other than what Azithan held around him.

"What is it?" Azithan asked.

Something troubled Fes, but what was it? He didn't quite know how to put his finger on it other than the fact that he detected something. It was a strange irritant, almost an ache that was within him. Whatever it was meant trouble.

Could it be that he detected the Damhur? It didn't seem as if he did, but maybe that was what he was picking up on. Perhaps that sense was what he noticed, and if it was, he needed to be prepared for the possibility of an ongoing attack.

While they waited, movement at the end of the street caught his attention.

He started toward it and realized that soldiers were approaching.

It wasn't the effect of a Calling, and it wasn't fire magic. The irritant suddenly made sense.

"Deshazl," he whispered.

Azithan looked over at him.

Fes nodded, pulling them off to the side of the street. "There are Deshazl soldiers here."

"Are you sure about it?"

Fes nodded. "I've been feeling something, and I wasn't sure what it was, but the longer that we're here, the more certain I am that's what it is."

And if there were Deshazl, that meant that there would be Damhur. There was another possibility, but it was one that seemed much more unlikely. Was it possible that they could be Asharn?

"We should—"

Azithan didn't have a chance to finish. An explosion of power erupted near them, toppling the remains of the wall they leaned against.

Fes spun off to the side, ducking his head out to see three strangely dressed people stalking along the empty street. Power surged off them. Deshazl power.

Fes focused and used his own Deshazl magic to send a surge of power at them. It bounced off them harmlessly. Two of them withdrew swords. Dragonglass blades.

Fes nodded to Jaken. "We're going to need your skill here."

Azithan began to pull upon power, letting his magic swirl around him. "I can help."

Fes shook his head. "Not against this. They have dragonglass blades, and they are Deshazl. Any spell that you throw at them will be destroyed."

He leaped forward, Jaken following him.

They crashed into the Deshazl soldiers.

They were skilled. Jaken managed to take on two of them, drawing them away, and Fes was appreciative of the fact that he did, leaving Fes man to man with one of the other soldiers, battling as well as he could but knowing that he would need to end the fight as quickly as possible.

Would he be able to position the Deshazl soldier in such a way that Azithan could intervene? Deshazl could be overthrown by fire magic if they weren't aware that it was there. He turned, drawing the Deshazl soldier toward him, putting his back to Azithan.

A spell exploded, and the Deshazl spun, slicing through it before it managed to strike him.

The speed that he managed was impressive. Fes

wasn't sure that he would even have been able to do anything quite like that.

He twisted, preparing for the next attack, and managed to block just as the soldier turned toward him. His sword blazed much faster than Fes could follow and much quicker than he could handle.

He needed to distract the other man long enough that Azithan could get another attack in or he wouldn't last long.

How?

His opponent had already shown how much more skilled he was than Fes, and even when Azithan had attempted to attack, the soldier had cut through that spell, and in the space of what should have been an opening, Fes had not been quick enough.

Could he draw upon his Deshazl connection in a way that could unsettle the soldier?

Fes focused and sent power toward the ground.

He didn't think he could use his magic on the man. The soldier had already shown that he was skilled enough to be able to deflect that magic. Maybe exploding the ground in front of him would be enough of a distraction.

Somehow, the soldier knew what Fes was doing. He danced off the side—and directly into the path of Azithan's spell. It blasted him back, and Fes darted forward, smacking him with the flat of his sword, following with a kick.

With the man unconscious, he turned his attention to the other two soldiers, wanting to see if Jaken needed his help, but he had already dispatched both men and was turning back to Fes.

"They are not unskilled," Jaken said.

"I would suggest that they are *quite* skilled."

Jaken frowned. "If they used the dragons, why do these men remain?"

"Survivors," Fes said. "Fire mage survivors."

Azithan's eyes widened, and he hurried off, leaving Fes and Jaken to follow.

They didn't encounter any more of the soldiers until they neared the base of the temple. There, five soldiers made their way toward Fes and the others. From the graceful way they stalked toward him, Fes suspected they were all capable.

It was more than that. Dragonglass weapons were sheathed at their sides. With weapons like those, there could be no other explanation as to what they were.

Farther along down the street, he caught sight of another cluster of soldiers.

How many were left?

If they were all coming from the temple, did that mean they had destroyed the fire mages within? Did it mean that anyone who still might have the potential to serve the empire was gone?

"This might be more than we can manage," Fes said softly.

"I don't know that we have much choice," Jaken said.

Azithan pointed at the buildings on either side of the street. Stone rained inward, collapsing on the Deshazl. It distracted the Deshazl making their way toward them, enough that Azithan shifted his spell, turning it toward them now, and with it, he flipped a burst of magic that struck the nearest two. They weren't able to react in time, caught underneath the speed of Azithan's magic, and went flying backward.

The odds were suddenly better. Considering how much difficulty Fes had the last time, he didn't know if the odds were in their favor or not, but at least he thought they had a chance.

"I will take—"

Jaken never had a chance to finish.

Almost as if one, the three men launched themselves, the jump taking them all the way to Fes and Jaken, the power within it telling Fes that they had used their Deshazl ability.

Fes brought his sword up, barely managing to block in time.

The nearest attacker was even more skilled than the last guy Fes had faced, and he was forced back, unable to even think about drawing upon his Deshazl connection.

The man gritted his teeth as he fought and swept his blade toward Fes in controlled attacks. One after another came, a flurry of blows.

He wasn't going to be able to deflect the next attack.

He tried to raise his sword but failed.

From somewhere near him came the sense of fire magic, but what did Azithan think that he could do to help? He wouldn't be able to fight fast enough—or strong enough—to stop this attacker. Fes tried summoning his Deshazl magic, but it didn't come nearly as quickly as he needed.

It seemed as if time stopped.

Everything came all at once. The sword blazed toward him. Fes expected the dragonglass sword to crash into him. A fire mage spell exploded, but not from where Azithan had been standing.

Could Jayell have come into the city?

If she did, there was nothing that Fes could do to protect her. She would have sacrificed herself. The fire mages were helpless when confronted with this type of magic. And he didn't *want* Jayell to fall. She deserved better. She deserved more than what he had brought her into, and as much as he had wanted to keep her safe, would she suffer because of his mistake?

The sword neared him.

As it did, the stirring of Deshazl magic within his belly lurched forward, but even as that happened, Fes knew he wouldn't be fast enough with it and that the power that raged within him wouldn't be enough. The sword would strike him, and he would die. He would fall this close to the fire mage temple, still not knowing the nature of his magic or how he could best utilize it to help those he cared about.

And then the soldier was thrown back. The spell struck him from two sides, seeming to crash upon him, crushing him in between it.

Fes blinked and lurched to his feet with Deshazl magic blazing within him. He looked for the soldier, but he was lying nearby, his neck at an awkward angle.

What had happened?

Azithan was facing the two men fighting Jaken, and spell after spell erupted from him, trying to delay their attack to give Jaken a chance to slice through them. He gave him enough of an opening that Jaken could cut down one of the attackers.

Where had the spell that had saved Fes come from?

He turned, looking for the fire mage who might have done it, worried that Jayell had come into the city. If she had, he would need to protect her, and he didn't know if he could keep both of them safe, not with this many people of power in the city.

Instead of Jayell, he realized that there was another

fire mage—one who he thought rivaled Azithan in power.

"Elorayne?"

Power exploded from her, shooting down the street. A snarl contorted her face, and she threw spell after spell, and it took Fes a moment to realize that she tossed them at other Deshazl. "Are you going to stand there, or are you are you going to fight?"

Fes raced along the street and reached another cluster of Deshazl.

With Elorayne near him, her spells distracted the Deshazl long enough that he could slip in and use his Deshazl magic to explode the ground, throwing the men into the air. He carved through the Deshazl, powered by his magic and the distraction of the fire mage.

Another group of attackers came, and Elorayne used a nearby building and heaved it at them, throwing it with more force than Fes had expected. The entire structure collapsed, spilling stone across the street and throwing the Deshazl off to the side. They didn't get up.

And then the commotion was over.

Fes turned back toward her. She held a pair of dragon pearls in her hand, clutching them tightly. Both pearls glowed softly with a deep purple that reminded him of the dragon he'd seen in his dreams.

"What happened?" he asked as they reached Azithan and Jaken. They were finishing up with another grouping of Deshazl. Azithan turned to Elorayne, and a grim look came over his face as he nodded at her.

"They carved through our protections." She held Azithan's eyes as she said it, and there was something in her expression that told Fes how unlikely they had thought that would be.

Given how arrogant the fire mages could be, Fes wasn't surprised that they were shocked that anyone had been able through their defenses and to them. At the same time, he suspected that with the number of relics they would have used, the nature of their defenses would have been impressive enough so that there shouldn't have been any way for attackers to have gotten through.

"How many?" Azithan asked.

"After the dragons destroyed everything, probably a hundred poured into the city. All of them immune to our spells."

"Deshazl?"

"From what it seems," she said. "Yet, they're with *them*, aren't they?"

Azithan looked around the city, his gaze lingering on the destruction, seeming to hesitate every time there was another explosion, sadness filling his eyes. "I don't know. We were attacked south of here. Fes led the resistance, and we thought that we managed to push them back, but perhaps we were wrong."

Fes couldn't help but feel surprised at the credit

Azithan gave him for leading the resistance. He had participated, but he had very nearly succumbed to the attack and had almost become a part of what had taken place. Had Elsanelle been even a little more forward with her participation in his training, he might not have been strong enough to resist. The dragon might have been captured sooner.

"How much was lost?" he asked.

Elorayne shook her head. "It's difficult to know. The temple is lost and within it..." She turned to Azithan. "Was this about destroying us?"

"I think this was about acquiring our relics," he said.

"They weren't successful. We managed to move many of them."

Fes frowned. "You moved them?"

Elorayne glanced back at him. "After the last attack on the temple, he recognized the need to remove the relics from the temple itself. They were unsafe. For centuries, we have considered ourselves protected, and we thought that we could store all of our relics within it, but with that attack, the emperor himself suggested that we move those relics."

"Where did you move them?"

She glanced Azithan, who nodded. "We divided them. Some went to the capital, protected within the palace, and some went to bunkers, while others went other places."

Fes let out a relieved laugh, unable to help it. "I can't believe it."

"You can't believe what?" Azithan asked.

"All of this. I think that they expected the relics to have remained here. Hell, I expected that the real relics had remained here. Did you know this?"

"I didn't know whether the plan had been enacted or not," Azithan said.

"They would've still managed to get away with many items of power," Elorayne said. "We resisted as much as we could, but we have kept many here. This is where we continue to train, and such items were necessary for our training."

Azithan swept his gaze around the city. "We need to withdraw from this place. Any who still have any potential must come to the palace to continue their studies."

"Is that really safe?" Fes asked.

Elorayne glanced at him.

"Look at what happened," Fes said. "Think about what might happen if Toulen manages to attack."

"Toulen?" Elorayne chuckled. "Toulen hasn't been a threat to us in many years."

"They haven't been a threat, but they ready for an attack. They have a certain type of magic that enables them to use totems against the empire."

Elorayne's eyes widened slightly. "The totems are the key?"

"The totems are used for training," Azithan said. His gaze swept around them and Fes realized that Azithan continued to hold onto a connection to power. "Apparently, they have decided that they will align themselves with the Damhur."

"If they do that, then we are in much more danger than we realize," Elorayne said.

"Gather all that we can and come with us. We need to get the fire mages, anyone with the potential to assist us. And from there, we need to protect the empire."

CHAPTER EIGHTEEN

The capital loomed in the distance. Fes had seen it many times from this vantage but never had he approached with such trepidation. Even the last time he'd come, intending to try and find whether any in the empire might be able to help, he hadn't been nearly as nervous as he was now. Everything within him was tense.

And they approached the capital with people of power. It wasn't even that he came alone. Several dozen fire mages walked with them, the horses having been destroyed in the attack on the city, leaving them forced to travel by foot. A small cluster of people, only few who managed to survive the attack, came along with Fes and the others.

As they traveled, he had worried about whether the capital had been infiltrated by people of Toulen. The slight smugness within Theole as they traveled left Fes even more worried. He wouldn't have been quite that smug had he not been convinced that the attack had already taken place—and been successful.

Would they find the city in ruins?

When they reached the capital, it looked no different than it had any other time Fes had been there. There was activity in the streets and occasional flashes of color from the Dragon Guards patrolling through the city. He listened, straining to see whether he would detect any signs of fire magic, and periodically, spells would explode near him, near enough that he wondered whether they came from the fire mages with him.

They had been cautious with their fire magic. They had not wanted to use their spells, wanting to conserve the power they had access to. If they didn't, they would quickly find themselves weakened, and there weren't enough dragon relics for each of them to have more than one or two.

There had been no sign of the dragons. Nothing to indicate that the Damhur intended to use them in another attack. The temple must have been enough for now.

Jayell nudged her horse to ride alongside him. "Nothing seems quite off, does it?"

Fes stared, trying to get a sense of what activity might be down in the city, but there wasn't anything that was clear. Maybe there wasn't anything off. Maybe they would reach the city and find that it was unharmed. If that were the case, every fear that they had would be unrealized.

"I'll admit that it seems almost… normal."

Normal didn't necessarily mean it was safe. What if all of this was for show?

They had been willing to attack the fire mage temple, which meant that they weren't afraid of the empire and the power the empire possessed. There would be no reason for them to be fearful of attacking the capital, either.

Waiting to attack would give the empire a chance to prepare. The Damhur might be many things, but they never struck him as foolish. Giving the empire an opportunity to prepare wasn't something they would do.

"None of this makes sense," Fes said.

Azithan approached, and Fes cast a glance over at Theole. He was surrounded by three fire mages at all times, now better defended than he had been when they had left Toulen. Theole wouldn't be able to do anything even if he were to want to.

"I feel nothing unusual," Azithan said.

They had paused periodically for Azithan to use his strange probing sort of magic, allowing him to touch the ground, sending a surge of power through it, before standing and getting back onto his horse. Every time he did, he seemed more at peace, as if whatever it was he detected wasn't what he had feared he might.

"I still think we need to be ready for the possibility of an attack."

Azithan glanced over at him. "It's possible that we managed to get here before they attacked. It's possible that the attack was thwarted. And it's possible that there never was going to be one."

Fes thought of the totems that had gained popularity throughout the city. It was difficult to believe that there wouldn't be any sort of attack, especially with those totems spreading as they had. They made for a perfect vessel. Unsuspecting people throughout the capital would suddenly be assaulted by sculptures that they thought of as little more than expensive trinkets.

"We should be ready for anything," Fes said.

As they descended the hillside, making their way into the city, tension continued to build throughout Fes. Others seemed to recognize his stress and they remained silent, giving him space. Jayell was the only one who stayed close.

Jaken and Azithan led the procession down into the city.

As they neared the outskirts of the city, Fes glanced over at Jayell. "This is a mistake."

"Coming back to the city?"

"What if *we* are the reason that something happens

with these totems? What if they were nothing useful until we bring Theole and Indra and her mother and brother along with us?"

"You can't really think that the four of them would be able to animate that many totems."

Fes hadn't thought that was possible, but there was something about Theole's posture as they rode, almost an arrogance that remained within him. He wasn't concerned about coming to the capital. He didn't seem worried about the fact that he was now a prisoner.

What was it that they intended to do?

Fes jostled through the line of riders and reached Indra, sidling up near her. "What does your father plan?"

She looked over at him. These three fire mages surrounding him were different than they had been before. All of them had some potential, and each of the three held a spell, pressing in on a barrier of sorts that pushed against Theole. The fire mages didn't use a similar spell on Indra, though there was a part of Fes that wondered if perhaps they should. She was at least almost as much a threat as Theole. What would happen if she suddenly decided to use her ability to animate totems near unsuspecting fire mages?

"My father doesn't have anything planned. We were traveling deeper into Toulen when you came across us."

"You weren't. You were traveling toward the outskirts of Toulen when you first came across me. It wasn't until later that you headed more inland. What were you doing when I came across you?"

Indra frowned. "As far as I know, we were setting our defenses."

Fes glanced over at Jayell. She had chosen to ride near Fes, staying alongside him as he questioned Indra. "What's your sense?"

"My sense is the city seems fine," she said.

Fes couldn't shake the strange, unsettled sensation in the pit of his stomach. It was almost a sense of nausea, though he didn't know quite why that should be. As far as he knew, there was no reason to feel that way, and it wasn't even that he detected anything other than the occasional spell from a fire mage.

They turned along one of the main thoroughfares through the city. Walls of buildings stretched high on either side of them, most of them shops with painted signs hanging out front. The streets weren't crowded, and as they went, people scattered out of the way, giving them space to pass. They made an imposing patrol, dozens of fire mages along with the captain of the Dragon Guard, and then a handful of others who didn't quite fit within the empire in any other way.

As they turned onto another street, Fes looked down it, thinking about his friend Tracen. They were near enough that he could stop and visit, but until he understood just what was taking place—if anything—he didn't want to leave these people alone. They were his charges, and he took that responsibility seriously these days.

In the distance, the palace became visible. In reality, the palace was visible throughout the city, situated in the middle so that almost all roads headed directly toward it, but as they neared, it became even more difficult to shake the weight from the palace. There seemed to be a presence, a sense of power that emanated from it, and it was a sense that Fes couldn't shake.

Whatever it was that troubled him seemed to come from there.

Fes frowned and spurred his horse forward, racing toward the front of the line as quickly as he could. When he reached Azithan, he motioned for him to slow. Azithan glanced over. "I think we should have some of these people go elsewhere in the city."

"The palace is safest," Azithan said.

"It would normally be safest, but what if it's not currently?"

"Do you detect anything?"

"Just a strange sense. Almost a hunch," he said.

Azithan glanced over at Jaken, who frowned. He had been frowning for much of the last few days, almost as if he regretted having been dragged on this assignment.

Jaken shook his head. "I don't detect anything, but then I'm not nearly as sensitive to them as Fes. If he picks up on something…"

It surprised Fes that Jaken would make such an admission.

"Tell me what *exactly* you detect."

Fes shook his head. "I'm not sure that I can tell you exactly. It's vague, and I've been aware of it since the city came into view. T The deeper we move into the city, the more I feel it. It seems to be coming from the palace, which leaves me troubled."

"I don't detect anything from the palace," Azithan said.

"Neither do I, and I don't know if that's what bothers me or if there's more to it. Either way, there's something off, and I think we need to be prepared for the possibility that all isn't quite what it appears to be."

"If we arrive with several dozen fire mages, we might raise eyebrows," Azithan said carefully.

Jaken tipped his head in a nod. It wasn't so much that they would raise eyebrows. There was no reason that several dozen fire mages couldn't come to the palace, but at least he was willing to listen to Fes.

"I know several good places where they could wait for word," Fes said.

"You don't want to come with us?" Azithan asked.

"I'll come, but we can send them off, and if nothing is going on, then we can send word to them, and they can join us in the palace. If something is going on, then they don't need to be involved."

"If something is going on, we might need their help," Azithan said.

"We might, but if we bring everyone with us, it puts them all in danger. If we approach more carefully…"

Jaken nodded. "It does make sense."

Azithan smiled. "It seems the two of you have decided to work together."

He turned his horse and headed back to Elorayne and said something to her. Within a few moments, she had guided the rest of the fire mages away, leading them off and down the street before they disappeared. The stragglers from the village around the fire temple went with them.

"Where did you have them go?" Fes asked.

"You're not the only one who has safe places throughout the city," Azithan said.

Fes chuckled. "We should have had them take Theole."

Azithan studied Indra's father. "I think Theole needs to visit with the emperor."

For his part, Theole sat comfortably in the saddle, almost as if he weren't a prisoner. There was something leisurely about the way that he looked around, and his eyes seemed to drift everywhere. Was he able to detect the totems within the city?

Maybe they should have knocked him out, forcing him to travel through here while unconscious. It might have been safer. Fes wouldn't have minded the opportunity to knock him out, and after everything that he had done to them, it wasn't as if Theole didn't deserve a little violence done to him.

If he were attempting a Calling, Fes would detect it. He had recognized the other times, targeting the totems, so he should be aware of it now. There was no sense of anything other than the occasional blast of fire magic.

Even that was not coming from the direction he expected. It came from deep within the city, though not near the palace, and not in the same direction that Elorayne had led the fire mages.

"How many fire mages are in the city at any given time?"

"It varies," Azithan said. "But Elorayne tells me that several have been traveling here, carrying the artifacts. It's possible that there have been several dozen already stationed here."

Maybe that was all that he picked up on. Then again, maybe there was something else that he had missed.

"What is it?" Azithan asked.

"Probably nothing."

They continued on toward the palace, and as they did, something within Theole's demeanor began to change. The casual, almost relaxed nature faded, and an edge of tension began to settle within him.

If nothing else, Fes thought that was better. He didn't want Theole to be relaxed. He wanted him to be nervous about what he might experience when coming face to face with the emperor, but he also worried that there might be another reason for his sudden change. What if Theole was nervous not because he might soon be judged by the emperor, but because he thought that whatever assignment he was going to take would soon be fulfilled?

Was taking him to the palace the wrong move? They had checked him for totems, and there wasn't anything else on him, but maybe Theole didn't need totems to animate them. Perhaps he had some other way—or maybe Theole knew that the emperor was Deshazl.

If he did, and if he knew that the emperor was susceptible to a Calling, then it could be dangerous to bring Theole face to face with the emperor.

Fes would be there. Azithan would be there. The emperor would be safe.

Positioning his horse so that he rode alongside Theole, he forced the other man to meet his gaze. "You've been quiet."

"Is there something you would have me say?"

"Is this not what you want?"

"If you want me to acknowledge what is going to take place here, you will fail."

"So you admit that something will take place."

Theole looked over at him. "We've already acknowledged that."

"When will it happen?"

Theole smiled tightly. "I don't have the answers you seek, Fezarn."

"If you tell me what you know, I will promise that I will keep Indra safe regardless of what happens."

"Indra doesn't need your help to remain safe," Theole said.

"She's in the empire. She is from Toulen. And the people of Toulen have decided to end the peace between our peoples. She very much needs someone to ensure her safety."

Theole studied Fes for a moment. "You've already demonstrated that you will do anything to protect my daughter. I don't need to do anything—or say anything—for you to continue what you have already begun."

Fes would argue, but there was no point in it. Theole was right. He had already demonstrated that he would do anything to protect Indra. Even now, would that change? He didn't feel as if Indra were responsible for what happened, and he didn't blame her for what her father had done, so of course, he would still try to help her.

When Fes said nothing, Theole's smug expression crawled back across his face and he turned so that he could look out toward the palace. They reached the gates surrounding the palace and Jaken was waved through. Dragon Guards remained stationed, the maroon and gold colors of their attire almost welcoming, but Fes felt uncertain.

They left the horses in the stable, and Azithan guided them to the palace. Once inside, a sense of heaviness seemed to fall around him. As it did, the strange irritant, that weird sense of nausea Fes had been feeling, intensified.

With it, he began to recognize the source.

It was Deshazl magic.

He glanced at Jaken, but the Dragon Guard seemed oblivious to that.

The sense of the Deshazl magic was near—near enough that it had to be coming from within the palace.

Fes hurried up to Azithan, and pulled on his sleeve, forcing the fire mage to lean in. "Be ready."

"Be ready for what?"

"Be ready for Deshazl."

Fes frowned. "The Damhur?"

Fes shook his head. He didn't know. Was it the Damhur—or had the Asharn returned?

CHAPTER NINETEEN

The continued sense of Deshazl magic filled Fes. His body thrummed with the energy, building with power. The last time he'd felt anything like this had been when he had faced the onslaught of Damhur. There couldn't be nearly that many Damhur in the palace this time. If there were, how would they have gone unnoticed and undetected, reaching the inside of the palace without raising an alarm?

Unless they *had* raised the alarm and now they hid within the palace.

It was a possibility Fes hadn't considered. What if the Damhur had overtaken the palace but had not revealed themselves to the city outside? If that had happened, then he could see how no one would be aware of them. And if they had done that, the entire palace might be filled with Damhur—or their Deshazl.

He grabbed for Azithan, who stalked through the palace with a deliberate intensity. Even Jaken marched quickly, seeming to ignore the strangeness that Fes detected.

Could he be the only one who picked up on this?

"I don't know where they are, but I can—"

The power filled him, racing toward him.

Not just racing toward him, but attacking.

Fes instinctively slammed up a wall of Deshazl magic, holding his hands out in front of him. When the attack struck, it smashed into his wall of Deshazl magic, and somehow, his magic managed to hold.

Jayell glanced over at him, and Fes raised his hand, motioning for her to create a barrier. Her magic might not work against the Deshazl, but it should work against the Damhur. If it came down to a fight, he would much rather have Jayell with him and ready for the possibility of an attack.

"We should have kept the fire mages with us," Azithan said softly.

He wasn't wrong, but now wasn't the time to have that kind of conversation. If they would've kept the fire mages with them, the number traveling to the palace would've been ungainly. This way, there was the possibility of navigating quickly.

"We can take the tunnels within the walls," Fes said.

Azithan motioned for them to follow and he scurried off down the hallway.

Fes continued to hold his magic pressed out from him, the barrier a solid sort of wall that prevented an attack. Magic slammed into that barrier, but where was it coming from?

An explosion near him caused him to stagger.

As he did, Theole pressed his hands out from him, sending the power of a Calling toward Fes, slamming into him. Fes resisted, but he was only able to withstand so much, and as he did, Theole grabbed the rest of his family and pushed them around a corner.

Fes lunged after them, but another explosion slammed into him.

"We need to go get them," he said.

Azithan looked along the hallway. "They're gone."

"They can't be gone. We're in the middle of the palace."

"But we aren't alone in the palace. If they have help, they might have known the moment we arrived," Azithan said.

Could that be what he'd been detecting? Had they used power to identify the arrival of Theole and his family?

Fes thought that unlikely. They couldn't have been that coordinated, and couldn't have expected that they would have brought Theole into the palace. Whatever was taking place was something else. It had to be.

"What do you intend for us?" Fes asked.

Azithan pulled them into a narrow doorway.

Fes expected some sort of elegant hallway, perhaps a sitting room of sorts, but instead found nothing more than a long, narrow closet.

Azithan pushed his way to the back, moving supplies out of the way, having a mop flop over onto Fes, before reaching a section of wall. He paused. Power steadily built from his hands, and he pressed that power into the stone causing it to glow. As it did, Azithan pushed. Something clicked within the wall, and the section of wall slid off to the side.

Azithan pushed Jaken into the opening and looked back at Fes and Jayell. "Hurry up," he said.

"Why would they have needed access into a closet?"

"The passageways were meant for the servants," Azithan said.

"We need to find the emperor."

"If the palace has already been invaded in this way, we might be too late."

Could they have already lost the palace? If they did, the next thing would be the city. If the Damhur had the necessary forces to control the palace, it wasn't much of a stretch to believe that they had the forces required to overthrow the city. With the dragons to attack, it would be a simple matter to destroy everything.

Fes stepped into the darkness.

Jayell held something out in her palm. It started to glow softly, casting a gentle orange light that pushed back the darkness. Azithan shuffled them behind them so he could seal the door closed. As he did, he cupped his hand over the top of Jayell's. "We need to limit the possibility of exposure until we know what is here."

Jayell nodded. The power she'd used within the dragon relic extinguished and she squeezed it in her hand, taking Fes's hand with her free one.

Azithan squeezed past them, joining Jaken.

"Don't worry, Jaken and I have good eyesight in the dark."

"You two might, but I don't."

"The sense of power is coming from… there." He pointed in the darkness before starting ahead, not sure if they would follow, but knowing that he needed to see where the sense of Deshazl magic came from.

They made their way along the hallway, moving carefully but quickly. With each step, Fes worried that they were making too much noise. They walked with a shuffling sort of gait, and it was loud, the sound practically bouncing off the walls. He worried that a fire mage spell would crash into the passageway, chasing after them. Even that would be unnecessary. All they would need to do would be to send a Calling after them. It might be enough to draw Jaken out.

There was no sense of a Calling. The heavy pull of the Deshazl magic continued to draw him along, almost as if it demanded he find it. It was different than a Calling, different than any Deshazl magic he had detected before.

The passageway turned, and Fes hurried forward, now moving more swiftly. The rest followed him. The passageway ran into another intersection, and Fes pointed. Jaken nodded and slipped his sword out of his sheath a little. The sound seemed far too loud, a soft ringing of his blade as it was freed from the sheath, and Fes noticed that the blade itself seemed to glow a little. Azithan and Jayell didn't seem to notice, leaving him wondering if he was the only one who could see it.

Fes withdrew his sword from the sheath and noticed that it glowed with the same soft light that he saw from Jaken's sword. He had seen that sort of glowing light before, though in the past it had been when he was in the heart of the forest.

They reached a section of the wall where Fes paused. He leaned forward, pressing his head against the stone as if listening. Power seeped out of him, drifting into the wall itself, and the section of the wall began to glow softly.

"What is it?" Azithan asked.

"This is where I detect the power." He looked at Jaken, who didn't seem to have detected anything.

"Then this is where we must go." Azithan nodded at him and pushed, the wall sliding over, giving them an opening to step into.

Fes and Jaken leaped forward.

Fes kept his Deshazl magic pressed out from him, maintaining that shield in place.

They stood in a great hall, though it was a room Fes had never been in before. The hall was empty. As he surveyed the room, he noticed faint blood streaked along the floor, signs of a battle that must've been waged here. A statue in one corner had toppled over from a pedestal in the center of the room, leaving the outline of a dragon now fallen.

No Deshazl awaited.

And yet… there was something about the statute that drew Fes. He hurried over to it and lifted it, setting it back into place. The statue was made out of dragonglass and somehow carved to look like a dragon. It was impressive in detail, apparently having been made by someone who had actually seen a dragon, but how had they managed to work with dragonglass in such a way? As far as he knew, nothing could shape dragonglass, unless one of the dragons had made it.

"Fezarn now is not the time to be worrying about

statues, even one that has always been a mystery to the empire."

"Why a mystery?" Fes asked.

"This one has been here since the founding of the empire. There are others of more detail and size, but this one—this small statue—has a place of importance that others do not."

"Why not move it?"

"Why should it be moved? The ancient emperors saw fit to hold it in esteem. All who have followed have done the same."

"Why?"

"It's believed symbolic to the founding of the empire."

"Something about this is strange," he said, not taking his eyes off it. He ran his hands along the surface, tracing for signs of power, but couldn't figure out why it seemed to call to him. Maybe it was nothing more than his imagination.

But no—he could feel the power within the statue. *This* was the power that he'd been detecting.

How?

Jayell crouched next to him, and as he studied the dragon, he said, "I don't know what it is. There's something powerful about this sculpture."

"The *sculpture* is powerful?"

Fes nodded. "I don't know how to describe it any

better than that, but the sculpture seems to call to power. It's like the dragon, only..."

It was different. Fes hefted the sculpture and found that the weight was manageable. He tucked it under his arm, holding his dragonglass sword in his other hand, and turned to Azithan.

"You cannot take that, Fezarn. It is—"

"I'm taking it, Azithan. We will deal with it when it's over."

"You intend to fight while holding that?" Azithan asked, annoyance in his voice.

"I'm not leaving it here until I understand what it is. This is what I detected—I'm certain of it. And if there's power within this sculpture, it might be beneficial to us to have it along with us as we face whatever it is that's out there."

"And when you can't carry the sculpture, do you intend for Jayell or me to hold it?"

Fes hoped it didn't come to that. For that matter, he hoped that he could get out of the palace without needing to fight. Maybe the emperor was fine, and all he was detecting was the emperor practicing Deshazl magic.

But if that were the case, then why had there been an explosion? Where had Theole and his family gone?

Azithan studied him for a long moment before shaking his head. "Can we now see if we can find out what might have happened to the emperor?"

Fes kept the dragon tucked underneath his arm. The more that he thought about what he was doing, the more foolish he felt, yet he couldn't shake the sense that he needed to have this sculpture. If nothing else, he wanted to understand what it was. Azithan didn't really try to dissuade him of that desire. He seemed only concerned about Fes getting slowed down, but holding on to the sculpture like this wasn't going to slow Fes down.

They reached the door to the grand hall, and Azithan paused, pressing his hand on the surface. Power surged from him, seeping out from his palm and drifting beyond, out into the space behind the door. Azithan kept his eyes closed, almost as if listening, and he held himself in that way for long moments.

Finally, he pulled himself back, glancing at the others. "I'm not entirely certain what it is that I detect on the other side of this wall, but we need to be ready for the possibility of—"

An explosion slammed into the door, sending Azithan staggering backward. He struck the stone floor, his head striking it and bouncing off.

Jayell hurried over to him and helped him back up. He blinked slowly, and a dragon pearl fell from his hand, rolling across the stone. The surface of the pearl glowed, but the light within it flickered for a moment before going out.

"Azithan?" Jayell asked.

He coughed and grabbed for his head, holding it in both hands. There was a glazed look to his eyes that reminded Fes of what happened when the Deshazl were Called.

"He's injured. You need to do whatever it is that you do to heal him," Fes said.

Jayell reached into her pocket and pulled out a dragon pearl. She pressed her hand against Azithan's chest, sending a surge of magic through him. The power filled Azithan, and Fes waited. He'd been around Jayell when she had used a healing spell before, but she wasn't as sure about her ability with them.

From the way Azithan stared blankly at the ceiling, whatever had happened when he'd hit his head seemed to have more than dazed him.

Jayell's jaw clenched, and she continued to push her spell through him. It built, growing with increasing intensity, power filling Azithan as she strained to heal him. Tendrils of power crept away from her hand, sweeping through him.

"I don't know what's wrong with him," she whispered.

"Keep working," Fes said. "You can do this."

Azithan rested his head on the ground and his eyes closed. His breathing became erratic.

Jayell grabbed another dragon pearl from her pocket and squeezed it, pressing power through it as she sent that power into Azithan. It swirled through him, filling him, but even that wasn't enough to bring him back.

Another explosion struck the door, and Jaken grabbed Fes, pulling him to his feet. "We might need to fight."

Fes stared at Jayell, wishing there was something he could do to help her with Azithan, but that was her fight. This was his. He kept the dragon underneath his arm and turned to the doorway.

The door slammed inward.

Fes hadn't been certain what he would encounter but had thought that most likely it would be the Damhur with their Deshazl, or possibly Asharn.

What he saw surprised him.

Servants.

Not only were they servants, but each of the servants had totems marching alongside them.

"The *servants* are from Toulen? That's how they were going to start the invasion." He could easily imagine what had transpired. Toulen had sent their people to infiltrate the palace, and in doing so, they placed themselves into a position where they could gain access to the emperor.

Clever.

Theole would have known, and that explained his arrogance. He would have known that there wasn't any way for Fes to have expected this attack. He had been worried about the Damhur and the Deshazl, but that wasn't what they faced at all.

And maybe there were some Deshazl here, but it wasn't quite the same.

What he detected was the power coming from the totems.

Fes slammed a Deshazl magic into the nearest totem. The creature staggered but the power of Fes' magic didn't do much more than that.

Jaken darted forward, his sword a blur as he started fighting, moving through the Toulen servants. Fes focused on the totems. He could let Jaken work on the servants, and he felt no remorse when they fell before Jaken and the power of his sword.

He had destroyed totems before, and he needed to do the same now, only to do so, he would need to find a way of getting his hands on either side of each.

Fes twisted, but the dragon sculpture was too ungainly to hold while still managing to get to the totem. And if he didn't get to the totem, the stone creature would push them back.

Fes set the statue down and twisted off to the side, slamming his hands on either side of the nearest totem. Power exploded from his hands and crushed the totem between them.

The nearest Toulen turned to Fes.

"You shouldn't be able to—"

Fes slammed his sword into the Toulen before he had a chance to finish.

He spun, reaching for the next totem, and pressed his hands against the creature, and again power exploded from his hands, causing the stone to crumble.

The Toulen servants turned their focus to Fes.

"Jaken!"

"You worry about the totems," Jaken said. "I will give you time."

Fes twisted again and reached another totem. This one was squat and had a massive head and a snarl on its face. Whoever had carved this one had some skill. He pressed his hands onto the surface of the totem. It was cold, different than the stone totems had been. As power exploded from him, slamming into the totem, the totem twisted but didn't crumble, not the same way as the other had.

Was it not stone?

A sinking sensation set into his stomach.

He could think of one reason why the totem might not crumble.

What if this was one of Tracen's totems?

He had worked in metal, carving the totems, and Fes remembered him saying that he put a little bit of himself into each one.

If that were the case, it would require that Tracen be here to animate them, wouldn't it? Unless there were others who could animate the totems, not needing the person who carved them.

He needed to try something different. He sent another explosion through the totem, focusing on its leg. Like before, the metal twisted but didn't crumble, and the totem continued toward him.

Fes made a quick survey of the remaining totems. How many more would be metal like this? Tracen had made dozens, certainly enough that they would overpower the palace when animated like this.

He used another blast of Deshazl power, crashing it into the other leg. Metal twisted and finally, the totem staggered, falling.

But it wasn't stopped. The other totems had all crumpled, the Deshazl magic exploding the stone within them, but without having any way of doing the same, this metal totem would keep coming.

That is, it would keep coming until Fes managed to stop whoever it was who held the Calling.

He turned away from this totem and reached the next nearest one, slapping his hands on either side of the creature and sending a blast of Deshazl magic through his hands. Stone exploded, and the totem dropped to the ground. At least that one was easier.

He turned again. There was only one totem remaining.

Three of the Toulen servants jumped in front of him, blocking him from reaching the totem.

Where was Jaken?

There was no sign of the Dragon Guard soldier. Had they gotten to him? Had they dragged him away somewhere?

Fes blocked the first sword thrust at him and spun, twisting his blade, bringing it around and cutting through one of the Toulen, sending the man staggering backward.

He pressed out with a burst of Deshazl magic, forcing the next man backward. It left him facing only one of the Toulen servants.

Fes sent power toward him, but it washed over him.

He caught his blade, twisting. He turned again, this time forcing the Toulen servant into the nearest totem. The man tripped over it and went staggering.

Fes ignored him for a moment while he slammed his hands onto the totem, sending an explosion of Deshazl magic between his hands. The totem twisted, but it didn't crumble.

Another metal totem.

He swore under his breath and darted back, kicking the Toulen servant. The man grunted and rolled away from Fes's boot.

Fes darted toward the totem, grabbing the leg and sending a blast of Deshazl magic through it. The leg twisted, the force of his Deshazl attack causing the metal to bend.

It staggered, toppling to the ground.

He didn't know how long he would be able to avoid it, but it gave him time to figure out what to do with the servant. He slammed his sword into the fallen man, preventing him from getting up.

Something crashed into him from behind, and Fes went staggering forward.

He turned, trying to lift his arm, but it didn't work.

One of the Toulen stared at him. He didn't recognize the man, but there was an expression of grim satisfaction on his face.

"Why?" Fes managed to get out. He coughed and tried to take a breath, but pain surged through him. How badly was he hurt? Would he be able to get to Jayell in time for her to heal him?

The two metal totems crawled toward him.

He didn't have the strength to reach for his Deshazl connection. It was there, distant, but injured as he was, he didn't think that he could grasp it and doubted that he would have the strength necessary to call upon that magic.

He tried bringing his sword up, but his arms didn't work the way they should.

The Toulen servant took a step toward him, the angry smile still twisting his face.

Fes staggered back a step. He caught his foot and fell, dropping onto his backside.

The Toulen servant stood over him, a plain steel blade

held in his hands. The blade started toward him, and Fes stared at it, determined to watch as he died.

Power slammed into the Toulen man. His eyes widened in surprise, and he went staggering off to the side, tripping over one of the totems.

Fes looked over and thought he saw Jayell approaching, but he couldn't be certain. His vision started to blur.

Hands lifted him, dragging him out of the hallway.

Heat bloomed within him.

Was that fire magic?

Fes could no longer tell. The only thing he was aware of was pain and the heat. They mixed together, surprisingly pleasant, and he let his eyes flutter closed. His breathing slowed. Visions drifted to him, almost like dreams. In them, he saw dragons. There were dozens and dozens of dragons, all of them flying high in the sky, patterns forming as they swirled among the clouds. In that vision, the dragons were free, finally able to soar as they once had.

The vision left him with sadness. The dragons wouldn't be able to fly freely. Never again would they be able to. Not as long as there were people like the Damhur—and now, those from Toulen—who thought to use them.

They would have to remain hidden. It was not only for their safety but the safety of others. If the dragons were captured and controlled, entire cities were in danger.

One of the dragons seemed to lock eyes with him. At first, he thought it was the blue-scaled dragon he had helped rescue, but that wasn't it at all. This one had deep purple scales, so dark they were almost black, and the entire surface of the dragon glowed with a white-hot flame. It swirled, smoke coming off its wings, and flames erupted from its mouth. The same dragon he'd seen in his visions before.

It was a powerful dragon.

What a shame that a dragon like that would never again fly freely. It was a shame that the dragons had remained hidden for as long as they had, forced into exile and nearly into extinction simply because people feared them.

Pain and heat slammed into him again. Fes moaned.

Was this what dying would be like?

If it was, and if he had visions for all of eternity, perhaps there were worse ways to be.

Another blast of heat worked through him. It seemed to happen in time with the dark-scaled dragon that watched him swirling toward him. Every so often, that dragon would get closer, and heat radiating from it would grow more intense. As it did, Fes could feel that heat filling him.

There was power in that heat. It was unlike anything

he'd ever experienced before, and he thought that he should recognize it, but it didn't seem to be fire magic. Could it be dragon magic?

"No," he muttered. It was the only sound that he could make.

Someone touched his face, smoothing his hair back, trying to soothe him, but he wanted none of it. He wanted only to be able to relax, to fall into peace, and to die—if that's what was in store for him.

If death was like this, if death meant that he could watch the dragons, then he didn't mind death. He would revel in it, and he would not fight it.

He took a deep breath, feeling peace.

Heat and power filled him, exploding through him.

The purple-scaled dragon dove toward him in the vision. It loomed closer and closer, that white-hot fire that trailed along it scales blazing even brighter, surging from red to a blue that was so bright, Fes needed to look away, and yet he couldn't look away. That power demanded that he stare at it, that he watch it, and there was nothing he could do to take his eyes from it.

The dragon loomed closer and closer, and with a burst of flame, it no longer had any color but the fire.

Its eyes remained visible as the dragon curled its wings around Fes, continuing to dive.

And then the fire reached him.

It happened faster than he could react, and he took a

surprised gasp of air, filled with heat and flame and power and pain.

That power ate through him, burning until there was nothing but fire and pain and power.

And then there was nothing.

CHAPTER TWENTY

When Fes opened his eyes, he half expected to see nothing but the dragons flying overhead, the same dragons that he had seen in his vision, and he wanted to know from the deep purple-scaled dragon why it had attacked him. Instead of dragons, he came face to face with Jayell. She looked down at him with worry in her eyes. One hand smoothed his cheeks, pressing his hair away from his face, and her mouth moved in a soft whisper, but he couldn't hear what she was saying.

He tried to sit, but his body didn't react.

"Jayell?"

Did he make any sound or was that only his imagination?

Her hand stopped moving, and she frowned at him.

Fire magic built and started to press upon him, but

Fes resisted, pushing back instinctively, even though he had no dragonglass with him to oppose the spell. The power of her fire magic spell slipped apart, dissipating with whatever it was he did.

Her eyes widened, and she looked down at Fes and seemed to realize he was awake. How had she not before?

"Fes?"

Her voice came to him as if through a long tunnel, echoing strangely within his ears.

Everything ached.

What had happened to him?

He remembered getting struck, the attack from the Toulen servant having caught him from the back, stabbing him, leaving him dying.

How was he alive?

Maybe he wasn't. At least, not entirely.

Or maybe Jayell had managed to get to him in time, saving him from certain death. Like Azithan had said, she was skilled, and though she didn't have much experience healing, she was growing more and more capable, and he didn't doubt that she would soon be able to rival Azithan for ability.

He tried sitting up again, and this time his body seemed to react. There was a delay, though, almost as if what he thought about didn't happen nearly as quickly as the way his body needed and wanted to behave.

"What happened?" His voice came out raspy.

Jayell frowned, shaking her head. "I don't understand."

Her voice still sounded muted and strange, and he wondered how badly he been injured. Could it be that he had been hurt badly enough that he couldn't hear?

"What happened?" He repeated it again, being cautious to do so carefully, trying to get the words out in a way that she could understand.

Jayell tipped her head to the side, frowning. "Are you asking what happened?"

Fes nodded.

"You were stabbed in the back. You had lost a lot of blood, and when we found you, we tried to heal you, but nothing was working."

"We?"

She turned over and nodded to a still figure nearby.

Fes couldn't tell who it was, but if another had been involved, she suspected that meant Azithan.

"You were fading, dying. There wasn't anything that we could do. We tried…"

Fes stared at Jayell. What was she trying to say? He had almost died? He remembered the feeling all too well and had a vague recollection of what it had been like, and thought that he could remember the sense of nothingness, but then it was gone. The sense had been replaced by visions of the dragon, and in those visions, he had managed to see his life flashing, and then the dragon had attacked, swooping into him.

That was the last thing that he remembered.

It had to have been nothing more than a vision, a brief surge of light and nothingness before his world had ended.

But there seemed to have been something to it. He remembered the sense of heat and power and pain, all of them combining together, surging within him. Those couldn't have been imagined—at least, not wholly imagined.

"You should've died," Jayell said. Tears streamed from her eyes. "Azithan and I tried to heal you, but it wasn't working. Everything we tried to do to bring you back was failing. It was almost as if something was pushing against us, something that tried to fight us, but I don't entirely know what it was."

"What do you mean something was fighting you?"

"Like I said, I don't have a good explanation for it. There was a sense of it, but then… then it was gone. When it was gone, the power that I was able to draw had disappeared."

"It didn't disappear," Azithan said, finally looking over. He studied Fes for a long moment. "It was absorbed. It did not disappear."

Fes frowned. His mind had a hard time grasping what they were telling him.

"We pushed our healing into you, and my experience with it has been extensive. I know what should happen when a healing is attempted, and this time, there was nothing like what I had expected. The healing was drawn into you, but it changed, not only getting drawn in but also practically swallowing it. I had no control over the healing, and the power of our dragon pearls was swallowed."

Fes looked from Jayell to Azithan, trying to understand what they were telling him, but none of it made sense. He remembered the nature of the injury, the stabbing into his spine that should have taken him. Whatever had happened had involved something unexplainable.

"I had a vision as I was nearly dying," Fes said.

Jayell glanced at him uneasily. "What kind of vision?"

"A vision of dragons." Fes closed his eyes, looking through the darkness, trying to re-create the vision, but it didn't come to him easily. The strange muted quality to sound had improved, but his throat still felt hoarse and ragged, as if he had been screaming.

"You've seen the dragons, so I suppose that's not too surprising." Jayell glanced over at Azithan, but he simply watched Fes, an unreadable expression on his face.

"It was more than that. At the end of the vision, it seemed as if a dragon attacked me."

Azithan frowned, taking a step toward him. As he did, Fes realized that Azithan had been injured. He staggered and wobbled with each step. "Why would a dragon attack you? You are Deshazl. You should have a partnership with the dragons. Isn't that what you have claimed?"

Fes shook his head. That was what he had claimed, and he believed that the dragons didn't want to harm him, at least not the two dragons he had experience with.

But that didn't change the fact that there had been the attack in his dream.

"Maybe it was nothing more than a fear of mine," he said.

Only, Fes didn't fear the dragons attacking him, not anymore. Perhaps at first, he might have, but he had seen the goodness within them. He had seen how the dragons wanted to work with the Deshazl, and how they wanted to fly free. That had been the vision, having that image, seeing the dragons soaring overhead, finally free. If nothing else, the dragons didn't want to be Called and controlled. They didn't want to abandon the world. They wanted to remain a part of it.

Azithan watched him. "When we thought you were going to die, something changed." He settled down next to Fes, dropping heavily to the ground near him, crossing his legs as he leaned toward Fes. "Power bloomed within you. I couldn't see it, but I could *feel* the effects of that power. I'm not entirely sure what it was."

"What sort of power?"

"I'm not sure. There was no power, and then all of a

sudden there was enormous power. It flashed within you, and after that, you… you appear to have been healed."

Could the *dragon* have participated?

Yet, the dragon was nothing more than a vision, his injured mind attempting to create something for him.

Unless it hadn't.

"Where's Jaken?"

Azithan nodded to the door, and Fes stirred, dragging himself up so that he could sit and look over. Jaken leaned against the doorframe. He had his sword unsheathed, and he rested his head, almost as if unable—or unwilling—to move.

"Is he hurt?"

"Only by the fact that he had to cut through people he cared about."

Fes stared at Jaken, beginning to understand. To Fes, they had been Toulen servants, attackers who had turned on him, but to Jaken, they would have been people he had known and cared about.

He should have thought about that sooner.

"How did they manage to infiltrate the palace so effectively?"

Azithan shook his head. "I don't know. They shouldn't have been able to, but they have been doing this for years. From what we can tell, they have plotted it a long time, and now was the time for their plot to be enacted."

"Why now?"

"Because the dragons returned," Jaken said. He looked over, and a haunted expression in his eyes sent chills through Fes's spine. "It's possible that they used the dragons against the city."

"There has been no evidence of that," Azithan said.

"Would you have known?" Jaken asked.

"I would have," Fes said.

Jaken watched him for a long moment and took a shaky breath. "I don't even know if my father still lives. These are people who have served us for years, some of them for generations."

Generations. How could they have been so calculating in their actions?

But, it made sense. When he had faced Elsanelle, she had alluded to plots that he could never imagine. She must've known about the Toulen invasion, and she must have known that there was a threat to the empire, which meant that all of this had been planned in a way that he didn't fully understand. Maybe he couldn't fully understand it.

"Where's the dragon sculpture?" Fes asked. It should be here, but had it been damaged in the attack?

"I don't know. You set it down before fighting," Jayell said.

He had, and he had done so near the doorway. Could it still be out in the hallway? If it was, there was a part of Fes that felt as if they needed to go after it. It wasn't so much that the sculpture was valuable. It was made of dragonglass, so there was some value in it, but it was more that there was power to the sculpture that he wanted to understand. It was that power that had drawn him.

Another surge of power caused him to lift his gaze toward the door. “We have to get to the emperor.”

“How?” Jaken looked over, pain filling his gaze. “How are we supposed to get to my father when the servants themselves attack us? They have numbers, but more than that, they know everything about the palace.”

“Even the access passageways?”

Azithan shook his head. “We’ve not used those for servants in many years. For the most part, they’re restricted to only those who serve the emperor most closely. We have wanted to have a way to ensure our safety and have not wanted to reveal those corridors, even to the servants.”

“Why not?”

“It takes but one person to reveal a secret, and then it’s no longer a secret,” Azithan said. “We’ve kept everything to ourselves so that we can ensure the safety of the empire.”

It was good the servants didn’t know about these passageways, but even without that knowledge, they knew enough to be dangerous. There were other ways through the palace, and the servants would have access to all of them.

"Is there another way to reach the emperor?"

"We aren't far from his quarters," Azithan said. "I had thought that we could find him more easily this way, and hadn't expected that we would encounter any difficulty, but..."

"But we did," Fes said.

Azithan nodded. If they ran the risk of confronting all of the servants, then there might not be anyplace in the palace that was safe any longer. And if that were the case, then they might need more help than they had realized.

He looked over at Jayell. "I think you need to go and summon the rest of the fire mages."

"You might need my assistance with this."

"Probably, but if we don't get help, we might not have a chance of getting the emperor to safety if we find him."

"We could all go," she said.

If they all went, they ran the risk of not being able to make it back into the palace again. It was going to be hard enough to fight their way through the palace against the servants who knew it, but finding a way to break in was potentially even more dangerous without anyone on the inside.

"You'll need us to distract them," he said.

"And what if we can't get them in?" Jayell asked.

If they couldn't get them in, then it was possible that they had already lost. With the emperor controlled, the next step was the city. For now, it didn't appear the city was any different than it had always been, but how much longer would that remain the case? How long would it be before the Toulen servants decided to change their tactics? And how much longer before the Damhur came with the dragons?

That was what Fes really worried about. It wasn't so much the people of Toulen that he feared. It was the threat of the Damhur—with the dragons and their Deshazl—that he worried about.

He managed to stand. He had expected to be unsteady on his feet, especially after nearly dying, but he was far more stable than he had anticipated. More than that, he felt good. Strong. When he reached for his Deshazl magic, it flared within him, hotter and faster than it had before.

Had nearly dying somehow restored him in ways that he hadn't expected?

"You seem off," Jayell said.

"Not off, just surprised," said.

"Surprised by what?"

"It's nothing," Fes said.

Azithan stared at him, a deep frown furrowing his brow. "It must not be nothing or else you wouldn't have seemed startled," he said.

"It's just—"

Another explosion blasted near the door, and Jaken staggered back, swinging his sword up in front of him.

Fes turned to Jayell. "Go after the fire mages. Bring them back and be ready for battle."

Jayell breathed out heavily. "And what happens if they won't—or can't—help?"

"Elorayne will ensure they help," Azithan said.

"And what if she can't? We lost much during the attack on the temple. It's possible that there isn't any way for them to help. We came to the capital because we didn't have enough dragon relics remaining to defend ourselves."

Azithan frowned. "Bring her this." He reached into his pocket and pulled out a dragon artifact. It was a length of bone, twisted and curled, coming to a point at one end.

Fes had seen bone like that, but only on a living dragon. A dragon horn.

Jayell gasped. "How is it that you have this? There aren't many."

"Trust me; it wasn't without great difficulty. Bring this to Elorayne, and she should be able to use it to ensure that you get into the palace."

"What if I don't make it out of the palace?" She glanced from Fes to Azithan, and there wasn't fear in her eyes, not as Fes would have imagined, but there was a certain resignation about the possibility that she might not survive.

"Then you need to use the horn."

"Azithan, there's only so much power within these relics. The dragon pearls store more than most, but we have a limited number until we can get to the stores."

"We have more than you realize," he said. "And the dragon horn is more powerful than most know."

He handed it to Jayell, setting it into her palm. "Much power is stored within it, and you can use it. Don't fear that you will drain it. When I first acquired the dragon horn, I thought the same, but over the years, I've come to realize that unlike other dragon relics, the horn seems to have an endless supply of power."

Jayell took a deep breath and gripped the dragon horn before turning to Fes. "If I don't make it back to you…"

Fes patted her on the hand, looking into her eyes. "You will. I know that you will."

"But if I don't, I want you to—"

Fes wrapped her in a hug and gently kissed her lips. All the time they had spent traveling together, and there had been no time for the two of them to reflect on the idea that they might want more. They had been battling almost constantly, and even in their quiet moments, there had been little more than the opportunity to prepare for the next attack.

"I know what you want me to know," Fes said.

She leaned toward him and kissed him on the cheek. "When I first met you, I thought I knew what I was searching for. I had wanted answers, and I thought that I would find them by following the priests, learning from the Path of the Flame, thinking that abandoning the fire mages was the only way that I would learn what I wanted."

"You don't have to explain."

"If I don't make it back, I want you to know that I appreciate the fact that you helped me. You helped me learn that while I might have questions, it's okay to have those questions."

She stood on her toes, and this time she kissed him on the lips. Fes kissed back, everything within him tingling from it.

And then she pulled away. She squeezed the dragon horn before stuffing it into her pocket and turning to Azithan. "How am I going to get out of here?"

CHAPTER TWENTY-ONE

The darkened passageway seemed to call them, and Fes crept forward, moving carefully. Each step seemed loud, though he knew it wasn't. Within the walls, there wasn't any way anyone could hear their passing. They were concealed, but for how long?

Jaken took up the rear position, and Fes heard him making noise, jostling about within the passageway, turning quickly, as if expecting an attack at any given moment. Maybe he did expect an attack, but so far, they had managed to make their way through the passageway without incident.

"How much farther?" Fes asked Azithan.

The fire mage shook his head. "We have to take a roundabout approach to find the emperor."

They had checked a dozen different places, and in

each of them, they had found nothing more than destroyed rooms, evidence that the battle had come through each area, but nothing more than that. There were no bodies, and there were no soldiers, leaving Fes to wonder what had happened to the Dragon Guard who should have been here and who should have been keeping watch. How many had already fallen?

The longer they searched, the more uncertain he felt. Jayell was doing something, heading out into the city, looking for the rest of the fire mages, and there was a part of him that wanted to have gone with her, but they would need to draw away the Toulen attackers, especially if they intended to sneak the fire mages into the palace. Fes wasn't sure that there would be any way of doing so without getting caught, but they needed to have an opportunity to defend themselves.

"What if they've already killed him?" Fes asked.

Azithan glanced past him, looking at Jaken. "If he's already gone, then we have to be prepared to do everything in our power to ensure *his* safety."

"I'm not sure that anyone will believe he is the emperor's son. He never made the announcement."

"As I've already told you, there are other ways of proving his connection to the emperor," Azithan said.

He left it at that, and Fes hoped that was true. If it weren't, and if for some reason they didn't have any way of proving Jaken's status as the emperor's son, there would be even more chaos within the empire.

At the next door, Azithan paused, pressing his hands against it, sending a surge of power through the door much like he had with each one before. Power built, and the door slid off to the side, revealing a storage closet much like the very first one that they had gone into to reach the passageways.

Azithan moved supplies out of the way to reach the door at the end of the storage closet. He paused, tipping his head against the door, listening.

"Why here?" Fes asked.

Azithan glanced back at him. "We need to see if we can't reach the emperor, and every other access point has been locked. This is one that might be less likely to have been lost to us."

He waited, leaning on the door for a moment before pulling it open a crack. Heat built from him, a deep and powerful fire magic spell. It might be Fes's imagination, but he didn't think that was nearly as much power to the spell as what Azithan normally used. Had giving up the dragon horn weakened him?

Fes pulled on his Deshazl connection. Each time he did, he found that the sense of magic within him was much more significant than what he expected. Why should he suddenly have a much greater connection to the Deshazl magic ever since his near-death experience?

He pushed out with that power, sending it out from the doorway, racing along the hallway, tracking with Azithan and his spell.

"I don't detect anything."

Azithan stepped back and turned to Fes, who cocked his head to the side. There was a strange pressure upon his spell. Azithan might not pick up on anything, but he did.

What did it come from?

He didn't think that it represented a threat nearby. The pressure was near enough that he suspected that if they went out into the hallway, they would encounter whoever was out there.

"There's something out there," Fes said.

"I didn't detect it," Azithan said.

"I do," Fes said.

He raised a hand, motioning to Azithan and Jaken. "Wait here."

Before they had a chance to object, he slipped out into the hallway, unsheathing his sword and pressing a barrier of Deshazl magic around him. It was much easier to do than it usually was.

Something else to the barrier felt different. Rather than merely a wall of power, it had heat to it. It wasn't something he should be able to feel when he used his magic; at least it wasn't something that he'd ever detected when using it before. The fact that he picked up on it now surprised him.

He would have to think more on that later.

The sense came from around the corner in the distance. Fes turned the corner and came face to face with three Toulen soldiers.

They hadn't expected him.

He crashed into them, cutting down two before they had a chance to react, ignoring their cries, and when the third turned to him, swinging a sword, Fes unleashed his Deshazl magic in a tightly controlled blast, catching the man in the chest and slamming him against the wall, where he hung for a moment before dropping, limp, to the ground.

Fes pressed out with his Deshazl connection, letting it sweep along the hallway. This time, there wasn't a sense of anyone nearby. He backed down the hall, heading toward the storeroom, and grabbed Azithan and Jaken.

Azithan frowned at him. "What happened?"

"There were three soldiers."

"Were?" Azithan asked.

"They aren't a danger to us." He watched Jaken, worried for the man, considering that the servants were people he had known and cared about, but his face was a blank mask.

Azithan took the lead once more, leading them along the hallway. Every so often, he would pause, pushing out with his magic. When he did, Fes followed, almost mimicking what he did, yet the way Fes used his magic was a little different. He listened for pressure against the Deshazl bubble he created, and when he felt it, he motioned to Azithan. Most of the time, Azithan had picked it up as well, but there were other times that he didn't.

They encountered a grouping of five Toulen coming around the corner. It was a patrol. All were armed, and two totems marched with them.

Azithan sent a blast at the totems, but his magic washed over them uselessly.

Fes leaped forward, pushing out with his Deshazl connection. He unleashed more power than he intended, and it sent all five of the Toulen soldiers slamming into the wall. The totems remained. Fes rolled off to the side of one and smashed his hands on either side of the other. It was cold and slick. A metal totem.

The last time he had been in front of a metal totem, he had very nearly not survived. He wasn't going to have nearly the same success destroying it as he did with the stone totems. Fes forced his hands in such a way that he could bend the metal, and as he pressed his Deshazl connection between his hands, the metal screamed, forcing the legs to bend awkwardly toward the totem's head.

It crashed to the ground.

Turning to the other totem, he avoided a kick and

pressed out with a blast of Deshazl energy. It buckled the totem. Fes grabbed the top and the bottom of it with both hands and sent another surge of power, crumpling the totem between them.

"What was that?" Jaken asked.

"What do you mean?"

He pointed to the crumpled totem nearest them. "That. How were you able to do that?"

"It's my Deshazl connection."

Jaken shook his head. "That's more than just your Deshazl connection. That's a different kind of power. I could feel some of what you did, but not all of it. And there was heat within it, something that I don't usually feel when Deshazl magic is used."

Fes didn't have an answer that would appease Jaken. He wasn't entirely certain what he had done, only that the magic *felt* like his Deshazl connection, but the power was more than he should have.

"Fezarn?" Azithan asked.

He was saved from answering by another cluster of Toulen servants coming toward them. There were no totems with them, and they startled when they first saw them, but then charged with a foreign shout.

Azithan sent a blast of magic in their direction, but it bounced off one of the Toulen attackers.

Not just Toulen, then. If the magic managed to

bounce off, it meant that he was Deshazl, or at least had some of the Deshazl magic within him.

Fes launched himself. With a snarl, he darted forward into his attack, swinging his sword wildly. He connected with two of the attackers, but they seemed to have anticipated his movement and trapped him in the middle of the five soldiers.

Fes spun the sword, letting it whistle in the air, but the soldiers forced him back.

Where was Jaken?

Fes managed to catch sight of him. Jaken had been forced down the hallway, battling with another pair of soldiers.

That left Fes alone.

Unless Azithan could help?

Where was the fire mage?

He couldn't see. He was too busy trying to keep a sword from smacking into him to be able to see where Azithan might be.

Fes spun, twisting so that he could avoid an attack, and his sword whistled through the air.

He did little more than push back his attackers, making them question their willingness to press the attack, but he didn't give himself any real space.

He needed to change that, but to do so, he would have to do something that might put him in danger.

Fes pushed out with Deshazl magic, exploding it in a circle.

It forced his attackers back and bought him a moment, long enough that he shifted toward them, slicing at the nearest attacker, cutting down one of the men.

One versus four was better than facing off against five, but he was still far outnumbered, and the way they moved spoke of training and experience fighting together.

Somehow, his Deshazl magic wasn't as effective as it needed to be here.

He sent another blast which swept out, striking the nearest attackers.

They staggered backward.

Fes darted forward, catching one of the attackers, pushing out with his Deshazl magic as he did, managing to cut him down.

Three were left.

They were skilled, and they danced toward him, darting forward and back, attacking in a rhythm. That rhythm distracted him, and almost too late he realized that one of the attackers set down a totem.

It began to writhe, quickly taking form, and suddenly three attackers became four.

Another attack came, and he was pushed back, and he

realized that each time they did it, they were setting the totem down as if attempting to distract him.

Now there were two totems and three attackers.

Another swirl of power and they feinted toward him, forcing Fes to sweep backward, and a third totem appeared.

Facing five attackers had been bad enough, but now he was facing six, including three totems.

He had to focus his energy on the totems. They would be the most dangerous, but to do so, he needed to allow himself to get close enough to them, and he wasn't sure that he could—or should.

Fes focused on the power within him, drawing it through him, surging it into the sword. He needed to focus that Deshazl magic, and he needed to be ready, but being prepared meant that he would have to lower his sword for a moment.

Heat and flame flared within him.

It was a different sensation that he had never felt when drawing upon his Deshazl magic.

What was this?

He didn't have a chance to think about it. He forced it out, pushing with everything he had, sending it in a blast away from him. Fes screamed as he did. Other screams echoed.

When the blast cleared, he looked around. The attackers lay scattered, some twisted painfully, their bodies broken, others not moving. The totems had changed, their metal forms dripping, no longer a threat. Had he *melted* the totems?

That seemed impossible, especially with the type of magic he possessed, but what other explanation was there?

Where was Jaken?

Fes found him standing amidst three fallen attackers. He gripped his sword, staring at Fes, a strange expression on his face.

"What happened?" he asked.

Jaken shook his head. "You happened."

"What do you mean?"

Jaken looked over. "I was locked in a battle, and then you exploded power out from yourself. I don't know what it was, but it took all of them down—and left me standing."

The melted remains of the totems seemed to draw Fes. More than anything else, that was what surprised him. He had used his Deshazl magic to powerful effect before, having had it explode out from him and strike attackers, so seeing how that magic worked and seeing it slam into the Toulen attackers wasn't altogether surprising.

It was the brutal way that he had apparently destroyed the totems.

That, as much as anything, surprised him. He had

never had that much control and certainly had never managed that much power. To destroy the totems like that meant that something in his magic *had* changed.

And it had all happened following his death.

Could the vision of the dragon have changed him in some way?

It didn't make any sense, but then again when it came to his magic, Fes wasn't certain that anything made sense.

Even now, he could feel the power within him. Always before, when he had used his magic, there hadn't been that striking sense of it, that feeling as if the power burned deep within him, not as it did now.

But what had changed?

Whatever was added had magnified his magic, amplifying it in a way that he needed to understand.

Considering what they faced and what they might continue to face, it seemed critical to Fes that he better understand what had happened.

"I can't explain it," he said to Jaken, who seemed to consider sheathing his sword before thinking better of it. He checked on the fallen forms of the Toulen scattered around them before looking over at Azithan.

"We shouldn't remain here for too long," Jaken said.

"Where do you think we should look next?" he asked.

"I don't know. Azithan seemed to have some ideas, but so far, we've encountered nothing other than these Toulen soldiers."

They would need to keep moving. If they waited here too long, they ran the risk of more servants coming across them. The more often they did, the less Fes liked the chances of making it unscathed. They had been lucky so far, but what would happen if they were come upon by dozens of Toulen soldiers? What would happen if there were more than only soldiers?

He wasn't prepared for the possibility that they could face a dozen or more totems.

"There is one place he might be," Azithan said.

Both Jaken and Fes frowned but Azithan ignored them, moving down the hallway, holding tightly to his connection to his fire magic. The deeper they went into the palace, the less certain that Fes was that fire magic would be the key to their safety. It was possible that getting to safety would involve himself and Jaken, but what if that wasn't even enough?

Could the empire already have failed?

CHAPTER TWENTY-TWO

They caught up to Azithan, and Fes held onto his connection to his Deshazl magic. He didn't dare release it, not with what they were dealing with, and not until he understood what else they might face. They encountered no one else in the hallway. He should have been thankful for that, but it troubled him that they didn't. Could they have already defeated most of the Toulen insurgents?

That seemed unlikely. More likely was the fact that they traveled in the wrong direction, and that wherever Azithan led them either wasn't where the emperor would be found, or away from the main part of the Toulen warriors. They reached stairs leading down, and Azithan swept along them, plunging them into darkness.

Fes followed cautiously, keeping his connection to his

Deshazl magic. As he went, he tried to understand the nature of that magic. In the past, his relationship to his Deshazl magic had been a sense of power deep within him. That sense remained, but there was more to it now, almost as if there was heat that hadn't been there before.

Could he have connected to one of the resurrected dragons?

If so, did it mean they were nearby?

If the Damhur used the dragon to attack, even his connection to it might not be enough. But if he *had* connected to the dragon, it might explain how he had destroyed the totems, but it didn't explain to Fes how he still had that connection. When he'd reached the dragon before, the link had been brief.

The only other explanation was the vision he'd had. *Something* had happened there.

Within that vision, he had seen the dragon, and the dragon had gone toward him, and at the last minute, Fes had felt the effect of that dragon and had noticed that power had surged into him. Could it be that the dragon had somehow lent him its power? If that were the case, what did that mean? And if so, which of the dragons had done so? Maybe it was their way of fighting the Calling.

"We are nearly there," Azithan said.

Fes blinked, tearing himself from the thoughts that had been racing through his mind. It did no good to continue to worry about those things. He needed to focus on the task at hand and help Azithan and Jaken reach the emperor.

Azithan pressed his hand on a section of stone and power built from him, slowly seeping out, growing more and more powerful as it did until it collided with the door. It began to glow. First with a soft orange glow, and gradually that glowing intensified, becoming brighter and brighter until the entire stone took on a white light.

"Where is this?" Jaken asked as they stepped through the doorway and into a much narrower staircase. Azithan continued downward, moving quickly. There was no light here, and even Fes's enhanced eyesight didn't help.

Fes turned to him. "You don't know?"

"I ceased knowing several flights ago," Jaken said. "I've been into the belly of the palace, but I've never descended this deep. There hasn't been a need."

"Few have traveled this far into the palace," Azithan said. He didn't slow as he descended, taking the stairs two at a time. The walls of the staircase were much narrower here than they had been in other places, and Fes's shoulders brushed against them as he descended. Every so often, he would glance over at Azithan, expecting the other man to offer more information, but he never did.

"And you think the emperor might be here?" Fes asked. That seemed unlikely, but what did he know? What if the emperor had come here, sneaking deep into the belly of the palace as a way to escape the Toulen servants and their attack?

"As I said, it is unlikely."

"Then why are we risking this, mage?" Jaken spoke, heat rising in his voice. "We need to find him, and taking this hidden route might be intriguing to you, but it does nothing to find my father."

"He isn't anywhere we've looked. With the number of patrols that we came across, we should have seen some evidence of him. The fact that we haven't tells me that the Toulen attackers don't know where to find him. It's time for us to look in places that they wouldn't know about."

"Would my father know about this place?"

"Your father is the one who showed it to me," Azithan said.

They continued to take the stairs, heading down deeper and deeper into the palace. The walls were made of plain stone with hints of moisture along it, almost as if water seeped through here, but there was no musty odor in the air. They traveled so deep that Fes began to wonder how they would find their way free again. Climbing back out would be difficult, and if they were forced to fight at all, they might not be able to get free.

As he began to fear that they would continue descending, the stairs abruptly ended. There was a narrow hallway leading off them that Azithan guided them down, and from there, they came to another doorway. This was different than other doorways. Made entirely of iron and heavily engraved, Azithan tested a lock, finding it locked.

"Is this it?" Jaken asked.

"This is the last place I know to look," Azithan said.

"And if he's not here?"

"Then it's possible they have him."

Azithan pressed against the lock, and a spell burst from his hand, sneaking into the lock and opening it with a soft click. As he pulled the door open, light bloomed from the other side.

"Jorun?" Azithan said.

There came no answer.

The fire mage stepped deeper into the room, the power of his spell leading him, radiating from his hand as it filled the space. It was a different type of spell than he had used before, different enough that Fes could feel the intricacies of it. It seemed designed to probe, though he wasn't entirely certain why and what it was for.

Azithan spun around slowly, his gaze drifting along the walls, and he paused when he looked at Fes, his gaze settling upon him. There was a hint of worry in his eyes.

"You thought you'd find them here." It was a vast room, and there were a few chairs along with a carpet that ran the entirety of the floor. A wardrobe at one end looked unused. A row of crates was nearby. Nothing about the room spoke of use.

Azithan nodded. "He's not here. I don't know where else he would've gone."

"Why here?" Fes asked.

"Because here is a hidden room designed to protect the emperor."

"Why would they need a hidden room within the palace?"

"They've always kept one on the off chance that the palace was overthrown. The emperor could come here and remain protected."

"This doesn't seem like a good place to remain protected," Fes said. "Anyone who needed to get to you would find it difficult, and what are the supplies? Without having anyone here, you would starve."

"Not only starve, but you wouldn't have any water," Jaken said, surveying the room. His gaze swept around it, almost appraising it, before turning back to Azithan. "Why would my father have come here? This would be dangerous to him."

"Your father would have viewed it differently. If he knew the palace had been compromised and knew that there wasn't anywhere else for him to go, he would have come down here looking for safety."

The light in the room told Fes that someone had been here. Maybe not the emperor, but someone had known about the space and had come here. And if it had been the emperor, where was he? Why had he gone now?

Unless he had come here and found another way out.

Fes began to make his way around the room, looking at the walls. They were all of stone, though darker than the rest of the palace. In some places, they were damp and smelled of earth. Fes traced his hand along them, searching for anything that might explain where the emperor would have gone. There was nothing.

"Maybe he was here, and they followed him," he said.

"The door was locked," Azithan said.

There was that. With the door locked, it seemed less likely that they would have dragged him out, locked the door behind themselves, and even left the light on within this space.

No… there had to be another explanation, though there didn't seem to be anyplace else the emperor could have gone.

Fes made his way along the carpeted floor, his gaze running along the walls, but found nothing that would explain what might've happened to the emperor. A part of him expected to come across a hidden access point, but there wasn't any.

What if it wasn't in the walls?

His gaze drifted to the floor and the carpet. It didn't appear to have been moved, but what if the emperor knew something about this place that Azithan didn't? The emperor had known of its existence and had told Azithan how to find it, so it was possible that the emperor had known of another way out of here, and it was just as likely that he had kept that information from Azithan.

Jaken crouched down next to him, watching, as Fes started to roll back the carpet. "What are you doing?"

"What does it look like I'm doing? I'm trying to see if there is anything beneath this carpet."

"Why would you think there would be?"

"Because there is no other way out, from what I can tell," Fes said.

"I don't understand," he said.

Fes paused, the carpet half rolled up. "Look around you. If your father was here"—he looked up at Azithan, who continued to hold out a dragon relic, letting it glow softly as he searched the room, the power from his spell pulsing off him—"and the longer that we're here, the more I believe he was, then there would have to be someplace that he would have gone. I agree with Azithan that it doesn't make sense that he would have simply disappeared. The door was locked, Jaken."

Jaken stared at Fes for a moment before helping him roll back the carpet. When they were done, Fes stood staring at the floor. It might be his imagination, but there was a section of the floor that looked a little different than the rest.

Fes traced that part of the floor. There was nothing

that he could detect that felt different, but he was sure that it was there.

Using his connection to the Deshazl magic, Fes probed it.

Strangely, he felt a reverberation. It came softly, little more than an echo of pressure against him, but it was definitely there.

"Azithan?"

The fire mage joined him, crouching nearby. He ran his hands along the floor, pushing out with a spell. As he did, his breath caught. "Why wouldn't he have told me about this?"

"Maybe he didn't want you to know about it."

Azithan frowned at Fes.

Fes shrugged. "What if he was worried that you might be involved in an attack on him?"

"Fezarn, you know that I would never—"

"It doesn't matter what *I* know. All that matters is what the emperor believed. And though he might have shown you this room, that doesn't mean he wasn't still willing to have another way out in case there was danger."

"It doesn't matter if there's another way out if we can't open it," Jaken said.

"That's just it. If we can figure it out, how was your father going to be able to do so?"

"He is Deshazl."

"He might be Deshazl, but he doesn't know how to use his connection to that magic."

Fes closed his eyes, trying to think through the possibilities. On a whim, he unsheathed his sword and used that to pry into the ground, trying to dislodge a section of the stone. As he did, he felt the floor move.

His breath caught. That was it.

He continued to jam the sword deeper into the stone, trying to get leverage, and each time he did, he managed to pry it a little more.

Jaken joined him, sliding his sword into the growing crack, and together they popped the stone section of flooring up.

When they were done, they sat looking into a darkened opening.

"He wouldn't have come here," Fes said softly.

"How do you know?"

Fes looked over at Jaken. "Look at how hard it was for the two of us to open this. If he were here by himself, there wouldn't have been any way for him to have opened it." Fes looked over at the rolled-up carpet. They might've found a way out of here, but that still didn't explain what had happened to the emperor. "And he wouldn't have been able to push the carpet back into place."

"Unless he had help," Jaken said.

"Who would've helped? Anyone who might have done

so would have needed to replace the floor and the carpet, but then they would have needed to lock the door behind him."

More than that, they would have needed to be trustworthy, and after an attack by the servants within the palace, Fes could easily imagine the emperor not trusting anyone.

"What if there were servants who weren't willing to attack?"

"You know the servants better than I do. Did you see any that seemed to hesitate?"

Jaken met his gaze, frowning slightly. "No."

Fes stared into the darkened hole, wondering whether they should risk descending into it. If they didn't, there might not be any way of finding what had happened to the emperor, but even if they went in there, there wasn't a guarantee that they would find him. It was far more likely that Toulen servants had come across him and managed to restrain him.

Maybe their time was better spent searching through the palace for the emperor, but Fes didn't think so. He didn't think that they would find anything if they went wandering through the palace, nothing other than more of the Toulen soldiers and totems that they would have to fight.

This was the first place that had finally started to offer a chance for success.

"I'm going down," he said.

"Fezarn, I'm not certain that is the best idea."

"Probably not." Fes smiled up at Azithan. "But I don't have any other ideas."

He lowered himself into the opening, gripping the stone. He felt around with his feet until he found what appeared to be a ladder descending deeper into the ground. He shifted his position until he could get his feet locked onto the rungs, and from there, he climbed down into the darkness.

As he went down, the earthy odor that he'd noticed before intensified.

He didn't like the idea of this. What would he find down here? It was dark enough that he couldn't see well, and even if he could, he wasn't sure that he was making the right decision. Above ground, Jayell was searching for help. What would happen when she got to the fire mages and brought them back here? Would they still be able to help? Maybe it would be better to wait.

Fes continued down. Sound from above made him look up, and he realized that he wasn't alone. Jaken followed him.

He nodded to the other man and they continued down, moving quickly.

The ladder was carved into stone, and there was a surprising amount of grip available. Fes was thankful for that, for if it weren't there, he would have slipped and likely would have fallen into the darkness. Every so often, he paused, looking to see whether there was any sign of anything else that he might recognize, but there wasn't anything.

Down and down they went.

Fes's arms and legs began to burn, and with each step on the ladder, he started to question what he was doing. Eventually, he would have to make his way up, but curiosity took him, and now he wanted to know where they were going.

"How much farther do you think it is?" Jaken asked from above him.

"I don't know," Fes said.

"I can't believe this has been here," Jaken said. "It seems to keep going."

Fes nodded but wondered whether Jaken could even see it. In the darkness, there was not much that he could even see, leaving him struggling to see much more than directly in front of him. Everything was a haze of gray and darkness.

Eventually, that began to change. A faint light drew him, and he realized as he went down that the light came from far below. Knowing there was an end—at least knowing there was something else that he would find—gave him renewed strength. Fes continued down the stairs, moving more quickly. His arms and legs were burning, but he ignored them, focusing on the endpoint, thinking only of the light far below that grew gradually closer.

As he descended, he knew that he was close. Slowly, the light became something more. It became a brightness, the light filling everything around him.

And then there was nothing.

Fes hung suspended on the ladder, his legs kicking freely. "Hold up," he called to Jaken.

He swung, debating whether to drop. From here, he couldn't see the ground, though there was enough light that he thought he should be able to. If there was ground beneath him, where was it? How much farther would he have to go? Going back up wasn't an option. There was something down here. He only needed to find it.

Fes hung and then pulled on his Deshazl magic, wrapping himself with it. If nothing else, he could use it to create a barrier.

He dropped.

Dropping to the ground left him falling freely for a long moment, kicking his legs as he descended. He tried not to think about where he might land—or *if* he might land—and let himself fall.

And then he struck the ground.

He let out a relieved breath. At least there had been an endpoint.

He looked around. Everything here had the soft

glowing light, almost filling it. It made it difficult to see clearly.

He should have known better than to descend into a space where he didn't have any idea of where he was going, but now that he was here, now that he had finally reached the bottom, he wondered what was here. There had to be some purpose for this, but as far as he could tell, that purpose didn't make any sense.

"Is it safe?" Jaken hollered from high above.

"I think so," Fes said.

Suddenly, Jaken dropped next to him. He looked around, squinting against the darkness. "Can you see anything?"

"Not that well," Fes said.

"Odd, isn't it?"

"Only if you think that we should be able to see something because of the light."

"That is why it's odd," Jaken said.

Fes smiled. He was thankful he wasn't alone and appreciated that Jaken was here, even if now that they were down here, there might not be any way to get back to safety. How were they going to reach the ladder high overhead?

"Maybe this was a mistake," Fes said.

Jaken glanced over. "Now you say that?"

Fes pointed, and Jaken followed the direction of his

pointing, looking up at the space they had descended down through.

"Yes. That will pose a challenge."

Fes chuckled. "Are you always so understated?"

Jaken shrugged. "It does no good to get excitable about this. We made our decision. Now we must figure out what else we will do."

Fes laughed to himself. He hadn't expected Jaken to be quite so practical.

"There has to be something down here. There's some reason for this space, though it's not the easiest place to reach."

"Perhaps that's by design," Jaken said.

"Why, though? What reason would there be to make it so difficult to get down here?"

"It's possible that something is stored here," Jaken said.

"Why do you think we can't see anything?"

Noise above them drew Fes's attention, and he looked up to see Azithan descending the ladder. He could barely make him out, only clearly enough when he watched Azithan drop down, joining them. He did so with a little less grace than either of them had managed and came to stand near them, looking around.

"I take it that the two of you have already realized where we are?"

Fes and Jaken shared a long look.

"We haven't," Fes said. "We can't see anything."

Azithan glanced at both of them, an incredulous look on his face. "You can't see anything?"

Fes shook his head. "There's bright light, but nothing else around us."

Azithan frowned. "Interesting."

"Why is that interesting?"

"It's interesting because I can see quite well," he said.

Fes grunted. "If you can, then tell us where we are."

Azithan turned and pointed. "The hall continues in that direction.."

"It only goes in one direction?" That didn't seem to make a whole lot of sense to Fes, not considering where they were and what they had come across. There had to be something else here, some other explanation that would make sense, but what was it?

"There is a wall behind us, but nothing else," he said.

Fes frowned. "Have you been here before?" he asked.

He didn't think that Azithan had. The fact that he hadn't known this place existed made it unlikely, but there were things about the fire mage that Fes didn't fully comprehend. It was possible that Azithan had been here before. If he had, maybe he would know how to get them out.

"I have not," he said. "It is interesting that this is here, and more interesting that it is so difficult to reach."

"That was sort of our take."

"Shall we go?"

"Go where?" Fes asked.

"To see where this goes."

"Since you appear to be the only one of us who can see where we're going, I think you're going to need to lead."

Azithan nodded as if there had been no other possibility. He started ahead of them, and Fes followed. As they went, Azithan paused every so often, peering into the strange light. What was he seeing? They would pause for Azithan to look around, and when he seemed to find something, he hurried forward,

Jaken watched, and he had a troubled expression on his face.

"What is it?"

"This. All of this. I am not quite certain where we are, but something about it feels off."

"Other than the fact that we are so far beneath the earth that I have no idea how we intend to get back out?"

Jaken glanced over at him. "Such as that."

"Azithan?"

The fire mage raced forward, and every so often, Fes expected him to pause and come back and join them, but he continued racing in front, almost as if drawn forward. And maybe he was. It was possible that there was something Azithan detected that Fes did not. If that were the case, they needed to follow and say nothing, but if

Azithan were aware of something, it would be helpful for them to share.

"Do you see anything?" he asked.

Azithan shook his head. "The hallway continues through here."

"If it continues, then are you sure this is the right plan?"

Azithan turned back to them. "You would have us go back?"

"I would have us at least consider where we're going."

"We need to keep moving through here," Azithan said. "I don't know why, but I have a feeling there is something important up here."

"I'm not sure that your feeling is what we need right about now," Fes said.

Azithan glanced at him. "Then trust that I suspect we will discover all that we need to know by continuing onward."

Fes shook his head. "I have a hard time trusting anything, especially when it comes to what we're facing here."

Azithan stared at him but didn't say anything more. He continued on, hurrying through the darkness, leaving Fes and Jaken to follow.

The farther they went, the more the glowing around them seemed to intensify. Fes wasn't sure, but that seemed important, though he didn't know quite why. What was it about that glowing that was important?

He still couldn't see anything clearly through it. Whatever it was pulled him and seemed to draw Azithan with it.

Slowly, it became even more intense, brighter and brighter as they went, leaving Fes to fumble forward. No longer could he easily see where he was going.

He grabbed onto Azithan's shoulders and kept close. Jaken did the same to Fes, holding on as they moved through there.

"I don't like this," Jaken said.

Fes glanced over at him, smiling. "I don't like it, either, but Azithan seems to know where he's going."

"Azithan might be able to see where he's going, but I can't."

Fes looked forward. Did his ability to see have anything to do with fire magic?

He unsheathed his sword, contemplating carving through a spell, but that wasn't what he detected. It wasn't a spell so much as it was an energy that was all around them.

The longer he went, the more he felt sure that there was more to this than he realized. It was more than just the energy and more than just a spell. It was power, but what kind of power? What did it mean for him?

Maybe it meant nothing.

As he staggered forward, he stared, looking into the brightness all around him.

There was something familiar about the light glowing all around him, and it wasn't until Azithan stopped that Fes realized what it was.

"Dragon relics."

Azithan turned, prying Fes's hand free from his shoulder.

Fes leaned toward him. "That's it, isn't it? This is all about dragon relics."

"That is what I suspect."

"What kind of relic glows this brightly?"

"Not a relic. Many relics."

"Many? Why would there be many relics?" Fes caught himself, thinking that he understood. They had run from the attack on the fire temple and had come to the capital wanting to find a way to safety, assuming that fire mages might be able to protect them, and had discovered the stores were gone. But maybe they weren't. Perhaps they still had reason to hope.

"This, I believe, is the long-lost dragon throne," Azithan said.

Somewhere nearby, Jaken gasped.

CHAPTER TWENTY-THREE

"What's the dragon throne?" Fes asked. He wished he could see it, but even his hands in front of his face were no more evident than anything else. He couldn't make out any sign of dragon relics, though there *was* a sense that powerful relics were nearby.

"It's nothing but a myth," Jaken said.

"It's not a myth."

The voice came from somewhere nearby, but Fes couldn't see where. There was movement and the sound of footsteps. With them, he suddenly became aware of another presence.

"The dragon throne is not a myth. The emperors throughout time have all known of its existence."

It was the emperor.

He was here.

"How is it that you're here?" Fes blurted.

The emperor laughed bitterly. "When the attack began, I went the only place that I could think of going. I should have left word about where I intended to go, but you had been gone, and there was no word of when you might return."

"The door was locked," Jaken said.

The emperor pressed his lips together while regarding Jaken. "You don't think I have made preparations for that possibility?"

There would have to be something more to how the emperor had gotten here and hid, but before he had a chance to ask, Azithan stepped forward.

"What happened?"

"An attack that my fire mages, Dragon Guard, and soldiers could not stop. The servants..." As he trailed off, Fes heard much the same disappointment in his voice as Jaken had in his. "I came here for safety."

"What is this?" Fes asked. "What's the dragon throne?"

"It's supposed to be a fully preserved dragon," Jaken said.

"Fully preserved? As in skin and scales and everything?"

"Nothing quite like that, Fezarn," the emperor said. "The dragon throne represents a dragon that was brought deep beneath the palace, preserved here for the possibility of an emergency. When I first learned of it, I had wondered how such a relic would ever have managed to have been brought here completely intact. Now that I know of the connection between the dragons and the early empire, I think I understand."

"What do you mean by intact?"

"Azithan?"

"I don't think I should do this," Azithan said.

"Just draw enough power away that they can see."

A spell built, and it came with enormous power, so much so that Fes shook with it. The light within the chamber faded. It was only a fraction, barely more than a little, but it faded enough for Fes to make out shapes. He could see Jaken standing nearby, sword clutched in hand, as useless with it as Fes would be. He could feel and see Azithan. The power of his spell was enormous, but Fes had the sense that there was even more power available to him if he were inclined to take it.

Finally, there was the emperor. He looked well, certainly better than Fes had expected after everything he would have had to have been through. Still dressed in his robes of office, the only sign of what he'd been through was the tightness around his eyes and a smudge of dirt or soot on his forehead.

Behind them, Fes saw bones.

There was no other way to describe it. It was the remains of an enormous dragon. As the emperor had said, the bones were completely intact. Fes could easily make out the shape the dragon once had taken and could see the horns curling up, horns that were even longer than the one that Azithan had given to Jayell.

Power radiated from the dragon bones.

It was the source of everything. It filled the space around them with light, leading to a powerful glowing, bright enough that he could barely see through it, even knowing it was there.

"There's so much power here," Fes whispered.

"It's an intact dragon," the emperor said.

"What does that mean? Why does it cast so much light? The dragon relics don't usually do that."

"Not unless they're used," Azithan said.

"Is this relic being used?"

Azithan shook his head. "I can't tell. It… It is impressive." He turned to the emperor. "And it's more than one dragon."

"This is too much for a single dragon. It would be enormous," Azithan said.

"My father told me that this dragon came here to protect the city. It watched over us."

"Your father believed that even though the stories have long said the empire destroyed the dragons out of fear?" Fes asked.

"The stories might have said that, but those who know have never believed that the empire feared the dragons. How could we, with our fire mages? We have benefited from them, and it seems as if the dragons have benefited from us."

"With this here, we will be able to protect ourselves," Azithan said.

"Perhaps," the emperor said.

"You don't think this will work?" Azithan started forward and stopped near the dragon. He held his hand above the jaw, barely there.

"I'm not certain whether this will work or not. The dragon relic is unique, as you said, and I'm not certain we should use the dragon throne in such a way."

"They attacked the temple," Azithan said.

The emperor gasped. "When the servants began to attack, I knew there was a coordinated plan, but I didn't know the extent of it. I would never have expected them to attack the temple."

"The servants didn't attack the temple. That was the Damhur with their Deshazl. As you've seen, the Deshazl have an ability of cutting through fire magic, and they used that to their advantage."

"So the Toulen are working with the Damhur."

"Apparently, the people of Toulen and those of the Damhur are connected, much like the fire mages are connected to people from the Damhur. Much like Asharn and the Deshazl share a connection." Fes still couldn't believe how connected everything was, but it made a certain sort of sense. With everything connected in such a way, the ancient war truly had never ended.

"We are woefully underprepared," the emperor said.

"We thought we would have allies, but they have failed us," Fes said.

"The people of Toulen have never been an ally. We have managed an uneasy peace, but nothing more than that," the emperor said. "Any belief that they would provide help is..."

Fes ignored him, as he was drawn to the dragon remains. It was strange, the brightness glowing out from them unlike any other dragon relic that he'd ever seen. The power within them clear to him, clearer than daylight. It troubled him that there would be such brightness. Why should there be unless someone was using the dragon throne, drawing power from it? Instead, when Azithan had attempted to draw upon it, it had dimmed.

He started to make his way around the dragon throne. At one point, he rested his hand on what would have been one of the leg bones. When his hand touched the bone, power pulsed back, reverberating against him.

Fes jerked his hand back. What was that?

He moved on, worried that he might be disrupting the power balance, and brushed against a rib bone. Much like before, there came a pulsing reverberation of power, and it echoed within him.

He frowned. There was something to this power that

he didn't fully understand, but it was clear that power was still within the dragon.

What exactly did it come from?

More than that, why should he feel it so clearly?

It was more than just an awareness of the relic. It was an awareness of the power within it. None of that made any sense to Fes.

As he walked back toward the front of the dragon, standing in front of the massive jaw, Azithan watched him. "What is it, Fezarn?"

Fes shook his head. "I'm not sure. I can feel power from the bones."

Azithan nodded. "There *is* power within them. It makes sense that you would be aware of it."

Fes looked over at him. "There might be power, but I've never felt it from dragon relics before."

Azithan glanced at Jaken and then the emperor. "Can you feel the power within this?"

Jaken joined Fes and reached out, touching the dragon bones. He held his hand in place for a long moment before finally taking it away and shaking his head. "I don't detect anything."

The emperor did the same, and he left his hand in place for even longer than Jaken had, staring at the bones. "The first time I learned of the dragon throne, I wanted to feel the power of it. It was then that I knew I wouldn't have any potential as a fire mage," he said softly. He kept his gaze locked on the dragon. “There have been emperors who were fire mages. It has helped maintain our position over the years. I thought… I thought that coming here would free some part of me and would allow me to reach that magic, but…” He shook his head, leaning forward, his hand still resting on the dragon. “I felt nothing. My father was disappointed. He wanted me to reach for power much as he could, and when I failed, I think in his heart he felt as if I failed him.”

“Not all emperors have been fire mages, though,” Jaken said.

His father looked over. “Not all, but he blames my mother for my lack of ability. Were it not for her…”

“Your mother was Deshazl,” Fes said.

The emperor nodded. “She was. I don’t understand why I couldn’t have both abilities, but at the time, I was little more than a disappointment. Not able to reach for fire magic and dependent on other fire mages for safety.”

Fes sighed. He couldn’t imagine what that might have been like for him. “How old were you when you came here the first time?”

“I was fifteen, and of age to come into power. There was no power, and…”

“Why haven’t you brought me here before?” Jaken asked.

The emperor sighed. “You were tested differently. I feared that you would take after me, and rightly so.”

"Is that why you encouraged me to train with the Dragon Guard?"

The emperor nodded. "I don't have any particular abilities, at least I didn't think that I did. And I didn't train, giving me no way of protecting myself. I was not going to repeat that mistake with you. I made certain that you had all the training possible, wanting you to be as skilled as I could help make you."

"And my testing?"

The emperor dragged his gaze away from the dragon. "Azithan ensured that you were adequately tested."

"I can see that neither of you feel the power from the dragon," Fes said. "Which still doesn't explain why I can." He looked over at Azithan. "What is it that allows me the ability to detect this power?"

Azithan shook his head. "I can't explain that. You are Deshazl. And as far as I know, you haven't shown any ability to use fire magic. Not that I haven't tested you." Azithan smiled. "One of the first things I did before entrusting you to recover the first dragon relic was to test you. I didn't need you claiming the relics and using them."

Fes grunted. He hadn't known that Azithan had tested him, but wasn't surprised by that. "Why can I feel the magic now?"

Azithan shook his head. "Perhaps because you are so attuned to the Deshazl magic. Maybe it's because you have touched the dragons. Or maybe it simply something else that we don't understand."

Fes reached toward the dragon again, bracing himself.

As before, power pulsed back, pressing into him. It came as a blast, almost enough to unsettle him, and he held his hand still, determined to understand why he should detect it. His understanding of the Deshazl magic was the same as Azithan's, and because of that, he shouldn't be able to detect the fire magic or the potential within the dragon bones.

Power beat upon him.

As it did, Fes was reminded of his vision.

Why should the power he felt remind him of what he had known in the moments before he had nearly died?

He pulled his hand back, looking up at the dragon bones. Why should he detect such power from the dragon bones? There had to be some reason.

"Fezarn?"

"Azithan, I still feel the power coming from the bones, but..."

It was strange, and Fes couldn't fully explain why he should be aware of that power, nothing other than the fact that he was Deshazl.

Yet, the more that he attempted to reach his hand out, the more he tried to touch the dragon bones, the more certain he was that it was something else other than his Deshazl connection.

Could it be the fact that he had nearly died?

That seemed an odd reason to be aware of such ongoing power, but what other answer was there?

He decided to reach for the dragon throne again.

As he did, he held his hand in place, determined to see what it was that he detected. It had to be more than merely his Deshazl connection. Fes held his hand in place, fighting against the urge to withdraw.

Power pulsed against him, but it was more than that. There was a familiarity to the way that it did, and he recognized that power. He had felt that power before, he had known it, but why? This dragon had long ago passed from this world.

Despite that, there still was the sense of life in the power within the dragon. He knew that it shouldn't be there, and he knew there was no reason to be aware of that sense, but he couldn't shake what he felt. He couldn't shake the belief that there remained a part of this dragon that wasn't completely gone.

Was that why the bones still glowed?

"The dragon's not gone," Fes said.

Azithan frowned. "Fezarn, not only is the dragon gone but the skin and scales, as I believe you said, are no longer. There is nothing but the bones."

Fes looked over at Azithan. "I understand, but that's what I'm picking up on. That's why I can feel the power within the dragon."

The emperor stared at Fes as if he were mad. "The dragon throne is from the dragon that was lost when the empire was founded. These bones—and this throne—have been here since the very beginning. Whatever you think you detect, it's wrong. The dragon is gone."

Fes couldn't shake the sense that the dragon wasn't gone in the way that the dragons they had used in the past might have been. The bones were clean of tissue, there was no sign of the scales, and there was nothing that should explain what Fes felt, but in spite of that, he felt it with a certainty deep within. There was something more to this dragon than there should be. It was not gone.

And if the dragon wasn't gone, was there some way to bring it back?

They had wanted help, and what help could they have other than a dragon like this?

It seemed impossible, but then again, so much of what Fes had been through over the last year seemed impossible. None of what he had experienced should have happened. He should not have any sort of magic, and yet he did. He should not be able to do many of the things that he could, but despite that, Fes managed to reach power that made no sense to him.

He touched the dragon bones again, holding his hand in place. This time, he was ready for the strange reverberation, and he listened, hoping that perhaps the dragon would explain what it was, as if to still speak through the generations.

As the power echoed within him, Fes continued to feel it, aware that magic was within the bones. Why should he be so aware of that magic? What was it that took place that allowed him to detect the power within the dragon bones? As it pushed against him, Fes instinctively reacted, pushing back.

When he had felt the reverberation of magic before, he hadn't pushed back. This time, when he did, his Deshazl magic reacted. It surged up from deep within him, power that was different than he had used before. The power surged forward, coming from the depths within him that he had rarely attempted to reach.

With that power came a sense of heat.

That heat was familiar. It was the heat and pain and power that he had felt when he had very nearly died. It was that heat which had kept him alive.

Fes pulled his hand back, staring at the bones.

Was it the remains of the dragon—this dragon throne—that had saved him?

Jayell and Azithan had mentioned power that had filled him, and they had mentioned how he had survived something that should have killed him. Maybe it came from this dragon throne.

If it did, Fes wondered why it had changed him.

He tried to think about what it was that he had experienced, thinking back to that vision, trying to reach through those memories, drawing on the sense of power that he had when consumed by the dragon power, and remembered the way the dragon had surged, growing brighter and brighter, until eventually it was nothing more than light that had joined with Fes.

That mattered, somehow.

He reached for the dragon throne again, resting his hand on the bones, a question rising within him.

Could it be that this dragon throne deep within the bowels of the palace had somehow been responsible for restoring him?

If that were the case, what did it mean that he had the vision of heat and flame surging within him? What did it mean that he had felt as if the fire from that dragon had joined with him?

That had to be significant somehow, but why?

That power surged within him again, echoing, reverberating against him, a familiar sense that he thought he should know. It continued to slam into him, and like he had before, Fes pushed against it, sending his magic against that power. He pulled on more strength, drawing as much as he could.

The sense of magic continued to grow, building. It was more power than he had been able to summon prior to nearly dying. Could he have been meant to come here?

"Fezarn?"

Fes ignored Azithan, focusing only on the dragon throne. The power of the bones filled him, different than any other dragon relic he had been around. This was more than the scattered remains of dragons—he was sure of it. And as he had told Azithan, he thought that whatever it was he detected meant there was a different sort of power here.

It was the kind of power that he needed to reach. It was the kind of power that he needed to understand. Somehow, he would have to know what it meant. That knowledge was critical.

And it was more about restoring that power than using it.

It always had been.

Why hadn't he seen that before now?

But then, he had. When he had seen the dragon rise, reborn through the effort of the Damhur, he had known the truth deep within himself. He had felt the force of the dragons, and he had known that they must return. Now that he had spent time with the dragons, he felt that even more clearly. Somehow, Fes needed to ensure the dragons were restored. That was his purpose as Deshazl.

Was that the reason for his magic?

Maybe the dragons had gifted the Deshazl, though he didn't think that was entirely it. They were born of the same magic, the power that flowed through the Deshazl also filling the dragons, and it was that power which Fes thought to connect to. He was meant to connect to the dragon. That was what the vision had told him.

Fes pushed, sending his magic back against that of the dragon throne.

The magic poured out of him, heat and fire and power that he had never possessed before flowing from him and moving from him and into the dragon throne. For a moment, Fes thought that he was losing his own magic in the process, but that wasn't it at all. It was almost as if his magic joined with that of the dragon throne, blowing out from him before rejoining him. The powers mingled together.

Someone shouted, but Fes ignored it. He remained focused on the task, keeping his hand on the dragon, thinking back to the image of what he had seen in his vision.

The dragons could be reborn. He had seen it happen before.

Fes poured power from him, and it joined with that in the dragon bones, and…

Something changed within him.

Power exploded.

Fes had no other way of explaining what it was. It was a mixture of pain and fire, much like his dying had felt. And much like that, there was a surge of blackness, and for a moment, Fes thought that he *was* dying, but through that sensation, he had another sense: that of the dragon.

Awareness of it surged within him.

Fes gasped.

The bones began to move.

Was that because of him, or was that because of something else taking place?

He continued to pour out his magic, and it was as if the dragon bones—the dragon throne—guided him. Fes could no longer withdraw his power, even if he were to want to. Given what he detected, he didn't want to. He wanted to let that power flow out from him. He wanted to be filled with it. He wanted to have that magic spill out, growing stronger and stronger as it joined with the dragon bones.

The light around him changed.

It took Fes a moment to understand why and what he detected, but it was more than merely the light changing. It was the dragon bones themselves. The power that had surrounded the bones no longer glowed the same way. It shifted, shimmering, and slowly—gradually—there came a darkening.

"Fes!"

He blinked and felt torn back.

Fes shook, trying to free himself from whoever grabbed him, and realized that Jaken and Azithan had their hands on either arm, pulling him backward.

"Let me go!"

"Fezarn," Azithan said. His voice was tight, and there was almost a Calling within it.

That Calling sent Fes into a rage. He thrashed, throwing Azithan off him, and turned to Jaken, prepared to attack him. They would Call him? They would use that magic against him when all he wanted to do was help and save the dragons?

Jaken stared back at Fes, and he realized that Jaken didn't want to fight him.

There was something else.

Movement.

Fes turned toward the movement, realizing what it was that he saw.

The dragon throne was gone.

In its place was a deep purple-scaled dragon.

CHAPTER TWENTY-FOUR

Fes could scarcely breathe. He stared at the dragon. There was no doubt in his mind that this dragon was the same one he had seen in his vision. *He* had done this?

"What… what did you do, Fezarn?" Azithan whispered.

"I don't know. I felt power against me, and I tried to resist it, and as I did, I felt my Deshazl magic—magic that has changed since I nearly died—flow into the dragon throne."

"You *raised* a dragon," the emperor said. He stared at the dragon.

They all did.

The dragon was enormous, much larger than either of the two dragons that Fes had seen, and heat flowed from it. The scales were such a dark color that they might as well be black, though Fes knew from his vision that wasn't the case. The creature glowed softly, an orange sheen that seemed to radiate from deep within as if parting through the dragon's scales.

Somehow, Fes *had* raised a dragon.

He should be pleased, but all he could think about was what had happened to the other dragons. He should feel nothing but relief at raising one more, in bringing back into the world a creature like the dragon, but he felt none.

Only sadness.

What would happen if the Damhur managed to learn of this dragon?

Would it be used?

If they had come to the city with the Toulen attack, then it was possible that they would try to Call this dragon. He would *not* fail another dragon.

This was an old dragon. Fes felt that with great certainty. Maybe it was even what had once been called an Elder dragon, such as his namesake. With power like that, he didn't want the dragon to be used. The dragon deserved to fly freely, much as it had in Fes's vision. But then, in that vision, there had been other dragons.

Could it be that he had seen a glimpse of the past? Could the dragon have gifted him with that, allowing him to know what it once had been like?

The dragon roared.

The sound rumbled, and everyone took a step back.

"I begin to think this is unsafe," Azithan said.

"The dragon won't harm us," Fes said.

"Are you certain of that?" Azithan asked. "There have been exactly zero dragons in the world before a few months ago, and all of a sudden, now there are three. Two of them have been claimed by the Damhur, and now there is this one. It seems to me that the dragons are far more dangerous than what you believe."

Fes couldn't take his eyes off of the enormous dragon. It looked back at him, the orange eyes practically glowing.

What did the dragon think of it?

"You called to me," Fes said. He locked eyes with the dragon, uncertain whether it would answer, but suspecting that it knew what he said. The other dragons had understood him.

"There was a need," the dragon said. His voice rumbled, making the stone of this tunnel practically shake. Fes trembled beneath the sound, but needn't have. The dragon remained motionless, completely non-threatening, and watched Fes and the others.

"Do you know what happened with the other two dragons?"

"They have been used."

"Unfortunately, they have," Fes said.

"You were to have protected them. Dragons protect Deshazl. Deshazl protect the dragons."

The same sense of guilt that he'd felt when the other two had been called struck him. "I tried. I did everything that I could to protect the dragons, but the Damhur are too powerful."

"And you are not?"

"I did what I can," Fes said.

"It was not enough."

Shame filled Fes. The dragon was right. Everything he had done had not been enough. He hadn't managed to save the dragons, and he hadn't managed to protect them from the risk and threat of the Damhur.

Would the same thing happen to this dragon?

"No," the dragon said.

"No what?" Fes asked, frowning.

"They would not be able to control me."

"You knew what I was thinking?"

"You were responsible for bringing me back. There is a connection between us."

Fes frowned. "I don't understand."

"You are the reason I'm awake. That is the reason that there is a connection between us."

Fes stared at the dragon, unable to take his eyes off the enormous creature. There was something majestic about him—and he was sure this dragon was male. Not only was there the enormity—far larger than any of the other dragons he'd encountered—but there was something powerful about the way the dragon looked at him, a sense of age and authority.

"We have lost other dragons," Fes said.

"They are not lost," the dragon said.

"They are lost to us. The Damhur have claimed them, and because of that—"

The dragon leaned forward, steam rising from his nostrils. His wings started to unfurl, and Fes glanced around, worried that there wasn't space enough in this chamber for the dragon to stretch, but he needn't have. This chamber seemed made for the dragon.

And maybe it was. It was possible that the entire reason for this chamber's existence was to support the dragon, and now that it was back alive, it was possible that the dragon would be stuck here.

"They are not lost. They might be influenced, but they are not lost."

Fes glanced at the others with him. Azithan couldn't take his eyes off the dragon, staring at it while Jaken and the emperor stood off to the side. What were they thinking?

"What about you? Fes asked.

The dragon snorted and rose, filling the space around him. "I am safe."

"You're only safe because you're here, but what happens when you leave this place?"

"When I leave, I'll be safe."

Fes frowned, shaking his head. "When you leave, you run the risk of the Damhur Calling you, and—"

"I'm safe," the dragon said again, his voice a low growl.

Heat flared up in Fes's mind, and with it came a strange sensation, an awareness of the dragon that he shouldn't have.

It wasn't that he knew the dragon, but he could feel what the dragon felt, and more than that, he had a connection to that power.

It was that power which had joined with him.

With certainty, Fes knew that was what had happened. When he had lain dying, the dragon had joined, filling him. When he had seen the flames shooting toward him, that was because of the dragon. That joining had saved him—and had given him greater strength than he had otherwise.

But how?

An image flashed into his mind, a memory. It was the dragon sculpture.

Fes blinked, looking over at the dragon. "That was your doing?"

"That was me."

"What?"

Azithan stepped forward, and he looked at Fes. "What is it?"

Fes shook his head. "The dragon."

"I can see the dragon, Fezarn."

"He says that it was him in the sculpture."

"How is that possible?"

The dragon shifted, looking at Azithan before his gaze settled on the emperor and Jaken. Something in his voice changed, and Fes realized that he was making it so that he could be understood by all of them. He already knew from the other dragon that there was something in the way that the dragon spoke that allowed them to determine who could understand them, and it seemed that this dragon somehow knew how to make himself better understood to the others.

"There came a time when we were failing when the people you call the Damhur were controlling my people, and we found a vessel to place ourselves in until the time was right for our return. Not all of us were susceptible to the Calling, as you call it, but enough were to make it dangerous. The most powerful among us allowed ourselves to leave, separating our minds and power from our bodies, knowing that in time, we would return."

"All the dragonglass sculptures contain dragons?" Azithan asked.

Fes glanced over. "What do you mean by *all* of them? How many dragonglass sculptures are there?"

Azithan stared at the dragon. "Many."

The dragon lowered his head, steam billowing from his mouth and nostrils. "They were a vessel, nothing more. There were some who were tasked with keeping our frames together, protecting them so that when it was time for us to return, we would be able to do so."

Fes stared. Could that be the role the Deshazl had played in it? If that was the case, then why had they become the dragon walkers? Why had they allowed themselves to claim the dragon relics?

"The others were raised by using the dragon hearts," Fes said. "A different method."

"The hearts summoned the dragons from the dragon-glass. The method was no different."

"Why would the dragons allow themselves to be used by the fire mages?" Fes asked.

"Fire mages. Yes. There were some who called themselves that who were granted the capacity to benefit from our power. It was done so for our protection."

"Only some?" Azithan asked.

The dragon lowered his head even further, meeting Azithan's gaze. "There were only some who were worthy."

Azithan stared before taking a step back, moving away.

"We need your help," Fes said, glancing from the dragon to the emperor. "The city is under siege from those who would harm it."

"Fes—"

Fes turned to look at Jaken. The Dragon Guard

soldier stared at the dragon, and there was a sense of resolve emanating from him.

"We can't use the dragon to rescue the city. The moment people see the dragon, they will think that the empire has failed them."

"Because the dragons have returned?"

It was the emperor who stepped forward and nodded. "The empire was built on the belief that we defeated the dragons."

"Defeated?" the dragon snarled, shifting so that its wings unfurled. "The dragons would not be so easily defeated. We chose our fate."

Fes raised his hand, stepping between the emperor and the dragon. "Even if the Damhur haven't used the dragons and attacked, it's time for that lie to end. The people deserve to know what happened. They deserve to know the reason the dragons disappeared. It wasn't because the empire defeated them in some battle. It was because the empire worked with the dragons, and the dragons chose to allow themselves to retreat from the world so that they wouldn't cause more damage. That is valuable."

"Fes, you don't understand. Defeating the dragons is the one thing the empire has been known for."

Fes stared at the dragon before turning to the emperor. "And maybe it shouldn't be. When people realize that the Damhur intend to attack, or even when they realize the truth about the Asharn, they will realize that there is something else to worry about."

He turned his attention back to the dragon. Regardless of what the emperor and Azithan said, they would need the dragon. With a creature like this—a mighty dragon that had chosen to disappear from the world—there was much they could do to push back the Damhur from the city.

And once they rescued the city, they could move on, ensuring that the rest of the empire was safe. But first, they needed to save the city.

"Would you help?" he asked the dragon.

The dragon stared at him. "Is this what you want?"

There was something heavy within the question, even more than what the dragon asked. It was the question Fes had been asking himself for the last year or more, ever since he'd been drawn into something that he had not known he needed or wanted to be a part of. In that time, he had risked himself, challenging himself to try to figure out what it was that he wanted.

He had seen the effects of war and had seen the way that fighting had affected those he cared about. He had seen the way that violence had ruined lives, destroying entire cities. And now that he had seen the fall of the fire mage temple, he had seen the destructive force that the Damhur and their allies could bring to bear. The empire wouldn't be able to stand against that—not easily.

But none of that was really what he wanted. What he wanted was something different. He wanted to have the ability to see what was in his visions, to see the dragons flying freely, and to know what it was like to once more have dragons soaring overhead, filling the skies.

"It's the first step in what I want," he said.

The dragon shook its head and lowered it down to the ground. "Then I will help."

Fes stared, wondering what the dragon intended, before realizing that he wanted Fes to go forward and to climb on top of him.

He took a step, but Azithan grabbed his arm, pulling him back. "We don't know if the Damhur have attacked in Anuhr. It could be that it's only Toulen for now. But the moment the dragon is seen flying, everything will change within the empire."

Fes looked over at Azithan. "I know."

"And what happens if people are scared?"

"People will be scared," Fes said. "They have lived with the belief for a thousand years of the dragons as something to be feared. And the Damhur would only maintain that fear. If they are allowed to continue using the dragon, people will remain scared of them, and will never know that the dragons are not something to be feared."

He started to climb onto the dragon, finding his way along sharp spikes on the dragon's back and paused to look back at the emperor. "This is our way out."

The emperor stared at Fes.

"Not just me, but all of us. Toulen may have taken the palace, and they may have infiltrated the city, but they won't win. They can't."

He felt it with sudden certainty. Whatever else happened, he wouldn't let the city fall to the Damhur or Toulen. He would free the city, and then he would work with the dragon to release the other two dragons. And from there… From there, he would end the fighting. He would help ensure the dragons were freed for good.

Jaken took a step forward, joining Fes on the dragon.

"What are you doing?" the emperor asked Jaken.

"He's right, Father. It's time the people know the truth. We've seen it. The dragons were used, but they were not our enemy."

Fes helped Jaken climb onto the dragon.

The emperor stared up at them. "This is dangerous."

"It's less dangerous than attempting to return to the palace and facing the people of Toulen who have infiltrated the empire for decades. They have prepared all this time, readying themselves for this attack. They would have thought about everything we planned. Because they were likely present during much of the planning, they would have known what we intend," Jaken said.

Fes situated himself at the base of the dragon's neck, holding himself study. "They would not have anticipated this."

"Azithan?" the emperor asked.

"I think… I think Fezarn continues to surprise me." Azithan approached the dragon and touched the dragon's back. He paused, running his hands along the dragon's scales, and his eyes went distant. When they opened, he smiled. "All my life has been spent using the dragons, taking their power, and doing great things with it. Perhaps it's time that the dragons do great things with us."

He climbed onto the dragon and took a seat next to Jaken.

The emperor stared at the dragon for a long moment. Fes wondered what debate warred in his mind. He was Deshazl, but he was something different, too. His Deshazl connection had given him power of the dragons, but his time within the empire had given him a different perspective, one that meant that he had lodged within him the ancient beliefs of the empire, beliefs that ran contrary to the truth. Fes didn't have nearly so much invested in those old beliefs, so it was much easier to move on. It was not the same for the emperor.

Slowly, much more slowly than Fes wanted, the emperor approached the dragon. "Will he allow me to ride?"

The dragon roared. "You are Deshazl. You may ride."

CHAPTER TWENTY-FIVE

The dragon knew a different way out of the palace. They crawled forward, moving along the ground, each step taking them deeper and deeper before the dragon was able to unfurl his wings. Fes clutched the back of the dragon, trying to maintain his grip, afraid to do anything else. No one spoke. Fes didn't blame the others for their unwillingness. He didn't feel as if he could speak.

Not only was he with the dragon, but he was riding him.

Never in his wildest dreams would he ever have believed that he could ride a dragon. He had been brought up to fear them, knowing them as dangerous and deadly creatures, and it was only recently that he had changed that belief, but even then, he had never thought that he would *ride* the dragons. Once meeting—and speaking—to the dragons, he would never have thought it possible. They were far too proud.

The dragon reached the edge of a ridge and stood there for a moment, leaving Fes to wonder what he might do. There didn't seem to be a way out, not heading in this direction, though it was difficult to tell. Sitting atop the dragon made it hard to know what might be in front of him. No longer did bright light surround everything. Now that the dragon had returned, there wasn't that same overwhelming brightness that there had been, but the dragon himself blocked his view, making it difficult to see.

And then the dragon jumped.

It happened quickly, leaving Fes barely able to breathe. The dragon dove, somehow descending within this space, taking them deeper into the earth than they had been before.

Someone near him gasped, and Fes shared that shock and surprise, but there wasn't anything that he could do or say that would redirect the dragon.

The dragon flapped his enormous wings, and they took off.

Fes couldn't see clearly, but they must be in some sort of enormous cavern. The dragon obviously didn't struggle to understand and circled, rising higher and higher, the speed of his movement almost dizzying. Fes held tightly to the dragon, gripping the back of the creature, terrified that he might slip.

Light bloomed in front of them.

At first, Fes thought that it might be nothing more than the dragon breathing fire, but he thought he would have seen that differently. This was something else, and as he watched, as the dragon soared toward the distant light, he saw it more clearly.

When they emerged from the cavern, there would be terrified people throughout the city. They needed to be prepared for that, but more than that, Fes knew they needed to be prepared for what would happen if they encountered the totems. Would the dragon be able to handle them?

The heat that came from his new connection to the dragon had allowed him to melt the totems and had allowed him to escape when attacked. He didn't need to fear surviving the totem attack.

No. He needed to fear something else entirely. He needed to worry about what would happen if the dragon were Called and controlled.

Even though the dragon didn't think that he could be Called, he had been gone from the world for a thousand years, long enough that the people who were able to Call might have honed that ability, gaining even more skill with their Calling. He would have to be ready. Somehow, he would need to protect the dragon.

Fes took a deep breath, wondering if the connection between himself and the dragon would protect him. He couldn't tell whether the connection would make a difference or not, but somehow, Fes had to think that it would, and that he could use that bond to prevent the dragon from getting Called, used by either one of the Toulen or the Damhur.

And what if he couldn't?

He would have to find some way, but he wasn't sure what that would be.

And then they were out and in the open.

Fes looked down, leaning off to the side of the dragon, and was shocked to see that they weren't anywhere near the city.

"Where are we?" he asked Azithan.

The fire mage shook his head. "I can't tell. Outside of the city, but it was difficult to determine how far we were going underground."

Fes twisted, catching sight of mountains in the distance.

The dragon plains.

That was the only explanation that he could come up with. They were close, and much closer than he would have expected, which meant that the dragon must have traveled quite a bit farther underground than he had realized. How was that possible?

"Did you know that Anuhr was connected to the

dragon plains like that?"

The emperor shook his head. "I would never have imagined."

They circled higher and higher into the sky. As they did, Fes wished that he could be on the ground and that he could look up at the dragon to see him flying. He had only seen the dragon flying briefly and had only seen this one flying in his visions. What must it be like to see the dragon in its glory soaring overhead?

They started to the south. Toward the city.

Land swept past them, blurring faster and faster. Fes tried to keep track of where they were going, but he couldn't follow, not easily. As they went, all he knew was that they traveled toward the capital. Everything was streaks of green and brown. Occasionally he caught sight of blue, and he suspected that came from the river running along the border of the empire and Toulen. Moments passed, and they reached the city.

Azithan tensed as he sat next to Fes. Heat built from him before fading.

"What is it?" Fes asked.

Azithan looked down at the dragon. "I'm not certain that I'm worthy of using these relics."

"What makes you think that? You've always used the dragon relics."

"I have always used them, but that was before I knew that the dragons permitted only certain people to do so. What if I'm not one they would have deemed worthy?"

Doubt out of Azithan?

That surprised Fes. The fire mage was, if nothing else, always confident and always seemed to know what he wanted to do. Having a sense of uncertainty from him surprised Fes.

"You could ask him," Fes said. Wind whipped past him, tugging on his clothing and his hair. Something was freeing about sitting atop the dragon, something that felt natural. Still, in all of his visions of the dragon, he'd never seen anyone sitting on them. There had been dragonwalkers, but had there ever been a dragon rider?

Azithan turned to Fes. "And what of the others? Elorayne and Jayell and all of the other fire mages we left within the city? Will they all be deemed worthy?"

"I think we have to worry about that later," Fes said. "First we need to ensure the safety of the city." He turned his attention to the dragon and thought of the palace at the heart of the city. Would the dragon know where to go?

Fes needn't have worried. The dragon turned, heading straight over the city, veering toward the palace at the heart of the city, and dove.

The dragon let out a massive roar as he landed.

"I guess he's announcing himself," Azithan said.

They had landed in the courtyard outside the palace,

and Azithan, along with the emperor and Jaken, climbed off the dragon. Fes hesitated a moment before jumping down.

"What will you do?" Fes asked the dragon.

"I will stay," the dragon said.

"What if—"

The dragon roared again. Heat burst along his scales, sending Jaken and the emperor back. Azithan stayed fixed in place, and a fire mage spell bloomed from him, creating a sort of protection.

"You will know if they succeed," the dragon said, fixing Fes with a bright-eyed stare.

"I need to be strong enough to stop them."

"You aren't alone."

"What do you mean that I'm not alone?"

Power filled him, but it boiled up from within Fes, not coming from the dragon. At least, it didn't come *exclusively* from the dragon. It was a shared connection, and Fes realized what had changed since he had nearly died. The dragon filled him with his power.

He gasped. He could draw magic from the dragon and could use that to fight.

He took a shaky breath and stepped back. The dragon pushed off from the ground, his massive wings catching the air as he circled into the sky. Fes stared, amazed at the sight of the dragon as he circled. That was what he had wanted to see. Seeing a dragon flying freely in the sky over the empire had been what he had longed for, and now that he finally was able to see it, he would have to head into the palace and fight.

Azithan rested a hand on Fes's arm. "If we succeed in securing the palace and the city, then you can return with him."

Fes shook his head. "When we succeed, there will be another task."

Azithan frowned.

"We will have to go after the other two dragons." And more than that, they would have to find out if there was any way to help the rest of the dragons trapped within the dragonglass sculptures. "I know the emperor doesn't want to engage in war, but I don't know that we have much choice anymore. I wanted allies. Well…"

Fes continued to stare for a moment before turning his attention away, and they headed into the palace.

Toulen soldiers greeted them immediately.

Fes pushed out, using his Deshazl connection, drawing heat and fire that he didn't have before. It exploded outward, striking the Toulen soldiers in the chest, throwing them back. Jaken surged forward, finishing them off.

They stalked through the palace. A pair of totems met them, and Fes poured out his connection to the dragon, emptying it into the totems. They twisted and melted, turning into little more than broken sculptures.

"You'll have to leave something for the rest of us to do," Azithan said.

Fes smiled. "If we managed to clean out the palace, I'm sure there will be plenty for you to do."

They continued to storm through the palace. Every so often, they were set upon by Toulen soldiers, but none of them posed much of a threat now that Fes drew power from the dragon.

They made their way floor by floor, working through the palace, cutting down all of the Toulen soldiers. As they went, Fes paused at the totems most of all, destroying them. The totems gave the people of Toulen greater strength, and without them, they had less of an advantage. Jaken and the Dragon Guards could handle simple soldiers, but they couldn't handle indestructible totems.

They reached the emperor's quarters and finally paused. They hadn't encountered any more soldiers, leaving the palace apparently cleansed of the attackers.

Azithan turned to the emperor. "I think it's time that you stay here. We will finish removing the Toulen threat."

"You would leave me in my quarters alone?"

"Not alone."

Heat built behind Fes and he spun to see a line of fire mages storming into the emperor's rooms. Elorayne led them, with Jayell marching alongside her.

When Jayell saw Fes, her eyes widened. "You... you survived."

Fes frowned. "You didn't think that I would?"

"The city has been under attack, and we almost didn't make it back here."

"Totems?" Fes asked.

"They are all throughout the city, Fes. That's why Theole looked so smug."

"How did you get back here?"

"It was not without risk. We lost two fire mages, but we're here. Now we can—"

"How did you manage to protect the emperor?" Elorayne asked, interrupting Jayell.

Fes glanced back at the emperor. He was whispering with Jaken, and every so often, he would glance in Fes's direction.

"The emperor was safe when we found him."

A massive roar echoed, and Fes hesitated, looking up. The dragon was close—close enough that he could feel the heat from the creature, and it was almost as if the dragon wanted Fes to know that he was there.

What happened? Something had angered the dragon.

Fes turned and started toward the door, but Jayell caught his arm. "Fes?"

"I need to go," he said.

"What is it?"

He looked back at the emperor and Jaken. "It's a dragon."

"The Damhur are here?"

Fes shook his head. "We found something within the palace."

"You *found* a dragon?"

"We found the remains of a dragon." He met Jayell's eyes, staring at her for a long moment. "That sensation you felt when I was nearly dying came from the dragon," Fes said. "Had it not been for the dragon, I *would* have died."

"A *dragon* saved you?"

"Somehow," Fes said. "The dragonglass sculptures are the remains of the dragons. They placed themselves inside the sculptures, leaving their residual selves within them. I used that and helped restore the dragon."

Jayell glanced over at the emperor before her gaze paused on Elorayne. "You did this?"

"Like I said, I don't know exactly what it was that I did, other than I used the connection I felt. As far as I know, there are other dragons that we need to find and restore."

The dragon roared again, and Fes hurried from the room. There was an urgency in the call. Racing through the palace, he went up, looking for a way to reach the dragon at the top of the palace. He'd never been here and didn't know whether there was a way to get to the dragon, but thought that there had to be. The palace had been built in a time before the empire. It had been built at a time when people must have wanted to work with the dragons.

With that being the case, he suspected that the top of the palace opened up to the outside even though he'd never been there. He stopped at a door and flung it open.

Soaring overhead, much closer than he had expected, was the dragon.

Why was the dragon not higher?

Fes looked around, and as he did, he thought he understood.

A Calling.

While he was in the palace, he hadn't been aware of it. The sense of the Calling had been faint, and with everything else that they had been going through, he had overlooked it. But this sensation was unmistakable.

Who was Calling the dragon?

Worse, was it working?

He wasn't about to lose another dragon to a Calling.

Fes stood on top of the palace, looking down at the base of the palace, searching for whoever it was who might be Calling to the dragon. That Calling had to be here, not within the palace. And whoever it was would have to be powerful.

Could the Damhur have reached the capital?

If they had, it might already be too late. There was

only so much that Fes and the rest of the Deshazl descendants could withstand, and if they had come, bringing with them others who could Call the Deshazl, there might not be any way for them to resist that magic.

The war might be over before it even had a chance to begin.

The Dragon Guards would have the ability to fight, but how many totems would they be facing? How many soldiers—Deshazl, all of them—would the Damhur bring with them? How many people of the empire would turn, forced by a Calling?

And if they managed to gain control of this dragon, there would be no fight. There *could* be no fight. How could there be when there was no way to resist the might of the dragon?

"You need to fight this," Fes said.

The dragon roared and turned his attention to Fes, looking down from where he swirled. The sense of the dragon came to Fes, and with it, he had a sudden awareness of the effect of the Calling. It was a powerful Calling, enough that the dragon struggled against it.

More than a single person attempting to Call.

Fes felt the power and pushed against it.

The two of them joined together, power building from him, the combined energy of their connection giving him the strength needed to push back the Calling.

All he had to do was reach for the dragon, to push back the effect of the Calling, and together…

Fes felt the pressure from the Calling.

It demanded that he obey.

As much as he wanted to fight, there was a part of him that wanted nothing more than to relax his barriers, to allow that Calling to overrun him, and to fall to it.

He couldn't.

The dragon needed him.

He knew how to fight the effect of the Calling. He had tolerated much more than this. Elsanelle was far more potent than whatever it was he faced now, even though there seemed to be more than one person attempting a Calling. He could—and would—resist.

Fes forced his connection to the dragon. Together they would survive this.

"Focus on yourself," he said.

"They do not control me," the dragon roared.

Movement on the ground caught his attention and Fes realized that movement came near the base of the palace. Five people stood in a half circle, all looking up at him.

"Can you bring me down there?"

The dragon swooped toward him. There was less control to his movements than there had been before. It was jerky, almost violent as he flapped his wings.

Fes grabbed onto the dragon, throwing himself onto

his back, and the dragon jumped, spiraling down toward the ground to come to a landing not far from the cluster of five. Fes jumped from his back, exploding his Deshazl power outward from him. It met resistance, and Fes continued to push.

"You will not..."

Fes trailed off as he realized who stood before him. The dragon roared, and surprisingly, no one moved. Through his connection to the dragon, he prevented the creature from attacking but wondered how long he would be able to hold the dragon back. For now, he didn't want him to attack, not until he understood what had happened... and why.

"Indra?"

She ignored him, staring at the dragon. Fes didn't need her to turn her attention to him to know that she was partly responsible for the Calling. It seemed to be directed by Theole, as he stood in the center of a line of five people from Toulen, along with Indra and her mother.

It pained him seeing her do this.

"Please," he said, taking a step toward her. He pushed out with his Deshazl magic, not wanting to attack too aggressively, but what choice would he have, as she stood in front of him, attempting a Calling upon the dragon? Fes needed to protect the dragon, to do whatever it was that he could to defend the dragon from the effect of the Calling. Didn't she know that?

"Indra. You don't have to do this."

She turned to him then. As she stared at him, he saw the pain in her eyes, the hesitation she had.

She didn't *want* to do this.

"You need to stop. I don't know if the dragon can be controlled. I know that *you* can't Call him."

It took all of Fes's concentration to prevent the dragon from attacking. They weren't in any danger—not really—but that might change.

The effect of the Calling shifted, turning toward Fes.

He resisted.

When he had been under siege from Callings before, he had always used his connection to fight it, and this was no different, only it was more difficult than he had anticipated. The dragon helped, the connection between the two of them giving Fes additional strength and the ability to resist, but somehow, the Calling continued to press upon him.

He couldn't move.

Theole took a step forward. "Once we have you controlled, we will take care of the dragon."

Fes looked over at the dragon and realized that he couldn't move, either.

The Calling that controlled Fes somehow weakened the dragon, too.

Theole stopped in front of Fes. "I never would have suspected that you would manage to raise an Elder dragon. If any would have managed it, I expected the Damhur, but they managed only adolescents. And now we have an Elder."

Fes fought, but the Calling was powerful.

He tried to shift, reaching for his Deshazl magic, but even that failed to respond to him. It was as if Theole managed to suppress it.

"And now that we have the dragon, we will complete our attack on the city."

"You. Will. Never. Have. The. Dragon." Fes barely managed to get the words out through his gritted teeth.

Theole watched him, a smile curving his lips. "You aren't strong enough to oppose all of us."

Fes focused on Theole. He was right. He wasn't strong enough to oppose all of them, but maybe he didn't need to. Indra didn't want this. Fes was sure of that and was sure that she only did it because she had to and because her father forced her into this alignment.

He kept his focus on Theole. As he did, he was able to tease apart the effect of his Calling. It was greater than the others, and while Theole was more powerful at the Calling than the rest, he didn't have nearly the skill of Elsanelle. It was only because he was augmented by Indra and her mother, along with two others Fes didn't recognize, that he even managed to suppress Fes.

Could he break free of Theole's connection?

There had to be a way.

Fes focused on him, thinking about his Deshazl connection, letting it burn within him. It was there but buried deep, and somehow just out of reach.

He needed to borrow from the dragon.

Between the two of them, they were stronger than the Toulen.

All he needed to do was hone his attack. He needed to reach for Theole and nothing else. He had let the man live far too long.

That power began to seep up from within him.

Fes let it come, drawing through him. There was pain, and he knew the effect of the Calling tried to prevent him from reaching his magic, but he didn't care. The dragon and Fes were too powerful.

Fes focused it.

In a blast of heat and energy, it exploded out from him, striking Theole in the chest.

The Calling disrupted, the dragon lunged forward. He snapped his jaws around two of the Toulen—both people Fes didn't recognize and turned his attention to Indra before Fes threw himself in between them.

"No!"

The dragon roared, swallowing the two Toulen that he had attacked. "These Damhur attempted to control us."

"I know, but she, at least, is my friend." He turned to Indra. "It doesn't have to be this way. You can work with us. We don't need war."

Indra stared at him. "But Father—"

Fes looked down at Theole. His shirt steamed where the blast had struck, and he saw no movement. For Indra, Fes knew he should feel remorse, but he felt none. He was gone, and the effect of his Calling no longer tainted him, no longer drew to him, giving him freedom.

"Your father no longer needs to influence your decisions."

Indra glanced over at her mother. She said nothing, and Fes waited.

"We can end this," Fes said.

Indra turned toward him and, finally, nodded.

EPILOGUE

Fes sat on the top of the tower within the palace, looking out over the city. High in the sky, the dragon circled, occasionally swooping, but for the most part, merely flying, soaring through the clouds. It was an amazing sight, and it was one that had caused chaos throughout the city.

"I don't think people fully believe yet," Jayell said, looking over at Fes.

"They will."

He stared up at the dragon. There was a bond between them, a connection that he could feel burning there. Fes could borrow from the dragon's magic, and the dragon could borrow from some of Fes's strength. It was a unique connection, and he had the sense that it had not been that way when the dragon had flown before.

Was it because of how the dragon had returned?

So far, the dragon didn't have any answers. Fes kept waiting for the dragon to provide him a name, believing that he had one, but there was none offered.

"You intend to leave."

Fes tore his gaze away and looked over at Jayell. There was sadness in her voice, and nothing he could do would change that. "They've been taken. I've been trying to figure out what I need to do. What I *can* do. And I've come to decide that my role needs to be that of dragon protector."

Jayell smiled at him. "I suppose that suits you better than a servant of the empire."

"Does it?"

She shrugged. "It does. You never really were suited to serving the empire. I think the empire would have used you, but I'm not sure that you felt the same connection to it."

That was true enough. He didn't feel a connection to the empire, though perhaps he should. The empire had provided him with a life, and those within the empire had helped him along the way. Even though he didn't always feel a part of this world, he had become a part of it.

"When will you go?"

"Soon," Fes said. "First, I intend to check with Tracen." He still didn't know how much of this Tracen had been involved in, but his metal totems had been all throughout the palace. Hopefully, he didn't know anything, but if he did… what would Fes do? Tracen had been his friend.

"And the dragon?"

Fes glanced back up. He was farther away now and heading toward the distant mountains. In the time since they had scoured the city, removing the threat of the totems, the dragon had circled over the city, every so often disappearing before returning. Fes still didn't know why the dragon went off but suspected it had something to do with his desire to find others.

"For now, the dragon wants to find the remaining dragonglass sculptures."

"But they're missing."

Fes nodded. Since recovering the palace, they had found that the sculptures had gone missing. They should have still been within the palace, but when the people of Toulen had invaded, laying claim to the palace and trying to capture the emperor, they had ransacked it, and somehow the dragonglass sculptures had vanished.

That was the other reason he needed to attack. If the Damhur discovered that the sculptures contained the essence of the dragons, they would be able to raise more of them. How long would it be before an entire army of dragons were Called and controlled by the Damhur, and sent across the sea to attack the empire?

"I thought we would find allies in Toulen," he said. "And I was wrong."

"Had you not gone, it might have been too late. The emperor would have been attacked, and—"

Fes sighed, motioning for Jayell to sit. She settled onto the ground next to him, looking out at the sky. From here, the entirety of the city was laid out in front of them, but Fes didn't care to look out at the city. It was what he couldn't easily see that he longed for.

"I think it was lucky, nothing more."

"Maybe," she said.

"You think it was something else?"

Jayell shrugged. "I don't know. There was a time when I would have believed that we all had a purpose, that we were guided by the ancient forces that had once guided the dragons. I don't know whether I believe that anymore."

"You don't follow the Path of the Flame."

"Ever since meeting you, I haven't been able to. That doesn't mean that I don't believe in some higher power. I have to, especially considering what we've gone through."

"Sometimes I wish that I could believe in a higher power," he said.

"You don't?"

"I don't do things for some mysterious power."

"Why do you do them?"

Fes turned to her and smiled. She took his hand, and they sat there, looking out over the city and then out beyond the borders of the city and into the empire, waiting for the dragon to return. "I once thought I did what I did for money, but even that wasn't true. It's always been for those I care about."

"And now?"

"Now I'll act on behalf of the dragons. Until they are restored, I think that needs to be my purpose."

"Why? You said you acted on behalf of those you care about."

"If I don't do this, if I don't help the dragons, then people I care about will suffer."

More than anything, he was determined to ensure that he wasn't responsible for the suffering of any more of his friends.

In the distance, the dragon roared. Fes sighed and found his attention drawn to the south. Somewhere out there, far beyond the sea, he would find Javoor. And within Javoor, he would need to find the dragons. Rescuing them would be dangerous, probably nearly impossible. And yet, if he didn't try, others he cared about would suffer.

He stood and reached out a hand to Jayell, helping her up. "Come on. The dragon is returning."

Fes didn't need to turn to know the dragon headed back south again. He could feel it. And he could feel the same burning desire within the dragon that he felt.

It was time.

Book 6 of The Dragonwalker: Dragon Rider.

Saving the dragons means risking himself.

The empire remains in chaos following the last attack. Fes searches to connect to the newly raised dragon, wanting to find him before the Damhur attack again, but when he finally returns to the capital, he's too late.

War has returned to the empire in full.

With dragons controlled by the Damhur attacking along the coast, the fire mages and Dragon Guard outmanned, Fes urgently needs to find a way to save the dragons—and help the empire. The search brings him to a foreign land where he uncovers ancient secrets in his quest. He fears delay; the power of the empire fire mages is limited and already failing.

Somehow he needs to find a way to victory, but how can one man stop a war that has raged for centuries?

ALSO BY D.K. HOLMBERG

The Dragonwalker

Dragon Bones

Dragon Blessed

Dragon Rise

Dragon Bond

Dragon Storm

Dragon Rider

Dragon Sight

The Teralin Sword

Soldier Son

Soldier Sword

Soldier Sworn

Soldier Saved

Soldier Scarred

The Lost Prophecy

The Threat of Madness

The Warrior Mage

Tower of the Gods

Twist of the Fibers

The Lost City

The Last Conclave

The Gift of Madness

The Great Betrayal

The Cloud Warrior Saga

Chased by Fire

Bound by Fire

Changed by Fire

Fortress of Fire

Forged in Fire

Serpent of Fire

Servant of Fire

Born of Fire

Broken of Fire

Light of Fire

Cycle of Fire

The Endless War

Journey of Fire and Night

Darkness Rising

Endless Night

Summoner's Bond

Seal of Light

The Book of Maladies

Wasting

Broken

Poisoned

Tormina

Comatose

Amnesia

Exsanguinated

The Shadow Accords

Shadow Blessed

Shadow Cursed

Shadow Born

Shadow Lost

Shadow Cross

Shadow Found

The Collector Chronicles

Shadow Hunted

Shadow Games

Shadow Trapped

The Dark Ability

The Dark Ability

The Heartstone Blade

The Tower of Venass

Blood of the Watcher

The Shadowsteel Forge

The Guild Secret

Rise of the Elder

The Sighted Assassin

The Binders Game

The Forgotten

Assassin's End

Made in the USA
San Bernardino, CA
23 May 2020

72213932R00253